Golden Scale

Luke Harris

Published in Australia by Silverbird Publishing
First published in Australia in 2015
This edition published in 2019.

© Copyright 2019, Luke Harris

Contact details: luke@workingtype.com.au
Website: www.lukekharris.com/

Cover design, typesetting: WorkingType Studio

The right of Luke Harris to be identified as the Author of the Work has been asserted in accordance with the Copyright, Designs and Patents Act 1988.

ISBN: 978-0-646-93938-4

Harris, Luke
Goldenscale
pp332

National Library of Australia Cataloguing-in-Publication entry
Creator: Harris, Luke K. (Luke Kenneth), 1969- author.
Title: Goldenscale / Luke Harris.
ISBN: 9780646939384 (paperback)
Target Audience: For young adults.
Subjects: Fantasy fiction.
                  Friendship--Fiction.
                  Race discrimination--Fiction.
                  Secrecy--Fiction.
Dewey Number: A823.4

To Freya and Lila

In the Lowlands

Two days later, warriors came down from the plateau. They clambered over rocks and filed through fern-shaded gullies. Each carried a long, fire-tempered spear. All were afraid.

'How far?' asked a young man.

'Half a day's walk,' guessed another.

'It is good down here,' said a man daubed with lines of white clay. 'And warmer. There would be rich hunting. We could bring our wives.'

'No,' said the eldest. 'This is not our country and we did not come to cause trouble. We stay only long enough to do what we must. Then we go home.'

At midday they emerged from a stand of trees and moved through high pale grass. They saw smoke in the distance, but no people. A little later, one of the men pointed.

'There it is,' he whispered. Silently they spread out.

'Can you smell it?' someone called, and everyone could.

'Is it still alive?' asked another.

'Alive or dead, we made this problem much worse,' an elder said. 'Now we will give it to the earth and leave it in darkness.'

Day after day they laboured, shovelling and carrying. Their digging sticks were replaced many times and their hands blistered. Eventually, even the lowlanders came out of hiding and helped. By the dusty end of summer, they had finished. A long, low mound of earth ran along a gently sloping ridge.

Wearily, they turned for home.

'We did the work of men,' said a youth. 'I will dance it for the women.'

'No. This is a secret tale,' said the leader-of-stories, 'Speak of it only in our company.'

Their world returned to familiar rhythms, but, as ever, tales outlived their tellers.

Part One

Sunday 26 February

1

Beth picked up a lamb bone and surreptitiously dropped it into Freddy's mouth.

'Mum, Sam's feeding Freddy,' she said. 'Bones. At the table.'

'Again? Stupid. He'll hide it under the cushion again. Get it back, *now!*'

'But Mum—' Sam protested. 'It wasn't me. You can't see from in there. She's lying—'

'*Now!*'

A battle ensued beneath the table for possession of the bone. The dog growled in triumph and ran from the room.

Sam returned to his seat. His mother stared at him for a moment and then went after Freddy.

'You are stuffed, Beth,' said Sam. 'You won't know where it's coming from, but it'll come.'

'Stop, I can't take it,' said Beth. 'The fear.'

Her father finally looked up from his *New Yorker* app.

'The tribulations of pet ownership,' he said.

'He's your pet, Dad,' Beth pointed out.

'On paper only. Let me finish my article.'

Sam rebelled. 'Dad! Not again! I could have stayed at Damian's place. Watching you read stuff on a tablet is dead boring. It's anti-social.'

'That's hilarious,' said their mother, bone in hand, 'coming from you. Same genes, kiddo. You'd starve to death online if I didn't call you to dinner.'

'I have to go study, Mum,' said Beth. So much of family life was repetition.

'*Study*!' Sam exclaimed. '*Right.* She's writing in her diary.'

Beth sighed. 'I. Do. Not. Have. A. Diary, full stop, the end.' All true — she preferred to call it a journal. 'If you've been into my room, you little …'

'Why?' Sam asked. 'Worried I was reading the non-existent diary?'

'No, because it's *my* room. You might have touched something. Hygiene issues.'

'One more word,' said their mother. She glanced at Beth. 'You're fourteen. Can't you pretend you're growing up? And Sam. *How* are stupid practical jokes funny?'

Neither of her children bothered to respond.

Beth pushed her chair back.

'I've finished,' she lied. 'I'll come back down later.'

Her mother held out her hands to bar exit. 'No. We are going to fight and eat as a family,' she said. 'Put the reading thingy aside, Dear.'

—•—

Beth thought of herself as an only child with one brother. For four years she had been free to entertain herself and her parents; then along came number two. Now approaching ten, Sam had long ago mastered the art of getting *way* under her skin.

His eyes were pale blue, his face smooth and well-formed, fringed by waves of dark, untidy hair. Nature had thrown in a snub nose, deep-red lips and an athletic, compact frame. Adults found few faults:

'He's so *clever* for a ten year old.'

'What an *amazing* vocabulary.'

'Such a sweet, *sensitive* little boy.'

Beth could understand the clever part. Sam *was* intelligent, so much so that he paid barely any attention at school and still aced every test he ever took. But sweet? Sensitive?

She frowned, watching the light fitting above the dinner table swinging at the end of its cord.

'Look at the light!' The others stopped eating.

Cutlery clattered. A cup rolled off the table and shattered. The house groaned. Beth felt an urge to run outside, but the violence of the tremors suddenly diminished.

They all sat in silence for a moment.

'Cool! Another earthquake,' said Sam, starting to his feet. 'I'm going to look for cracks.'

'Stand under a door frame,' said their mother.

2

Beth swept fragments of porcelain into a dustpan.

Her father put his iPad to sleep. 'Great article,' he said. 'Anyone fancy a cup of tea?'

'*Nick,*' said their mother, 'you are an alien.' She walked off. She returned a moment later. 'And I don't want tea.'

'What's up with your mother?' Nick asked, as she went out again.

'*Really,* Dad?' said Beth.

'But it wasn't as bad as yesterday. Nothing to worry about. The valley has never had anything above five on the Kanamori scale. Not since settlement.'

'Mum was pretty frightened.'

'The house is well-built,' he said. 'We should do the dishes.'

Beth helped her father clear the table.

'What's wrong with the place, Dad? No-one else is getting these tremors.'

Nick ruffled her hair.

'Ground's settling a little. Nothing serious.'

Why doesn't he want to talk honestly about the tremors? Does he think he'd frighten me?

Nick let the water drain from the sink and dried his hands. He kissed her on her forehead. 'Ask me again tomorrow. Mission of diplomacy to your mother. Wish me luck.'

She bit back another rejoinder. He should be arranging for building experts and calling in the local council, but instead he offered only a weird air of distraction.

3

Beth treated her bedroom as a nation state. No entry without permission, intruders deported.

She kicked a wedge under her door. Shelves loaded with books lined two of the white-painted walls and her bed lay against the third. The fourth wall was mostly glass, and overlooked the tree-filled backyard. The wooden shutters were always closed at night. She tended to picture some freak standing in the yard and staring up. She wasn't afraid of the dark, just creatures that might take advantage of it.

Her books were a bit of a mess; science fiction, zines, thrillers, horror, short stories, travel books and graphic novels, all mixed up. She loved paper books, even how much space they took up.

Beth spent a few moments picking up books toppled by the tremors and straightening pictures. Out of habit, she assessed herself in the dresser mirror. She was ungraceful, gangly, her nose too flat and dark brown hair disorderly. She was uncoordinated ... hands and feet too big ... she grimaced.

A sensible distance short of beautiful — her uncle said. *You should be happy — beauty is a curse in the guise of a gift.*

She ached to be a little more perfect. Self-criticism was an impossible habit to kick. Fourteen was supposed to be just a beginning, but too often it felt like the end.

'School tomorrow,' said her mother through the door.

'News I can use,' Beth muttered.

'What?'

'Nothing.'

Beth sat at her desk and looked at her closed laptop. In some other universe she was backpacking through Mongolia or navigating New York City, but here she was stuck in Goolgoorook. Formerly a small country town, Goolgoorook was rapidly being digested by the nearest mega city: Sydney. Each year new housing tracts, more kids at school, big box retailers and fast food outlets in the main street and traffic all day. Someday people would forget Goolie had ever been anything but a suburb.

Their house lay on a gently sloping one hectare block. The far end was wooded, the portion closer to the road had been cleared for dressage by a former owner. If Beth opened her window she would hear a) Mrs Schmidt's cats killing birds, b) the Danner boys at war/playing cricket, c) Mr Economides shouting about soccer or d) the buzz-cut Leung kids riding their screaming motorbikes in the local reserve. It was getting hard to pretend she lived in the country.

And yet: Goolgoorook was still different. Beth knew the place as few others did, from a small platypus colony upstream from Collyers Brewery to high rock outcrops in the Jugamai hills. Most of her friends were absorbed with messaging and social media updates, worried about their status and hanging at the local skate park, so Beth had the local outdoors almost to herself.

Goolgoorook lay halfway along the flat-floored Jugamai valley and had once been the centre of a dairy-farming community. Now, real estate prices and rates soared. The dairy properties were broken down into hobby farms and small suburban allotments.

Beth had a good view of the northern portion of the valley,

lights scattered along the main roads and up to the edge of the hills. There the lights stopped, replaced by a dark void, the southern portion of Ooralloo National Park. A place of mystery, hopefully never to be subdivided, paved or sewered.

Remembering Sam, Beth knelt to retrieve her diary. It was hidden within the carved-out shell of an old math textbook.

A sharp rap at the door startled her and she slotted the diary back into its hiding place.

'I'm already *in* bed,' she snapped.

'What a good little girl. Hope you've hidden your diary.'

'Bugger off, Sam.'

'They've gone to sleep,' Sam said. 'Old people need their zeds.'

'So do I, Sam.'

'Cool cracks in the cellar! *Big* cracks.' Silence for a few seconds. 'Come *on*.'

Beth picked up her steel ruler, ready to defend herself. Cautiously she leaned down and removed the wedge. The door swung open. Sam stood in the hallway.

'Come on,' he said. 'I'm not going after you. Though you deserve it.'

She went along, downstairs into the frigid cellar.

'Mum won't like us being here.'

'*Mummy won't like it.* Awwww,' he taunted.

4

The cellar was long and dark, with red brick walls and a concrete floor. 'The lights are out,' Sam told her, switching on his torch. 'Be careful you don't electrocute yourself.'

Toys were strewn across the far corner of the cellar. Two electric drills lay on the floor, cords entwined. Sam laughed. He swung the torch beam in great arcs.

'Stop that,' said Beth sharply. 'You're making me dizzy.'

'Is this cool or what?'

'Dad will be pissed.'

'I'm the only one who uses this stuff to make anything,' Sam said. 'I should be in charge down here.'

'Making what?' asked Beth. The idea of Sam with power tools alarmed her.

'Whatever I like.' He held up a hand. The torch beam settled over the back wall. 'There's the *real* damage.'

Beth swallowed. Cracks? They were chasms. Three of them, each stretching right across the wall. Each ran vertically, splitting bricks. The widest was broad enough to take her arm. 'The house could collapse,' she said, alarmed.

'No chance,' Sam scoffed. 'Cellar walls don't hold up the house.'

'You're a builder?'

'No, I listen to Dad sometimes. When it suits me.'

The earth beyond the wall had spilled through the cracks. Beth wrinkled her nose at the smell, a mixture of damp soil and compost.

'Graveyard dirt,' Sam said. 'Hemming Heights was once a cemetery. The developers forgot to move some of the bodies.'

She glared at him. 'Seen it. Crap movie.'

Beth shivered, sniffed at the air. Something smelled wrong down here, something that made her flesh creep. She felt a strong urge to get out. 'I've seen enough. Torch on the stairs.' Surprisingly, he complied.

'You won't say anything to Mum?' asked Sam. 'Or Dad? I'll be stuffed if he finds out I've been into the underworld.'

'We have to say something. But I'll say it was me.'

Beth climbed the stairs so quickly that she hit her head.

——◆——

Beth found it difficult to sleep. She visualised the cellar and tried to recapture the strange way she had felt down there, and finally unconsciousness came.

She floated through dreams. The last of them, and the only one she could remember clearly, saw her alone on a snowy mountain top. A cold wind cut her clothes, stinging her hands and face. Without warning, an elegant black shape fell from a tree and stood before her. A huge penguin, with a needle-sharp orange beak and clawed feet, sleek with well-groomed black and red feathers.

'Ah!' it hissed. 'You are the traveller.'

'No,' cried Beth. 'A writer.'

'Write about me, then,' it commanded.

The bird began to squawk. Beth could not understand a word. Finally, it toppled into a crevasse.

Monday 27 February

5

She awoke dry mouthed and stupid with fatigue.

Beth had tried sleeping on her side or on her back, but it made no difference.

She trudged off to the bathroom and stayed in there leaning on the edge of the bath until someone knocked.

Her father ruffled her hair as she emerged. She grimaced threateningly at him.

'Early start today,' he said. 'Powerlines damaged on the Jugamai plateau. Buggered if I know how that happened — weather was perfect last night.'

Beth sighed. 'Take me with you, Dad. I'm sick.'

'Schoolitis?' He grinned. 'I used to get that.'

———

Freddy wagged his tail and wet the tablecloth with his nose, tormented by breakfast smells. Beth took pity and passed him a crisped strip of fat.

'He'll get bladder stones,' said Sam. 'Salt's bad for him.'

'So is starvation.'

'I can't see any of his ribs.'

Beth scratched behind Freddy's ears.

'You think you *own* that dog,' said Sam.

'I *do*. I feed him, shovel you-know-what—'

'He *owns* you. Two big meals every day, sleeps all the time.'

'But he's stuck here.'

Sam shook his head. 'Security beats freedom. Dogs have bred humans to feed and protect them.'

'You and your sad little theories.'

They ate in silence for a few minutes, Beth pretending to read emails on her phone, Sam scribbling pictures in a tattered notebook. She wanted to look, but he shielded the pad with his free hand.

'You know,' she said after a while, 'All of the tremors have happened at night. Every one of them.'

'But we're not here during the day,' said Sam, still drawing. 'Maybe there *are* tremors during the day.'

'Nope. We'd know,' said Beth. 'Something would move or fall over while we're out. But nothing does. Why do you think that is?'

Sam didn't reply, but his pencil slowed. Beth raised an eyebrow, amazed at getting a point across.

'Bye,' said Abbie, pausing at the doorway to the hall, toast in one hand, attempting to shrug herself into a coat. 'Be careful today. Put the milk away.' She paused. 'Don't go down into the cellar. Your father says the tremor damaged something down there. I don't even want to know. Maybe he'll do something about it. Let me know if you see any flying pigs.'

6

Cold air rushed past as Beth navigated her long driveway. She flew down from Hemming Heights towards Goolgoorook on her mountain bike. Mount Jugamai reared to the north, its stony peak already sunlit.

'Beth! Beth Ormonde! Wait!' panted a plump girl, pedalling hard. 'Oh, can't you slow down!'

'Irene.' Beth reluctantly moderated her descent.

'Did you watch *Soul Suckers* last night?'

'Downer. You know, I tried. Dad destroyed our TV. With a cricket bat. He was so out of control, but he's been like that since joining the cult. He's completely against anything with the Devil in it.'

Irene almost careered from the road. 'That's *mental*.' Her breath puffed in white punctuation marks. 'What cult?'

Beth sighed. 'Who have we got today?' she asked.

Irene giggled. 'Mr Flack first-up.'

'Oh. Outstanding.'

Students plunged through the gates of Ooralloo Secondary College like vegetable scraps spiralling towards a drain.

———

The College was made up of three parallel red brick buildings. Designated A, B and C, the two storey structures were linked by covered walkways and surrounded by cracked concrete and tatty sports fields. A dirt access road circled the school, dusty in summer and muddy in winter. Ten old Atlas oaks were spaced along the entry avenue, creating a misleading impression of grandeur. A Moreton Bay fig spread its branches behind C Block. Its deep shade belonged to the Year 12 students.

The school hall was the only modern building, a confection of glass and corrugated iron hastily built with money thrown at the school by the Federal Government.

Beth saw Sam cutting through the high school grounds with his usual pack, Pete Biscoff and the Dankovitz twins.

'Man, he *is* a cutie, ain't he?' said Jo Aarons, falling into step alongside her. 'Chicks will dig him later on.'

'So I hear,' Beth said. 'It's just camouflage.'

Jo was tall and slender, with long black hair. Her mother Indian and father Anglo, her skin copper and face a meeting of high cheekbones, hazel eyes and a white-toothed smile. She was the only beautiful girl Beth had met who was indifferent to her own appeal. Other pretty girls sometimes made a show of modesty but Jo was completely sincere.

They made tracks across the frosty lawn.

'It's Irene day,' Jo reminded her. 'Every week I blank it out, then ...'

'I know. You're *so* lucky she lives up your way. Hey, Mrs Neville wants me to try athletics. Again. Dark skin means faster runner. Proven fact.'

Beth tried to imagine Josie engaging in a sport, any sport. 'No bloody way. Fight the power.'

'I said I had a heart murmur. And flat feet.'

'I'll write your certificate. Hey, did you feel the tremor last night?'

'What tremor?'

'At about ten past seven. Like last week, only worse. Smashed a plate and split some bricks in the cellar. Mum cracked it because Dad wasn't doing anything.'

'I went to bed at six, said Jo. 'Headache. Out of it all night. Sorry. No broken plates, though.'

The first bell sounded and students began to mope their way to class. Beth related her penguin dream to Jo.

'Sounds like a case for Freud.'

Beth laughed. 'I'm just an innocent girl.'

'You say. In some places we'd be married off already.'

'Yeah, to some dirty old peasant.'

'Speaking of olds, my dad is going overseas,' Jo said, watching the running, jumping, texting and teasing energies of the emptying schoolyard, 'to Indonesia for a few months. Some lecturing gig.'

'He only got back the other day. What about your mum?'

'Sort of unhappy. But Dad's old fashioned. When he's gone … she's like a bird out of a cage. Does all this stuff she puts on hold when he gets back.'

'But you miss him, right? You're sad?'

Jo shook her head, shrugged. 'Not really. I dunno.' She never spoke for long about her family. 'Let's go.'

———

'I've got a treat,' said Mr Flack. He was a large man who moved with surprising speed. Prone to mercurial changes of mood, he was nevertheless popular. 'Indeed, a very interesting surprise for you all.'

'I'm an elephant seal,' whispered Simon Dodds.

'Who said that?' demanded Flack. 'No wait, who cares?'

He shuffled through a pile of papers on his desk, finally pulled one free.

'An excursion!'

'To Sea World,' Simon added.

'That's *it*, Dodds!' Flack boomed. 'I have your coordinates. Right now they place you far up a certain creek in a certain canoe.'

Simon stared at his desk.

'Sans Mr Dodds, the rest of us will be travelling up to the Ooralloo Plateau next Tuesday. We'll be visiting the Aboriginal cultural centre up there.'

Someone sniggered.

Flack's face froze. 'If it's not one idiot,' he said, 'then it's Len Crabbit.'

Beth loathed Crabbit with rare enthusiasm.

Crabbit met Flack's stare squarely. The expression on his narrow, thin-lipped face was pure insolence.

'Change of plans. Simon, who is just a clown, will be going, and Mr Crabbit will be staying here. With his friends. Fit in with your plans, Len?'

Crabbit's chair scraped back and he walked from the room without a backward glance.

'Right,' said Flack. 'He'll return — unfortunately. Isn't another school in the whole region that'd take him. You didn't hear that from me.'

'What are we supposed to do up there?' Dodds asked. 'I don't even like witchetty grubs.'

Flack sighed above general tittering. 'Broadening your

horizons, Simon. A group of elders have invited us. They will talk to us. We will study ecosystems up on the plateau. I encourage all of you to keep an open mind. There's an outside chance you might learn something.'

After that, Flack spent an hour talking about the Ooralloo Plateau, its heathlands, snow gums, and fields of granite boulders — a subject which Beth secretly found interesting. Jo ignored it in favour of drawing an elaborate picture of an elephant. 'Picasso's grade four teacher told him to stop doodling,' she whispered to Beth. 'Lucky he didn't.'

The recess bell rang, and twenty-seven chairs scraped back. Flack passed them permission forms as they left.

———

'I was expecting Crabbit to say something really off,' Beth said as they dawdled on their way to Phys Ed.

'He was thinking it. Flack didn't let him get started.'

In Crabbit-world, black people were subhuman, Jews ruled the world through secret councils, Asians were better in Asia and white people in danger of racial pollution. All picked up from his bong-hitting, heavy-drinking father and friends.

'Shut up,' said Jo, 'there he is.'

Crabbit watched Beth and Jo walk past the end of B Block, and hissed at them.

'Aarons, she visiting her relatives up at Ooralloo. Dey make big corroboree and sniff all the unleaded.'

Jo stopped. 'I'd be proud to be Aboriginal,' she said. 'but thank God I'm not you.'

A chorus of curses and insults spewed forth.

Beth felt the familiar sense of vertigo she experienced when really angry. She knew she had to get away before she did something radically stupid. She clenched her fists, vibrating with rage.

Taking Beth's arm, Jo hustled her away. 'Forget it. Zero percentage,' she said.

Beth seethed. 'Zero — that's my level of respect for that scum. Good comeback, though.'

'He loves shitting people,' Jo said. She looked back. 'Every day,' she said, 'people look at me like Len does. Makes me crazy. But other times, *screw you*. Why would I care what you think?'

'Is that a Richard Feynman reference?'

'He's da man.'

—•—

By some cosmic stroke of good luck, the soccer match organised for Phys Ed was overmanned and they were allowed to sit on the sidelines.

At recess they found a seat next to the tennis courts and sat in a lozenge of sunlight. 'We're marked, now,' said Beth, picking at her lunch. Crabbit's posse of thugs clustered under a weeping willow, snapping branches and carving misshapen swastikas into the trunk. As usual, the teacher on duty was nowhere to be seen.

Jo made a rude gesture towards Crabbit's homeys. '*I'm* the chocolate girl.'

Beth felt uncomfortable. What was an Anglo girl supposed to say that didn't sound patronising?

A tennis ball rolled along the ground near Beth and smacked

into the chain-link fence. A shiny-haired boy ran for it, tripped and rebounded from the fence. He smiled through the mesh at the watching girls, then flung the ball to his opponent. He looked back. 'Hello Jo. Beth.'

'Hi Thor,' they chorused, and he waved and ran back to his game.

'What do you think of him?' Beth asked Jo. They had covered this topic many times before. Jo always avoided committing herself.

'He's got an idiotic name.'

Beth grinned. 'They used to call him Thunderpants at primary school. Never seemed to bother him. Do you think he's fit?'

'What does *fit* even *mean*? Nice smile.'

'You like him?'

'A bit. I like my dog, too.'

'Bet he's well liked online. You'll have lots of competition.'

'I don't care,' said Jo.

'He's older than he is,' said Beth, 'if you know what I mean. Seems fairly intelligent. Good natured. And his wrists are nice.'

'Wrists. Right. And?'

Beth shrugged. 'He's pretty clumsy. The others laugh at him. He's a natural outsider.'

'Dunno why you're promoting him to me. Sounds like you should buy the product.'

'Shut up,' said Beth, blushing. 'You never take this sort of stuff seriously.'

'If lerve happens to me, I will. I promise. But I'll leave the god of thunder to you.'

7

During Geography, they did whatever they felt like, which wasn't the work in front of them. Ms Honeycutt despised electronic devices, so tablets and laptops yielded temporarily to paper and pen.

Beth drew imaginary buildings with domes and spires. Jo kept her head down and wrote in her diary. Beth imagined her style would be fairly intense and heavy on psychological insight. The implications of a trip to the 7-Eleven would probably take several pages. She smothered a smile.

Sarah Crabbit sat at Beth's elbow.

'Bloody hell,' she said. 'I'd rather be training.'

'Your brother,' said Beth, still thinking of the morning's events, 'is a—'

'Waste of space,' Sarah agreed. 'I'd apologise for him,' she said to Jo, 'but what's the point?' Even in Year Nine, she was the tallest girl in school, hair kept very short and dyed red, a striking sight on a dim winter's day. Sarah played several sports, all of them well. 'I'm going to hook up with the darkest-skinned African guy I can find just to piss him off.'

Ms Honeycutt finally joined the land of the semi-living and shuffled over to their corner of the room.

'What is this now, girls?'

Heads turned to watch their possible disgrace.

'We're discussing the oppression of the poor by the West,' Jo said. 'And the role of protest in subverting the system.'

'We're thinking of organising an Occupy Goolgoorook protest,' Beth added.

Honeycutt smiled. 'Good for you!' She strode to the front and chalked 'inequality of income' on the board.

'Too easy,' said Sarah.

Jo smiled. 'She was a protester in the 1970s or something. Glory days.'

Eighth period was set aside for study, but Beth decided to leave early.

'Going to check on that tremor,' she told Sarah and Jo. 'I'm off to that Geophysics Institute. They handed out their card in Flack's class, remember.'

'It hit the bin a second later,' said Jo. 'I'll hang around here.'

'Sorry about your dad.'

'Hey, he's not. Come to dinner soon. Just you and Sarah.'

8

Beth ducked out of the school yards before someone could spot her and cycled across to the University Laboratories near Ha'penny Street — a newly subdivided area packed with industrial parks and corporate glass-box offices. The geophysics department of Western University was a little hard to locate — eventually she found it up a flight of stairs in a building shared with an insurance company.

She knocked and waited for half a minute before turning the handle and entering. She found herself in a large room filled with rows of desks topped with large flatscreen monitors. She could hear the low mechanical hum of many computers operating in the same space.

'Wait,' someone called. A hand emerged above one of the monitors, followed by a head. A young man with untidy black hair and a nose ring.

'Are you delivering something?'

'I'm from the school,' Beth said. 'Doctor Graydon came and spoke to us. He said we could drop in if we liked.'

'Uh. We don't get many visits. Not from kids.'

'I'm at high school,' Beth said, offended.

'I'm Niall,' he said, loping over. 'I'm doing my postdoc here. Did you need info for an assignment?'

'I'm interested in earthquakes,' she said. 'Not for class.'

'We do a bit of that,' allowed Niall. 'Mostly modelling stuff for the big miners, but some straight seismology.' He smiled at her. 'Pretty dry stuff.'

'There was an earthquake at my place last night,' said Beth. She felt like an idiot as soon as the sentence left her mouth.

'Where are you from?'

'Up the hill,' said Beth. 'Hemming Heights.'

'Oh. I haven't heard anything in the news.'

The door opened behind her and she turned to see Doctor Graydon at the threshold. He frowned at her.

Niall made introductions and Beth repeated her news of the earthquake.

'Huh,' said Dr Graydon. *'Earthquake.'* He smirked at Niall.

'Dr Graydon ...'

'Call me Paul.'

'It really *did* happen.'

Graydon took a step back. 'Hey, no foul. You're the first student to visit, you know. People seem more interested in social media.'

He offered her a can of some caffeine-rich soft drink. She politely declined.

Graydon was short and stocky and well into middle age. His hair was suspiciously dark. He leaned over a monitor and rattled through a series of screens. Presently he stopped and pointed.

'Read through the records yourself. The higher the line, the bigger the shake.'

Beth peered at the skittering line.

'That data set covers July 17. He pointed to the time stamps running along the bottom of the screen. From midnight to midnight.' Graydon rolled his eyes a little. 'Go for it.'

5.25pm: a tiny spike in the graph, probably caused by an large vehicle crossing the nearby Ooralloo River bridge, explained the doctor.

5.45pm: another spike. Another vehicle.

6.12pm: a long procession of peaks and troughs, like the sharp Jugamai hills. This sample was more variable, including strong after-shocks. Deep, and very far away — somewhere out on the Pacific Rim.

6.47pm: all quiet.

Beth's stomach tightened as she approached the crucial hour. She peered at the line. Nothing. But then a little outburst of seismic noise, perhaps building to something bigger ...

7.10pm: a tiny bump in the track. She pointed to it, and looked at Graydon, who shook his head decisively.

'Two point, if you're lucky. Hundreds of them around nationally every day. Very shallow, epicentre probably close. Maybe a big rock fell from Mount Acute last night. Happens sometimes, especially if it's windy.'

Beth shook her head. 'Wasn't a rock. It's been kind of regular, anyway.'

'Well. Our network is accurate — we can pick up a moose farting in Alaska. When the Japanese tsunami hit, it was our measurements that helped set the magnitude.' He shrugged, as if losing all interest. 'Anyway, you've seen the line. You're lucky you had somewhere to check.'

Graydon crossed his arms. Case closed.

No big quake, not even a half-decent tremor to explain the mess in her cellar. But there *was* a tiny little bump on the line.

Graydon wandered off to his office.

Niall turned to Beth. 'Don't worry about the doc,' he said. 'He's an abrupt kind of guy.'

'Look, I believe what he says. I guess that means that whatever is happening is real local.'

Niall nodded and scratched his jaw. 'You need a surveyor to come up and have a closer look, really. Or a geologist. Like Doc Graydon. I'll have a word to him later, if you like.'

Beth raised an eyebrow. 'Thanks.'

9

Beth's home stood near the highest point of the Hemming Heights Estate. Newly built housing tracts sloped away on all sides. In the middle distance, Goolgoorook township, and beyond that, the red gum-dotted Bul Bul plains. The paddocks of her early childhood were mostly gone. She was used to the sight of families moving in, piles of bricks and builders scrap, muddy driveways, new lawns, real estate signs and giant houses on tiny blocks of land.

According to a note on the fridge door, Sam was out shopping with Abbie. There was no way Beth was going to visit the cellar alone.

A sour smell had spread throughout the house, strong one moment, gone the next.

'What *is* that?' she murmured, halting. The odour was complicated, vaguely familiar. The scent of the earth under the house, perhaps stirred up by the tremors? After a long pause, she went into the lounge. As usual. Horatio audibly bumped the glass wall of his home.

'Blub blub,' said Beth. She took a pinch of fish flakes and scattered them through a hatch at the top of the tank. A large silver perch, Horatio was fast and cunning. His tank extended four metres, taking up the entire length of one wall.

'Do you feel the earthquakes?' she asked Horatio. 'I'd rescue you if it got really bad.' She looked out through the lounge windows. A wide timber-floored verandah ran along the front of the house. In summer, mosquitoes permitting, her family sat on cane chairs and watched the light and the mountains.

Beth couldn't stop thinking about the cellar. Her parents had planned to build up a wine collection down there, but they drank it as fast as they bought it. Hence, the cellar's real purpose as a dumping ground for things unwanted. And now those cracks, and that smell.

She watched the news, and then the weather. She didn't like forecasts. The beauty of weather was its unpredictability.

The phone rang. *Thor?* Beth wondered, as if he would bother calling a nerdy Year 9 girl. He wouldn't even know her surname. And if he searched for her ... he wouldn't find a single interesting thing anyway. She had tried that. Just a sparsely populated social media presence. Checking out new services, abandoning them just as quickly.

The caller was Sarah, relaying school news. Miss Shurrock was off on maternity leave, with Ms Speck called on as her substitute.

'*Noooo!*' said Beth. 'She hates everything I do. It can't happen.'

Sarah's laughter rang over the phone. 'It has.'

Edith 'Fly' Speck taught basic maths and advanced boredom. Short and spherical, she frequently wore what looked like a pink nightgown, matched with blue velvet shoes. Her voice oscillated between a whisper and a horror-movie shriek.

Sam blew in the front entrance. He slammed the door, pitched his bag across the corridor and headed for the kitchen.

'Gotta go, Sar,' said Beth hastily. 'The incubus is here, so Mum is too.'

She hung up and flung herself onto the sofa just as Abbie stepped in and glanced her way.

'Hi Beth. Nice to see you so relaxed. Phone still warm?'

The Ormonde home was unlike most other houses in Gool-goorook. Beth's parents had a dream when they chose their vacant block, and no tardy builder or dodgy tradesman was going to ruin it. Mud brick by mud brick, one red gum timber at a time, from floorboard to ceiling joists to windows and wall coverings, they advanced. Finally they had the hand-made work of art they had always wanted. The process of building the house almost ruined them.

Beth often caught her father staring at some architectural detail with an air of satisfaction and her mother wasn't much better. Beth was proud to live in something that fell outside the usual conformity of the town, but she sometimes wondered whether her parents lacked balance.

The house had two wings that met at right angles near the front door. Painted with a white limewash, the house was pierced by full-length windows every couple of metres. A broad verandah ran around the entire house, roofed with corrugated iron and floored with salvaged red gum timbers. Several large gum trees dominated the garden, shading areas of lawn and native grass and carefully placed granite boulders.

The southern wing was essentially one large room supported by thin black cast iron pillars and timber beams. Floors were jarrah. The lounge area overlooked the back gardens, widening into a dining area and, further along, without an intervening wall, a kitchen. Bathrooms, the laundry, studies and bedrooms were in the northern wing, arrayed along a long corridor.

———•———

'I don't want to go down there,' said Beth. I *really* don't. There's no point in going.'

Sam smiled. 'It's OK if you're afraid. Courage is fear walking.'

'You're living proof of that,' she said.

Moments later they were down inside the cellar. What they saw shocked Beth. The far wall had partially collapsed, spilling bricks across the room. The smell Beth had noticed earlier was even stronger. *Sawdust? Rotting pumpkins? Perhaps licorice, or grass clippings. Or crushed ants.*

Sam leaned down to pick at the rubble. 'I think it's OK. What's behind the bricks?'

They picked their way through the rubble. They came face to face with a rough, dark vertical wall of earth. Beth made Sam point his torch at a dark patch halfway up the wall.

'A hole!' they said in unison. The torch did no more than illuminate the edges.

'Out of here,' Beth said urgently, and darted for the stairs. Sam followed at her heels.

Beth topped the stairs and ran straight into her father. She screamed. 'Jesus ...' she gasped after taking a deep breath.

'Flattering,' said Nick, 'but I'm an engineer, not a carpenter.' He placed a large hand on Beth's shoulder.

'Going underground?'

'Been,' said Sam. 'We heard something fall down.'

Beth saw a tiny shift in her father's expression.

'I'm not mad,' he said. 'Dramatic isn't it? Don't tell your mother.'

God. He's weak about this.

'Beth?'

'No. I won't tell her. Scout's honour.'

Sam tried to squirm away but his father's hand held him firmly in place.

'I'm thinking of filling the cellar in. We hardly ever use it.'

'That won't work,' said Beth, hearing her own words as if they had come from some other source. 'I mean, the tremors won't stop.'

Nick sighed. 'Things will calm down.' He released the two of them. 'Never thought I'd see you two collaborating on anything.'

Sam bolted for the front door. Nick raised his voice to reach the escapee. 'No-go zone. I *mean* it.'

'Why warn him and not me?' Beth asked.

'Because you're fourteen and sensible. I know Sam got you into this. I'm proud of you for going down there to look after him.'

———

'I am not sensible,' Beth said quietly, sitting on her bed. 'I'm unpredictable!' Yet admittedly there was very little recent evidence for that.

'Well,' she said sullenly. 'I'm going to be.'

Why not now? The cellar. Let curiosity win out over caution.

'Damn.' She wished her inner voices were not so pushy. 'Look, there's no way I can go down there on my own …'

What, you're a complete coward? A cliché of a girl? You really need Sam?

11

Beth crept past the darkened lounge. Nick and Abbie had long retired to bed. Beth's LED torch was small, its light surprisingly bright. She was wearing a thin jumper.

I'm going back. No, I'm not. She hesitated at the top of the cellar stairs. Eventually *go forward* won out over *go back.*

In the dark, the walls were much closer, crowding in until they seemed about to touch her shoulders. Her fears had no specific shape, just a diffuse cloud of dread.

Yet this locus of terror was only a small dark room. If she listened hard enough, she could hear an occasional car pass on the street outside. She was shaking so hard she found it difficult to keep the beam of the torch fixed on any one point. The irregular hole was visible in the earth beyond the broken wall. It looked much larger now.

An object glittered at the edge of the aperture. A bit of broken glass?

She leaned close. Embedded in a clod of soil, the thing was hard to make out. She hunted around for a stick, found a broken length of dowel and started poking away. Gradually she was able to free the object. She was no longer thinking, just doing whatever came next.

As she grabbed at her prize, a hot gust of wind came from the hole. She cried out, the air slapping at her hair and face. A scent came, thick as oil. It was the smell of everything alive and dead mashed together, the sea, bread, skin, cut wood, oranges, dung, dust and compost.

Then she was at the cellar door without any memory of having climbed the stairs. She had just the presence of mind to close the door quickly behind her, and then to remove her shoes.

'What?' she whispered to herself. She couldn't stop shaking, her teeth chattering. 'Nothing.' Hot gusts of wind did not come out of holes in the ground. *But they did.*

———

Sam found her in front of the television, volume turned down, her face set and mouth half open. His hair was in disarray.

'Mum will do her nut. Saw your shoeprints in the dust down in the cellar. Impressed, actually, I didn't think you'd have the guts to go down there alone.'

She grunted, shrugged. 'Leave me alone.'

'What's that in your hand?' he asked.

A dirty lump, half-forgotten, held tight and unglimpsed for the past hour. 'Just clay,' she mumbled. 'I'm going to make something.'

'OK. Abnormal behaviour. Possible alien abduction, brain swapping.'

'You should be in bed,' said Beth, coming to her feet and brushing past him.

———

Once in her room, Beth stood motionless, her hand still clenched around her find. Eventually, her mind began to work again. She spread a sheet of paper on her desk and placed the lump of dirt on the paper. The clod was soft and came apart easily. Inside, she saw a flat, roughly diamond-shaped object with rounded corners. A succession of tissues removed most of the mud.

A rich golden *thing* half the size of her palm lay before her, edges curled up into a delicate series of frills. It was covered with concentric engraved lines, like the whorls of a finger-print. A ghost of the cellar's aroma rose from it. It was about the thickness of a credit card. When rotated, it glittered. Heavy, she noted.

She scratched at it with her fingernail, but left no mark. Could it be plastic? Or some kind of artwork — a fragment of a carving?

I should get on the phone and tell Sarah or Jo about this. Tomor-row.

Beth clasped the object. It was warm in her hand.

Needs a name, she thought. *Oh God, I'm so gone.*

She yawned hugely.

She wrapped the object in crepe paper, sliding it under her pillow. She expected to dream, and was not disappointed.

Ms Speck led her to the front of the class.

'Beth has something to show everyone,' she said.

Beth raised her arm, but her fingers would not open.

Students jostled her, wrenching her fingers free. From within, a darkness erupted and spread, spangled with gold flakes.

Speck pounced, grabbing at the flakes like a contestant in a booth full of money.

'They speak!' Speck shrieked.

She showed Beth a diary, but the pages were all blank.

Speck blurred into a penguin.

'The author is dead!' said the bird before vanishing.

Part Two

Tuesday 28 February

12

The Jugamai plateau showed pale and sun-washed through her window. Last night felt like an hallucination, but the gold disc lay flat and real in her palm. Where had the tunnel come from? Perhaps an old wombat burrow covered over when the house was built. Maybe the wombat was the marsupial equivalent of a bower bird, bringing shining things home.

She showered and dressed, re-wrapping the object in an old T-shirt and stuffing it deep into her bag. *I need it close to me.*

She thought about her dream.

Mr Flack argued the standard case that dreams were just a working-out of the events of the day. Jo said dreams were fragments of a parallel world. Or they were parables, or warnings. The mind was a monster-filled wilderness. Humans were so proud of their brains, but they hardly knew how they worked.

———

A group of students read the note on the door of Room 108. *Notice to all Mathematics Students: Ms Speck is ill. Please report to Room 121 for alternate activities.*

'Sick?' said Frances Sahel incredulously. 'A relief teacher can't get sick! She hasn't even started.'

'Are you complaining? I'm not,' said Jo. 'She's in prison. Two years for combining leopard-skin print skirts and long socks.'

After recess, Mr Flack took their parental permission slips

for the trip to Ooralloo. Len Crabbit tried to hand him a form that appeared to have been savaged by a rottweiler, but Flack tore it up.

'Stay here and help the cleaners.'

Crabbit swore, and was banished once more.

Fleetingly, Beth felt sorry for Len, just as she felt sorry for all outsiders. *People laugh at Crabbit*, she mused, *but they're frightened of him, too. Frightened of what he might do.*

Beth didn't have much to say to Jo or Sarah, and they left her alone, used to her occasional bouts of introspection. She thought constantly about the thing in the bag. She waited until the end of class, debating with herself.

I don't want to share with anyone. But I have to know!

———

Gradually the students filtered out, leaving Flack at his laptop.

She felt a strong urge to flee, not stopping until she reached her room. Or the cellar.

'Mr Flack?' She swallowed loudly on a dry throat.

Flack turned to glance at her, his glasses catching the light, eyes momentarily invisible.

'Yes, Beth?' He smiled.

Beth leaned awkwardly on a desk. 'I found something — at my house. In the garden. Could you look at it?'

'Of course. I'm not much on plant ID, though.'

'Not a plant. Not at all. I know it sounds dumb, but can you promise not to tell anyone else?'

'That *is* unusual.' He stood. 'A conditional promise, then.'

'I can't show it to you otherwise.' Beth crossed her arms.

He frowned. 'If you like. I won't tell anyone.'

Beth drew closer, and opened her hand, palm up. He gingerly took the object from her.

Snatch it back! Don't let him touch it! He'll ruin it!

His nostrils flared. 'Queer smell, but quite lovely.'

'What do you think it is?' Her hands itched to reach for it. She clutched at the sides of the table to take away the urge to act, and still her knuckles turned white.

Flack tested it with his thumbnail, holding it up to the light. 'Well, I don't think it's metal, and it's certainly not plastic. Scrimshaw, perhaps?'

'Scrimshaw?'

'Carved whale teeth. Popular in the nineteenth century. This is too flexible, though. It could be a carving of some sort. Possibly from the tropics.' With obvious reluctance, he returned it to her outstretched hand.

'It's warm,' he said. 'Like a living thing.'

Beth quickly pocketed the object. She fought an urge to run from the room.

'Such an interesting smell. The scent of everything.'

Beth was taken aback to hear her thoughts so closely echoed.

'Bring this back on Monday, and we can put it under a microscope. Maybe take a tiny sample, do some spectroscopy.'

Beth nodded slowly. Inside she knew she would never consent to such a thing.

'You've helped me,' she said. 'I have to go.' She walked away.

She felt certain she had done the wrong thing. *People who see this thing will want it. But it's mine.*

———

'You're late,' Sarah said, halfway through a lunch of cold sausages and mash.

'What's happening today?' Jo asked. 'Give it up.'

'Asked Flack about my house,' Beth said. 'About the tremors, you know. Mum's worried.'

They were interested, so Beth went on to tell them about Dr Graydon and the seismograph.

Later she fell to rationalising her omission. *I didn't know why I left out Flack and the golden thing. Why not tell them? They're my best friends. But I need something strange in my life. Sharing it might make it disappear.*

'I'll see you on Sunday,' she told Jo on their way out of A Block. They planned to visit Ooralloo Shopping Centre with their non-existent money. Sarah was unable to join them; she was travelling to Ballandale for a netball tournament.

'You'll stuff yer knee, and then what good will yer be?' said Beth, imitating Sarah's father. 'No bloke's gunna want ya if yer a cripple! How are yer s'posed to carry tinnies from the fridge to his waitin' hand, eh?'

Her two friends wandered off and she felt relieved. If they weren't around, then she didn't have to worry so much about her little secret. She cut across the school grounds, intending to take a less conspicuous route home.

Len Crabbit stopped her outside the Year 10 common room. His face was red, hair hanging in greasy half-formed dreadlocks. Beth wondered if he was on drugs.

'Got me in trouble again, yer filth. Stinkin' snob up there on your hill. Where's darkie? Jo-sephine?'

Beth shook her head, worried that Crabbit might snatch her bag, and the disc.

'I've never got you into trouble. You do that all by yourself.'

'Keep away from my sister,' Crabbit hissed, face twitching, 'you *and* your friends.'

'Your shirt is dirty.' Beth pointed to a coffee-coloured patch. 'Try Preen for stubborn stains.'

'Get stuffed. I'm white. That's what matters.'

'Off-white,' she corrected, 'and none too clean.' She began to move away from him, unsure how fast he was able to run. Her heart was thumping.

'I know my kind,' he said, swaying on his feet, 'and so should you.'

'My kind? Vertebrates?'

He moved towards her menacingly, fists clenched at his side. She tried not to flinch. Mrs Snedden appeared from nowhere, a vision of middle-aged authority.

'Mr Crabbit, shouldn't you be somewhere? Now.'

Len glanced sideways at her, kicked the wall very hard and walked off. Beth's hands were shaking.

'I went to school with his father,' Mrs Snedden said. 'This one's taken after him — it's very sad, really.'

On her way home Beth cradled the object, stealing furtive glances. She didn't pay much attention to the paddocks she crossed, the birds circling overhead or the scent of the evening breeze.

13

She entered the house with a minimum of noise, doing a double-take as she glanced into the lounge. Sam was standing by the couch, Abbie and Nick sitting on it. Whatever his crime, he looked utterly unrepentant. Beth closed the front door quietly so as not to interrupt the tableau.

'— I designed a glider. We were building it in a big shed at Albert's. Based on a book.'

'And you built it?'

'I started to, but I ran out of duct tape.'

'*Duct* tape. So you took a roll from school.'

'I only *borrowed* it. When the project was finished, I would have taken it back.'

Nick looked at his son with benign regard. *Probably proud of the brat*, thought Beth.

'What's this about a pilot?' Abbie asked.

Sam looked away. 'We were going ... to ...'

'Mr Flack says you were going to launch Pete Biscoff off a cliff,' said Abbie.

'Not straight away!' cried Sam. 'Only after we'd practised. A lot of practice. He's the lightest, you know. And it wasn't a very *big* cliff.'

'Oh! Pity you didn't have the Grand Canyon for practice sessions.'

Sam shrugged. Beth *almost* felt sorry for him.

'You can return the cable and apologise,' said Abbie. 'And can you keep the crazy schemes to the realm of fantasy? Your sister's a dreamer — keeps her out of trouble, doesn't it?'

That's both of them, Beth thought. *I'm this vague little girl.*

Dismissed, Sam walked out past Beth, making a face at her. From the expression on his face, she suspected the glider had already been replaced by some other scheme.

Later, curled on a mama-san chair in a corner of the lounge room, she tried to read *The Once and Future King* but made little progress. She thought incessantly of the cellar.

Her father was pottering around pickling onions, judging by the smell. The setting sun painted the room red and gold.

Abbie came in and lay on the lounge. 'Tough day, Beth. A bit of news for you.' She hesitated. 'There's talk my office will relocate to the city.'

Beth lowered her book and stared at her mother. *I am not going to live in the freaking city.*

'Not likely, I hope,' said Abbie, 'but the department may close some branches.'

'You're *the boss!*'

'The boss has another boss upon her back to bite her.'

'OK. I'm never going to work for anyone,' Beth said.

Freddy scratched and whined at the back door, and Nick let him out. The second tremor of the week began moments later. A painting fell, and pot plants jittered and leaked soil. Seconds later, the house was still.

'Nick!' said Abbie, rounding on her husband. '*Do* something about this. I mean, *really* do something!'

'As I keep saying, I have no control over bloody subsidence!'

'Subsidence my Aunt Fanny! Why doesn't anyone else even *notice* the tremors? It's the *house*! It's bloody possessed!'

Nick rolled his eyes, but she was not to be deterred.

'There's a saying: when you have excluded all alternative explanations, what remains is likely to be correct. Or something like that.'

'You're being irrational,' said Nick.

'A woman, you mean.'

Abruptly, they seemed to realise they were about to go too far, and without another word turned and stalked off to different parts of the house. Beth shook her head and wondered if she could get out of dinner.

Saturday 4 March

14

Rutted and white with dust, Fivepence Lane branched off Dairy Road, running north past the Ooralloo reservoir. West of the road, a low rise paralleled the course of Ooralloo River and the spectacular Roaring Creek.

Beth cycled off the road and into the long grass, until her legs were sticky with seed heads. She sneezed and her eyes began to water. Though autumn had officially begun, summer was still everywhere, butterflies in the air, the ground hard and cracked. The warm midday air moved slowly, carrying with it a great and refreshing silence. After hiding her bike beneath a tree, Beth began to descend into the river valley. The slope became steeper, but she went on without slowing.

Saturdays were often expedition days, and she usually travelled alone. Today, she planned to walk from Argyle Falls to the old drive-in site, a route she had only travelled once or twice. Away from other people, she felt better, more herself.

On impulse, she took the golden disc from her pocket and dipped it into the cold waters of Saraband River. The disc seemed to writhe in the cage made by her fingers. She leaped up the bank and laid it flat on a grassy sward.

She stared at it for a moment as if she was about to develop an additional sense. But no, the disc remained still. *Imagination.* Yet she was not convinced — something *had* changed for a moment.

Fish leaped from the water, hunting bugs. Beth knelt to

splash her face. If there was something else to be found, then it would be down in the cellar.

The Argyle Falls were a trickle in February. Beth clambered down with ease. If rock climbing ever became a school sport, she'd be a contender. There was an art to walking alongside a river, rock-hopping and fish spotting, travelling efficiently. Always another bend in the river to round and pools to discover.

After an hour or two she saw Miles Simpson in the distance, waving a net at butterflies yet invisible to her. Skinny and awkward, Simpson was a couple of years ahead of her at school. She waved, but kept her distance.

A large gum tree provided shade in the grounds of the old drive-in, long closed, the entrance blocked with concrete-filled drums. Her mother and father had watched movies here, several centuries ago. Faded *Karate Kid* posters hung from the graffiti-covered projectionist's shed. Beth sat under a plane tree and looked towards Hemming Heights.

Would Mum really work in the city? she wondered. *Dad wouldn't be happy. She'd be home late, would have to leave early. They'd be tired, tetchy with each other. Even more than they already are.*

She wandered home along foot tracks, successfully kicking a rounded stone for over a kilometre until she lost it in the grass. That night, Nick streamed a Sci-Fi movie and they all sat down to watch it with chips and lemonade. Sam added commentary, and Beth laughed despite herself. *I'm not going mad. Not yet.*

15

Beth dreamed. She waited for the penguin beneath the only tree on a snow-covered steppe. She looked out over herds of bison covered with letters and numbers instead of stripes.

'So. Did you read my story?' the bird asked, falling from a tree, extending long claws and thudding to ground.

'Yes,' she lied.

'Of course,' it preened. 'My life. All of it. There's more!'

As the penguin spoke the dream transitioned into nightmare. She was in a small room, the walls covered with thousands of copies of her golden disc. The discs cast a weird light, making solid objects seem transparent. The discs sloughed from the walls, metamorphosing into crimson butterflies. Each was singing *Come with me, to the sea ...*'

'Beth,' said something, great and deep. The sound seemed to go on forever.

'Beth.'

The butterflies dissipated.

'Beth.'

Now the room began to fade.

'Beth, come to me. Follow your senses.'

Beth's eyes flicked open.

She was standing in the cellar. A single globe burned overhead. Her feet were bare and cold.

'Beth.' The voice was pitched so low she could hear it through her feet.

Her bladder threatened to give way.

I'm in the cellar. Not in bed. I want to be asleep.

'My thanks, Beth.'

'For what?' she whispered.

'Listening where others could not.'

A gust billowed out of the hole and flapped at her clothes. Beth sniffed burnt metal and sea-salt. She sneezed.

'Apologies,' said the voice. 'I breathe ever more strongly.'

'Am I awake?'

'I think you know the answer to that.'

She did, wishing she didn't.

'What are you?' she asked. If she could only close her eyes long enough, perhaps she would be allowed to return to bed.

'I am the rest of what you already have. You know this is so.'

Beth shivered, clad only in a thin shirt and a pair of boxer shorts. 'Sam, is that you?' she asked. 'If it is, please stop. You win.'

No reply; another gust came out and she fainted.

Beth woke to a pillow in place of concrete. She rolled over and stared up at the sunlit ceiling. She glanced over at her bedside clock.

'*Hell! Ten thirty.*' After stumbling out of bed she circled her room.

Beth opened a drawer. She stopped moving. The disc was still on top of the dresser, but it had been joined by two identical companions.

'Oh, fark.'

Beth backed away until she bumped into her bed and then sat down. She put her hands on her knees and groaned.

Sunday 5 March

16

'Where are you going?' Her mother sat on her banana lounge, a hand shading her eyes. 'Are you wearing sun cream?'

'Yes, Mum. Just to the shops.'

'Oh. If you see Sam, lunch is at one.'

Beth pedalled into town as if pursued velociraptors, stopping outside Hale's Locksmith and Shoe Repairs.

'I want a lock,' she said.

'Yeah?' said the attendant. Thin and tall, His beard and moustache were wispy. 'Too easy. What sort?'

'Strong. It's for a door.'

'Totally. I've got a few sweet little numbers.'

He pointed to shelves festooned with silvery deadlocks.

'Sorry, not that sort of lock. A padlock!'

'Oh yeah. With ya now.' He led her to the next aisle.

Beth took her time, ignoring any locks that looked flimsy. Her eventual choice was heavy, the locking bar clicking home with impressive finality. The body was brushed steel and the shackle was matt black. She parted company with thirty-five dollars, and smiled faintly. Jo would just die if she saw good money wasted on something so *practical*.

Beth unlocked her bike. With this on the cellar door, she'd be safe. Her only challenge was to lose the key somewhere she could find it again.

'Did you get me an ice cream?' asked Nick, pulling weeds in front of the house. He had created a pile of vanquished weeds about a metre high.

'It would have melted.' Better to tell him now. 'I bought a padlock for the cellar.' She pulled the unit out of her bag and offered it to him.

Nick wiped his hands on his overalls and peered closely at it. 'Why?'

'Like you said. Sam's been going down there. It's too dangerous for him. I know you've been busy, so I thought I'd help you out.' Such an easy, shameful lie. *I'm getting better at them.*

He nodded. 'Little rotter. Always with the crazy plans.'

I had the guts to put my hand down that hole! Not Sam. Be proud of me, not him!'

'Has to be done,' he said. 'It is dangerous, even if he thinks it's fun.' He removed his gardening gloves and turned back to her. 'Did you need any money?'

'It was on special.'

She followed Nick out to the shed, where he collected tools, and then back into the house. He bolted an anchor to the door frame, and another to the door, threaded the padlock through, and closed it. He palmed the key and smiled at Beth. 'Fort Knox. He'll have to come to me, now.'

Beth departed before she could witness her father hiding the key.

Sam arrived at one minute past one. His forehead featured a long scratch, and Abbie fussed over him. 'Mum! It's stopped bleeding.'

'What did you do?' Beth asked.

'I didn't do *anything*,' he said. 'Ken's sword broke when it hit my shield. I already killed him. He was cheating.'

'Lunch,' called Nick.

Freddy moved into position.

'Why's there a lock on the cellar?' Sam asked.

Beth almost choked.

'Just a precaution,' said Nick, steepling his fingers. 'We need to keep clear of it until I can get a building inspector over.'

Sam glanced at Beth, but said nothing.

'Beth, Dr Graydon said you paid his laboratory a visit the other day,' said Abbie.

'Did he call you?'

'Just to say he was impressed at your interest.'

Beth grimaced. 'I only went for a few minutes. He said anyone from school could go. And I did.'

'I told him he could come over,' Abbie said. 'To see things first hand.' She looked significantly at Nick

'What's the point?' said Beth. He couldn't detect the quakes on their records. Not a flicker.'

Nick shook his head. 'As long as he calls before he comes over. Don't want him poking around without us there.'

As the sun began to slide down the sky, Beth's fear returned in small increments.

She wished she could go back to her usual life, dreams and disappointment and friends. Now the house she lived in seemed threatening.

Was it possible that Sam really was behind all of this? She thought that was unlikely. Firstly, his practical jokes usually required instant gratification, and secondly, he lacked the resources to engineer the events that had followed her discovery of the object.

Just before dusk, they all took Freddy for a walk, and watched the sun set behind the Bul Bul Plains. Billabongs and creeks glowed silver, the grasslands a deep reddish gold.

'This is why we came here,' said Abbie.

'And why the developers love it.' said Nick.

———

Dinner was quiet. No squabbles, intermittent conversation and a generally distracted atmosphere. Sam was unusually pensive, chewing at the end of a pencil until it was splintered. *Waiting for something*, Beth thought. *We're waiting for the next tremor.*

But the evening passed without a single rattle.

Since I heard the voice, there have been fewer tremors.

On the way to her bedroom, Beth detoured to touch the

padlock, reassuring herself. If the voice had been real, what had it been asking her? She undressed, put on an old shirt and thermal underwear and crawled into bed. For half an hour she scribbled in her diary, trying to set down all of her disordered thoughts. No use.

A sense of dread kept her from sleep. Every shadow became an enemy, her bedside clock slowly slicing off pieces of the night. By 1 a.m., a dead, strange hour, she was going mad with worry. The house ticked and creaked. There was only one way to allow her mind rest — to check the padlock again.

She opened her door and stepped out into the corridor. Light from distant street lights leaked into the house through curtained windows. Twice she stumbled on furniture, almost upsetting an empty vase.

She could hear the fridge clicking on and off, and Freddy shifting in his wicker basket on the verandah. Her torch revealed the padlock, still in place. She hefted it, considered the thickness of the metal. *I don't believe in anything I cannot see, feel or touch.* She bit her lip.

If I'm losing it, then I can explain everything easily. But I don't think I'm mad. No-one around me questions my sanity. Yet.

Would a lunatic invent a voice which called her name and dragged her into the basement?

'Beth,' said the wind. 'Beth.'

The padlock fell open in her hand — without violence, the workings defeated.

'Help me ... I need your help.'

The door swung inward so quickly she teetered on the threshold.

'I have a place for you, Beth.' The voice was many things, bass, full of burrs, deep as the ocean.

'Leave me alone.' Beth felt mean-spirited, harassed.

'*I* am alone, Beth. Unless you assist me.'

'I don't want a part of this,' she whispered.

'We find ourselves in the world,' said the other, 'and we must act.' It paused for a moment and Beth thought she heard frogs and crickets and seagulls, all singing from the cellar. 'I am in a very difficult position, Beth. Asking is the only solution.'

Beth looked down at the barely visible flight of stairs leading down into the cellar.

'What are you?'

Seconds ticked by. No return to her bedroom. She jumped when the voice sounded again. 'You know my kind, Beth, or should I say, you once knew us. We are no longer real for you.'

19

The cellar light was on. Her left foot found the first riser, her right foot the second. 'I can't go down there,' she said.

'Destiny demands it, Beth.'

The cellar came slowly into view as she descended. A rubble-strewn floor, the naked light bulb, broken toys. She pretended she was ready to flee, but in reality her legs were far too weak.

'You're just the wind. A mistake in my mind.'

'The wind has learned to speak. I have listened to all of you so very carefully. For so long.'

Beth tangled fingers through her hair, and pulled. 'Damn this!' she whispered. She stepped out onto the cellar floor. If the globe blew its element she would scream loudly enough to wake everyone in the house.

'My gifts, Beth? Three golden objects. You have them in a drawer. You even carried one of them in your pocket for day or two. They were once a part of me.'

'Why me?' Beth asked. 'Why not go to Sam?'

'He is too young. Unreliable.'

Her mind felt divided between panic, fear, exultation, frustration, rage — the full spectrum.

'I want to see what you are. I *have* to see you!' Yet she feared it so much.

She wondered why she hadn't panicked yet.

'I'm trapped down here, Beth. Unable to move. That is why I need you.'

'How can I trust someone I can't see?'

'When you took the objects out of your house, you must have touched them. And felt their heat, their life. Touch them again, Beth, and know the truth.'

'But they're covered with engravings. Not natural, they can't be alive.'

'Carved by nature, Beth, into my flesh. They are the true marks of a dragon.'

Beth's hands fluttered. 'A dragon?' She laughed, a shrill sound.

'What your kind call my kind.'

'Too much,' she said. 'Sam?' she said with hope and desperation. 'Come on. This dragon stuff is worn out. I don't believe it.'

'Beth ...'

'Give it up!' she called into the darkness. 'I'll make your life hell!'

'Please lower your voice. You may draw attention.'

'I don't care,' Beth mumbled. She sat down in the dust, stricken. 'We make dragons in our heads. Like fairies and trolls. They don't live under my house.'

'There is something else in the place where you found my scales. It may convince you.'

'No!

'You're sane, Beth. Please look.'

She got up, shuffled over, peered into the hole in the wall. Something glowed dull-white in the gloom. This time she knew what it was, without being told. She tentatively reached in and drew it forth, holding it very gingerly. It was a tooth, as long as her forearm, very slender and curving to a needle-sharp point. It was surprisingly heavy and as warm as the scales.

'Oh, crap. I don't want it.'

'Take it. I am what I say.'

It breathes through the hole, she thought, *and that breath is the smell of all things.*

'I've got to go,' she said.

A low noise filled the room; an inhalation. Beth backed up the stairs, clutching the tooth.

You've got me. I don't know how, but you have. She knew she would be back. *He is giving me himself, but I also have to give something of mine. Give.*

'Help me, Beth,' the voice hissed, fading into silence.

Monday 6 March

20

Morning came as usual to Hemming Heights, but her world had changed. Doubts had been replaced by certainty. After her flight from the cellar, she had run to her room into her bed. The cellar was more or less directly beneath her bedroom. Only a wooden floor lay between herself and what lurked below.

She slept without interruption until just after dawn. After rising she sat at her desk and waited for panic and terror, but they failed to even make an appearance.

Beth looked at the scales, arranging them in a neat line on her study desk. *I have all these things, now, these gifts/obligations from below.*

She turned her attention to the tooth. The tip was so fine and perfect, the ivory-coloured enamel silken in texture. What kind of creature needed teeth like that? She pictured shark-like rows of the teeth along its jaw.

Like a deep sea fish, it lived in the dark, far away from noise and motion. Perhaps it had excavated a burrow and become trapped, or it might be waking from a long hibernation.

A freaking dragon. She had to stifle laughter. Dragons were for black clad tragics — people who read Rice and McCaffrey, who thought Tolkien was a prophet and Harry Potter the apex of literary achievement. She knew a girl one year above her who carried crystals in her school bag and practised white magic on the weekends. She would be beyond ecstatic if she was in Beth's situation. 'Bring on the elves,' Beth muttered.

Wrapped in an old woollen jumper, the tooth just fit into her backpack. She also took the scales, as a defence against doubt.

Abby and Nick were already on their way to work. Freddy refused to go near her during breakfast, and ran out the front door when she was about to leave. She wasted five minutes before finally luring him into the back yard. *He knows, too.*

Abbie drove Sam to school just before nine a.m. in a noble attempt to keep him away from his confederates. She said was receiving a stream of letters from Sam's school, all of which dealt with his misdemeanours.

The theory of dividing Sam from his mates was good, but about as likely to succeed as growing pineapples at the South Pole. Sam attracted trouble the way rock stars drew paparazzi. Beth was grateful that her brother was distracted from the cellar, but she did feel a pang of sympathy for him.

21

Beth walked to school. She didn't feel like riding. She wanted to carefully consider this new feeling, her new knowledge. She glanced back at the hill upon which her family's house perched. *Something real. There are no spirits*, she thought, *just life.*

She walked on. It was hard to think sensibly. *I should listen to something,* she suddenly decided. She pulled out her earphones and scrolled down to the latest song cycle from *Euphoria*, a weird punk cum pop-hip hop band out of Rotterdam. Hardly any of the other kids — even Jo and Sara — had ever heard of them. She sighed as howling guitars and up-tempo drumming filled her ears.

She was late, and walked straight to her biology class.

Mr Flack was out of the room making photocopies. Beth picked her way across to her usual spot. Jo looked at her coldly. Beth's sense of euphoria instantly evaporated. 'Oh, hell, Jo. Shopping. On Sunday!'

'Right. Shopping. Sunday. I tried calling you.'

'I'm so sorry. I didn't even check my phone.'

'Thought something must have happened to you. I waited on Hick Street for an hour. Len walked past twice and called me names. One of his mates spat at me. He missed.'

'Filth!'

'Yep. My best friend forgets all about me. Dickheads make my life a misery. So I went home. Did *you* have a good weekend?'

Beth cringed. 'You should have called.'

'I did, about ten times.' Jo retorted.

'Jesus, I'm sorry. You're overreacting.'

'You're unreliable, Beth.'

I should tell her about the dragon-voice. Then she'll understand. About the cellar and the dreams and how I've got a mission now, or will have soon, and she'll share it with me. As my best friend. I'll show her the tooth, and the scales, and she'll have to believe. Beth opened her mouth. Her lips moved a little. She tried again. Nothing.

'Fly-catching,' said Jo. 'Don't bother apologising again.'

Beth tried once more, shook her head. She had the words queued up but they would not cooperate. The creature was hers alone. She felt as if she had been hollowed out.

'Teacher!' warned Nadine Oobie from her post by the door, causing a flurry of book opening and simulated work.

'Sit down!!' yelled Mr Flack as he walked in with a stack of photocopied handouts. 'Bums on seats, pens in hand.' He gave the whiteboard a slapdash wipe.

'Dad's gone now,' whispered Jo, 'and Mum wants you to come over for dinner tomorrow night.'

Beth nodded, hoping she could redeem herself.

'Next time I'll tattoo it onto my arm with a ballpoint,' she promised. 'Without anaesthetic.'

'Tattoo artists don't use gas. That would be too easy,' said Jo.

———

After the class was over and the other students save Jo had dispersed, Mr Flack beckoned to her. 'Beth, I've got the micro-scope out of its case. Have you got your little object?'

She considered running.

'Ah — yes.'

'Let's have a look at them.' He signalled for her to follow, walking off towards the biology lab. Jo gave her a resentful look.

'I'll see you later,' Beth said.

Perhaps Flack can give me information without knowing anything himself.

Flack beckoned her into the biology lab and ushered her to one of the large microscopes normally reserved for senior students. He clamped the scale to the viewing platen and squinted into the eyepiece. Beth felt like elbowing him out of the way.

'It's definitely not artificial,' he announced, standing up from the microscope. 'It has a real biological feel. Growth patterns, unevenness right down to the smallest scale. I was hoping to see cell walls, but they're not obvious.'

Flack pushed a button on the side of the microscope and a projector threw a large image of the scale against a white screen, highlighting mazy lines and intricate patterns. Beth thought it looked like a far-flung empire seen from space.

'I don't know of any animal that this could have come from. Or plant. Quite extraordinary, really. Not that I'm any kind of expert.' He clasped his hands behind his back and waddled back and forth. 'Do you mind if I keep it here for a while? I could run some tests. Send a sample off for dating and spectrographic analysis.'

Against all good sense, she agreed. *I have the other two.*

22

The just-built school library was the pride of Ooralloo Second-ary College, networked, online and suffused with the smell of new carpet. At lunchtime the place was empty and quiet. Irene was sitting beneath a potted palm, reading *A Complete History of Australian Soap Opera*, and managing to look both lost and cheerful at the same time. Beth sneaked past her and sat down at a computer.

Right, she thought. *This is where I find out everything there is to know about a non-existent animal.*

She loosed her digital dogs. Imaginary or not, it dragons occupied a serious amount of database space, web indexes and library shelves. She narrowed the search to 'Books in this Branch'. This list was smaller, but most covered topics other than 'actual' dragons. Dragons were a popular metaphor.

I could do a better job at home.

But finally a genuine candidate: *Fire-Breathers — Dragons in Myth and History*, published at the turn of the century. Beth switched to the browser for a moment. Reviewers on Amazon praised it as a serious work, notwithstanding its 'many eccentri-ties and errors of fact'.

She jotted down the location.

Yet half an hour later, the book was not to be found — neither in its correct place, nor anywhere in the surrounding shelves. 'It's on loan,' Ms Davis, the chief librarian said, appearing to share her disappointment. 'Due back in two days. Here, I'll tag it on the system, and let you know when it comes in.'

Feeling deflated, Beth sidled past Irene and went back into the sunlight to find her friends. They were gazing out into the middle distance and hardly acknowledged her. Lunch was half over, games of cricket and handball reaching their peak out on the oval. Another chance to tell Sarah and Jo everything, but she remained silent.

Her mind constantly replayed the voice from the cellar, coming up with nothing. She was so preoccupied that she barely noticed Sarah's departure. Jo stood and straightened her dress.

'See you tomorrow,' she said.

Beth experienced a sharp pang of remorse. 'I've got problems at home, too,' she attempted.

'I'd take yours over mine any day,' Jo said.

23

The school day finally over, Beth trudged back up the hill towards home. However agitated her mind, she could not deny that she also felt warm, satisfied, even happy. *Happy for what I've found*, she wondered, *or because I have a feeling of power? Or both.*

The hills to the west were backlit with white gold, the tree shadows a deep blue. A cicada serenaded her. She found herself at the side gate of her house, let herself in and scraped her shins on Sam's bike. Hobbling towards the house, she made a fist of one hand and waved it at the house. 'How much bloody time can it take to lean your bike against a wall?'

Hearing her voice, her brother met her at the back door. They walked together into the dining area, where Nick was reading from his pad. He looked as if he was half asleep.

'Sorry — not. You should have looked.' He mimed a tear running down his cheek. 'Dad's taking us to the movies! To see a horror film!' he shouted. 'Better cry now and save me the embarrassment.'

She clipped his ear. Rather, attempted to and missed as he danced backwards.

'Dad! What about dinner?' she asked.

'We'll eat out,' said Nick, 'before the movie.'

'Where's Mum?'

Sam hesitated a moment. 'In the city. For an interview.'

'The city job?'

'Maybe,' he said, losing his antic expression. 'Or maybe not.'

Beth glowered. 'Don't be a little prick.'

'Umaah.'

'Do we have to move from here?' Beth asked her father. 'I mean, she can't commute all the way to the city.'

Sam looked pleadingly at his father. 'Dad? We wouldn't do that, would we?'

'For crying out loud!' Nick chuckled, his acting poor. 'Your mother and I were raised here. We're not that keen to leave.' He picked up a piece of junk mail and studied it intensely.

What if they break up, Beth thought. That would be like the sun shining at night. Her school was overflowing with kids whose families had gone to pieces. Children living with mothers, fathers, grandmothers, uncles, or stepfathers, sleeping in different places at different times of the week, fathers shacking up with a succession of girlfriends, mothers choosing new men as bad as the old. Beth knew well enough that families were flimsy, but she didn't want to find out from first-hand experience.

'Don't forget the movies,' said Sam.

'Pizza first,' said Nick, 'Seconded?'

'Thirded. Extra hot salami,' agreed Sam.

'Captain Chicken!' said Beth, but two votes to her one carried the resolution.

———

The Limelight Cinema began pushing popcorn in 1971. The foyer's carpets were a mess of interlocking brown and orange circles, and the walls were covered with a strange red velvet wallpaper that felt like velour. Only the dregs of the Hollywood barrel were considered for screening at the Limelight — the more lowbrow and plotless, the better.

Sam managed to wheedle money out of Nick for a Coke and a bucket of rancid popcorn.

They watched *Tsunami Summer*, a CGI-driven disaster flick. Insular townsfolk ignored all signs of an impending earthquake/tidal wave, and the hero scientist spent fruitless hours trying to convince them to leave. One especially obstinate old lady clung to a lamp post, insisting on walking her dog along the beach despite the impending apocalypse.

'She's gonna die,' predicted Sam, correctly. 'Grannies always die in these movies.'

'But the dog will live,' Nick added, and he was right too.

'All *right!*' Sam shouted when the tsunami finally appeared, smashing the simulated town to pulp. 'Surf's *up!*'

All through the noise and action, Beth thought of the tooth, and the scale, of Mr Flack, of the voice and the smell, over and over. Not seeing or seeking any alternative path, just finding many ways to remember the same event. She felt as though an ant had found its way into her mind, and was unable to escape, marching, marching …

Abbie was home when they returned, shoes off and drowsily watching a current affairs program.

'Hiya, said Sam. 'The movie was crap. Foodlike substances were OK.'

'Hi yourself, Sammy. Beth. Hon?'

'It was not utter crap,' Nick objected. 'Fine acting, especially on the part of the tidal wave. Great range of expression.'

'It's actually a tsunami,' said Sam. 'Caused by earthquakes, not by the tides.'

Beth groaned. Soon she excused herself and went to her room, and stood looking out the window, at her reflection over-laying the town's lights. She was home, the night had come and she was tense with anticipation.

She put on her tattiest pyjamas and lay down, but could not sleep. Each time she closed her eyes, she heard *that* voice, inside her head, in the beating of her heart, the thrumming of her blood.

24

She pushed herself off the bed, opened her door, and crept downstairs through the darkened house. Once again, the cellar padlock was open and the door yielded to her touch. She stood before the hole. Waiting. Her voice came out as a whisper. 'Why did you talk to me? Why not some other person?'

'Well? Why?'

'Ahhhh,' the creature murmured, voice papery and insanely low, 'Beth. I did not expect you so soon. I thought you would take some time to adapt.'

She shook her head. *He's a flatterer.*

'When I began my sleep, such a long time ago, the land above was occupied only by wandering nomads. Now, humans have made a city around me.'

'It's not really a city,' Beth said, 'not yet.' She frowned. 'You're older than Hemming Heights?'

'Yes.'

'Much older?'

'When we dragons are asleep, time essentially stops for us.'

'Like hibernation? Hundreds of years?'

'Maybe thousands,' said the voice. 'This time it was shorter, I think. Perhaps the construction of your home awoke me earlier than usual. Waking can take many years.'

'We must seem like moths,' said Beth after a moment. 'Blink and we're dead.' She wiped her forehead. 'Why do you call yourself a dragon? Why use that particular word?'

'That is my essence,' it replied.

'But dragons are imaginary,' she said. 'A myth. Dreamed up by adults to entertain kids. You could call yourself something else. Your real name, maybe.'

'There is a truth beneath all the layers of myth. Dim memories, ancient encounters, stories passed down. That is how my kind becomes your dragon. And that is why dragon will do. As a label, for want of something better.'

'But what are you really called?'

'Naming is a weak tradition among my kind,' the dragon said. For us, no two things on this earth are at all alike, so we have no need of names. We are what we are.'

She felt weaker than ever. One connection seemed certain. 'You're making our house shake? The earthquakes?'

'Yes. Unavoidable. My body is slowly stirring, warming up.'

'It frightens us. Especially my mother—'

'Again, I apologise. I have an unanticipated problem, you see. I can't win free as easily as I had hoped. Or find food.'

'What do you eat?' She imagined flocks of sheep.

'That depends on you, should you decide to assist me. Tubers. Lichen. Maybe ferns. Not the fronds — the heartwood — the trunk, you would call it. They bring me closer to the sun.'

'Will you destroy our house when you leave?'

'Of course not. I can emerge beneath your gardens when I am strong enough. I have a sense of the shape of your home. You have nothing to fear.'

Beth rocked from one foot to another, considering. The dragon was an unlucky creature in its choice of a sleeping place. But how many lies would it tell in order to obtain help? *I'm ready to help him without knowing anything. What else can I do? Don't let him dictate everything!*

'Show me something more ...'

'I don't know if that's a good idea.'

Beth said nothing. She waited, breathing the cellar's damp air.

'Very well,' the dragon said finally. 'Just once.'

A deep rumble reached up through the soles of Beth's shoes, and a steady rain of fine dust fell from the roof.

'Stand aside.' the voice boomed.

Beth crouched.

Seconds later, a red glow lit the hole. Then a narrow tongue of scarlet flame jetted across the room, fanning across the far wall. Beth's skin prickled at the sudden heat. Blue smoke eddied through the room. Then the flame and smoke vanished like a movie run backwards. The room was suddenly very dark.

'Have I injured you in any way?'

She was silent for what seemed like minutes.

'No. Shocked. Is what I am.' She stopped. *He could have killed me.*

A second later the upstairs fire alarm began shrieking, and the dragon cried out.

Beth was already halfway upstairs.

Having fumbled the cellar padlock shut, she got to the kitchen seconds before her father appeared from the bedroom wing, followed by Sam in his pyjamas, then Abbie.

'I was making toast,' Beth improvised, indicating the slice she had just managed to insert in the toaster. Her legs felt shaky.

'At two in the morning?' Nick asked. He waved a towel at the smoke sensor, and the shrilling stopped.

'Hungry. Didn't have enough for dinner."

Sam looked at her intently. 'Where's the burned toast?' he asked. 'In the bin?'

'I ate it.'

'But you reckon the black bits cause cancer.'

'I was *hungry*.' Beth glanced at her parents, who were staring at her as if she had three heads or a forked tongue.

'Smells weird down here,' said Sam. 'Like singed dog or something.'

After innumerable apologies and a half-successful attempt to mollify her parents, Beth eventually trailed off to her room. She lingered a moment outside her parents' door.

'She's worried about your new job,' came Nick's muffled voice.

'Nick, you shouldn't have told them. Unnecessary.' Abbie sounded weary. 'I might not get the job.'

'Or you might,' he retorted. 'I'd rather that it wasn't a complete shock to them. Anyway, Beth's a survivor.'

'She worries me,' said Abbie. 'Been odd for the past week. Always doing her own thing. That's the story of her life, isn't it?'

'Like me when I was young,' Nick said. 'I can see a lot of myself in her.'

'You were more sociable.' Abbie tried a new tack. 'Remember Sam's jibe about her diary? Maybe he guessed right. Maybe she's discovered boys. Or a *particular* boy.'

'All fourteen-year-old girls are interested in boys,' her father said dismissively. 'Or horses, and Beth's never looked sideways at a nag, thank God.'

Their conversation moved on. Beth sidled away.

If only it was just boy trouble, thought Beth, climbing into bed.

Tuesday 7 March

25

For the second day in a row she walked to school without bumping into Irene. She carried on a conversation with herself, half muttered, half aloud. *How old is he? Where does he come from? When did he learn to speak? How long has he been listening to us?*

During French, a class populated by near-strangers, she wrote out all of her questions, constantly glancing around to make sure no-one was watching.

After the last syllable of French she traipsed into Art — a good place to make a mess and to mix unfamiliar substances. Hoping to achieve an interesting spontaneous effect, she started with a large sheet of recycled paper, ripping it into dozens of rough-edged ovals. Beth dipped these in wood glue and scattered them over a square of linen. Gold flecked paint followed, dripped and dribbled Pollock-style. Enjoying herself, she fell into an easy rhythm, stopping after an hour or so to survey her work.

She stopped breathing. Her random textural piece had become a structured series of accurately formed overlapping scales, each marked with a complex fingerprint-like pattern, in the middle of which was an unmistakeable eye, red and perfectly circular with a great golden pupil. She couldn't look away. *I don't even remember putting those details on the scales.*

'That's very interesting,' said Mrs Hirschner, and Beth jumped, clutching at a chair.

'I'm trying to do something gestural,' said Beth, remembering something the H-Bomb had said a few weeks earlier.

'Hmphh. Looks more Oriental to me,' said Mrs Hirschner. 'Maybe you're channelling a Song Dynasty painter.'

Beth smiled. *Just channelling one of the critters they liked to paint.*

At the end of the lesson she rolled up her half-dry construction, tied it with string and carried it with her. She slouched across to the oval where the rest of the Phys Ed class were waiting. Beth took a seat on the grass next to Jo.

'Sar's away somewhere,' said Jo. 'Bullamanka. Out bush somewhere. Sports stuff. God knows which one. Underwater hockey? Cross country tennis?' She was a lot friendlier today, gently ribbing Beth about Hanford, and sharing a few squares from a block of chocolate.

Ms Larundel led the class out to the tennis courts. 'Play,' she commanded loudly, handing out equipment. 'No dropping or scraping the racquets, and find the ball when it goes out of bounds.'

Beth knew how to hold a tennis racquet, but not much more. Despite Ms Larundel's frantic mini lessons, the two of them put on a display of anti-tennis, where the ball hardly ever stayed in and racquets seemed to be all hole and no string. They missed so many balls and double-faulted so often that Jo could hardly serve for laughter.

'Bloody futile,' said Beth as they retrieved their bags from change-room lockers. 'Might as well teach a cockroach to tango.'

'You come up with the weirdest sayings,' said Jo. 'And right now I'm saying goodbye. Catch you in the a.m.?'

'Earth to Jo. Like, of course.'

She hadn't thought about the dragon for at least an hour.

Beth hurried home and began searching for a specialist nursery. Surprisingly, there were a large number of them, but only one was close enough to reach on her bike.

She dialled, her heart thudding.

'Hello? I was wondering if you sold tree ferns. *How* much? Are there any *smaller* ones? Do I get a discount if I buy three?' She took seventy five dollars from her cash tin, almost exhausting her reserves.

She pedalled into town as if she was leading a breakaway group in the Tour de France. Her lungs felt raw. When she arrived, skidding to a stop in a spray of gravel, she took a minute to bring her breathing under control.

As she rested, she glanced up and down the street. She could see grassy paddocks, factory buildings and a big concrete silo that one day would probably be perfect for conversion into warehouse apartments. Green Thumb Nursery occupied an entire block along Newbegin Road, opposite a long row of pastel shaded cottages.

She entered the nursery through an archway made of intertwined rose bushes and vines. A small, middle-aged man with tanned skin, dye-dark hair and an elfin face looked up from a line of potted seedlings. He smiled and wiped his hands.

'I know that face. You're Nick's daughter, ain't ya?'

Beth nodded. Everyone knew her dad. No secrets in a small town.

'I'm Serge Golokov. I remember when you was knee high to a grasshopper. Worked with y'dad. Hydro project up in the hills. Y'd be at high school now, yeh?'

Beth agreed.

'Town's changed since then, eh?' he said. 'She used to be

such a quiet little place.' He scratched his forearm ruminatively. 'More business for me, though.'

Beth nodded and looked around. There were only a few other customers, silver haired couples inspecting begonias and azaleas. *I can't do small talk*, she thought. 'I called just before. Have to buy some things.'

'Right-oh! About the ferns, right? Follow me.' They eventually stopped under an expanse of shade-cloth. Serge mopped his forehead.

'Hotter'n a shearer's armpit in here.' Pointing at a dense wall of greenery, he smiled. 'Say hello to my children. That beauty over there, she's the basket fern. Fishbone, eh?'

'What's that?' Beth pointed to a large spreading fern with a thick trunk. 'I've seen it everywhere in the Jugamai hills.'

'*Dicksonia antarctica*,' he said proudly. 'The soft tree fern. Good specimen, that one. One hundred dollars for you.'

She held up her hands. 'A little bit much, I'm sorry. I don't have a job yet.'

'Right then. We've got some smaller *Dicksonia*.'

'That's fine. It doesn't have to be fancy.' She bargained him down to twenty dollars for a *Dicksonia* stump, a prickly, rust-coloured lump covered with a mat of fibres.

'Wait right there,' he said, as she hefted the stump. He returned with two more. 'Take these as well. On the house.'

Serge tied the three trunks together with coarse orange twine, and helped her secure them crosswise to the bike's rack. She hopped aboard and almost tipped the bike over.

'Oof. They're heavy.'

Serge stood back and looked dubious. 'Maybe y'dad could pick it up, eh?' he said. 'Bit *too* heavy.'

'It's a present,' she said. 'So I've got to keep it quiet.'

'If I get any cheaper ferns, I'll let you know,' he called after her. 'Don't forget — lots of shade and water.'

Beth nodded. The ferns would get plenty of shade, but water wasn't likely to be a part of the plan.

26

By cutting through the primary school and crossing Golf Links Road, Beth was able to sneak into Hemming Heights without attracting attention. She arrived at the house red and perspiring. Climbing the hill back to Hemming Heights with her fern-laden bike had been torture. She pushed the bike the last few hundred metres, dropping it once and cursing the unwieldy fern trunks. She quickly unlatched the side gate and pushed bike and cargo into the back yard. 'Now what do I do with it?' Freddy barked softly. *Shut up*, she mouthed.

She didn't have a cover story for her sudden interest in tree ferns, so she really wanted to hide them away before attracting any attention. 'Here boy! Here Freddy Fred!'

Beth drew a scale from her pocket and held it out. Freddy yelped and fled to the far end of the garden. She went into the house, called for Sam and sighed with relief when no answer came. Beth had an idea that he and Nick were off fishing or some boys-only thing that she sneered at but really wanted to join. She grabbed several garbage bags, returned, slid the fern trunks into them and took them to the cellar door. As she had expected, the lock was open and the door slightly ajar. About to descend, she heard a key turning in the front door. She jerked to a halt, the bagged ferns falling from her arms and bouncing down the stairs before thudding to a halt on the cellar floor.

'What was that noise? Is someone here?'

Beth fumbled the cellar door closed, shakily pressed the

padlock together and raced for the lounge. 'It's me, Mum,' she squeaked, out of breath. 'I dropped a book.'

'Oh,' said Abbie, peering around the corner. 'Gave me a start. The side gate's open, Beth. And your bike is in the way. Show some care!'

'Sorry Mum.' Beth couldn't help smiling. Sam was right, their mother *did* sometimes talk in bullet points. 'When are they back?'

'They might have gone to the coast. Could be a while. Dinner's in the freezer. I'm out for a little while,' called Abbie from the parental bedroom. 'Giving a talk to a business group.'

Just go already, Beth thought. A minute later the front door slammed and she was alone again. She thought about going down to the cellar, but delayed that in favour of a snack. She couldn't face the dragon on an empty stomach.

The phone shrilled just as Beth took her second mouthful of a peanut butter sandwich.

'My parents aren't home, and nor is my brother.'

'You're coming tomorrow night, aren't you? I mean, do I have to remind you again?' Jo, tone icy.

Beth squirmed. She had indeed forgotten. 'Of course I am. I don't forget everything, do I?'

'Well, we thought … you might be losing interest in your friends.'

'Why would I do that?'

'Boys. What do *you* think? Or *a* boy, anyway.'

'My mother's beating the same dog. It's not that,' she said.

Beth wondered if the faint scrabbling she could hear was the dragon somehow consuming the ferns.

'Look, Jo. It's not a boy. Not a girl, either, or a fixation on shop mannequins or women's magazines or anything else.'

In the background, Beth heard Jo called to dinner. She exhaled. 'Catch you tomorrow, Jo. And don't forget the blinking excursion!'

Abbie walked in just as Beth hung up. 'Jo, was it? Say hello to her mother when you see her next. Two hours?'

'Mum, it's only a local call, anyway. Five minutes.'

'Oooh. *That* was the shortest conversation you've ever had with Jo.'

'Right. What about your business talk then? You were only gone for half an hour.'

'I went on the wrong night. It's next week. Losing my grip.'

Beth didn't have an answer to that. She made a mental note to thank the dragon for halting his earthquake schedule. Abbie had enough to cope with.

27

After dinner, Beth felt paralysed. She worried about the dragon, her friends, her mother. She watched Horatio for a while. He in turn seemed to be watching her. Did every animal under the control of humanity yearn for a wild life? The dragon was surely the wildest of all creatures and his desire for the open sky must be fierce indeed. Unstoppable, perhaps.

Coiled and cramped in his lair beneath their house, listening to them (*he must be able to hear everything*), learning their language, observing, waiting. *For me. Maybe he's been listening to me for years. My whole life. He needs help, and he asked me. Just me. He needs me more than anyone else. Without me, he would be trapped forever.*

'Gotta do some homework, Mum,' she said.

'Have to,' Abbie said automatically.

'OK. I *have to* do some homework. We're going to see the elders up on the plateau tomorrow, and I want to ask some good questions.'

Abbie nodded. Her face was unusually pale, eyes shadowed. She looked away from Beth, as if disturbed by scrutiny. 'Go on then,' she said.

An idea had just come to Beth, one that would require research. The dragon might pre-date European settlement, but surely he had arrived *after* the arrival of Aboriginal people. Fifty thousand years was just too great a gulf of time for him to cross. He had therefore been *observed* by people.

She opened *Aboriginal Cultures of Eastern Australia* on her tablet. She scanned the table of contents until she found the Gugamai. The Gugamai people spoke Pijanti, one of a group of similar languages found along the east coast. They had been in the area for at least ten thousand years, probably longer. They ate starchy foods, bitter fruits, nectar, lizards, snakes and the occasional kangaroo.

A small patch of text leapt at her. *'One of the favourite winter foods of the Gugamai was the core of the soft tree fern, Dicksonia antarctica. After removing the outer covering, a core of white starch was revealed. Early settlers described the taste as 'like a bad turnip', but Aboriginal people were rather more positive. The starch could be eaten raw, but was usually roasted.'*

Was this a hint that the dragon had been in contact with Aboriginal people? After all, the creature's favourite food was also a traditional indigenous staple.

Beth re-read the whole chapter and took notes.

From within the bubble of her concentration, she noted the return home of her father and brother. Sam knocked at her door a few minutes later and went away after she had ignored him long enough.

She went back to her reading. An hour passed and the house grew quieter. Beth lay on her bed and tried to be calm, but found she couldn't stay still any longer. 'Here I come,' she muttered, and left her room.

The smell inside the cellar was ever more pungent. Beth upended a box, and sat a little to the side of the chasm. Bricks melted and split by the dragon's flame lay scattered around her.

When it finally came, the voice rose like a hot February wind. 'I'm not going to eat you.'

Beth swallowed on a dry throat.

Silence, then a low clicking like two small stones striking one another.

'You are beginning to accept me, I hope. You really have nothing to fear.'

'Did you like the ferns?'

'They were adequate. Not particularly fresh, though. Desiccated.'

She flushed. 'It cost me twenty dollars. I can't afford that every day!'

'You purchased it? Is it possible to purchase a plant?'

'Of course! Do you expect me to snatch them from national parks? That's illegal, you know.'

'You cannot obtain food there?'

'It's illegal,' she said primly. 'You can be imprisoned.'

'Well. I can eat other foods, if it is more convenient.'

'Such as?' She imagined giant mushrooms from deep in the forest. Whales. Marinated tree bark or sap ...

'The dry food you set aside for the wolf.'

'Wolf? What wolf ... Oh. Freddy, you mean!' She smiled. 'You'd eat *dog* food?'

'I ate three bags of it when first I awoke. Stored in the room in which you sit. High in protein, even if very stale. I drew it in with my breath.'

'He's not a wolf.'

'He smelled like a wolf. At times I have enjoyed hunting with wolf packs.'

'Oh,' said Beth. How would they communicate?

Dry pet food wasn't that expensive ... particularly the no-name stuff ... but if the dragon ate too much ...

'I'll see. I'll need money. Mum only buys one bag every two weeks.'

Hearing her voice, Freddy yelped, and scrabbled at the cellar door.

'Your *dog* smells me. Perhaps he is trying to save you.'

'I'd better go.'

'Indeed. I thank you,' came the sonorous voice. Beth stood still, not really seeing, just contemplating. After a while she turned and trudged up the cellar stairs. *How am I fitting this into my life so easily? How can I eat dinner with my family, talk to Jo, then go and chat with an imprisoned magical beast?* If she was crazy, she hoped it was only a partial madness.

Freddy backed away from her as she emerged, his muzzle wrinkled into a snarl. After a moment, he rubbed against her leg like a cat.

'You don't like me, then you do. Make up your mind, wolf.'

Beth lay on her back, gazing at the shadowy ceiling. *He can unlock the cellar without touching the lock. He can see me without seeing me. I'm helping him without any thought of possible consequences.*

After scribbling a mess of thoughts into her diary, she entered sleep like a canoeist arrowing over a waterfall.

Part Three

Monday March 13th

28

Len's friends stayed away from the excursion to Ooralloo.

'Excellent,' said Mr Flack, rubbing his hands. 'Let 'em stew.'

He looked caught Beth's eye when she boarded the bus. 'I want to talk to you. Soon.'

Embarrassed, she nodded and found a seat next Sarah. They were then joined by Jo.

After a few minutes, Sarah got up, mumbled something to them and moved down to the other end of the bus, striking up a conversation with one of her sporting mates.

'What's up with Sar?'

'She's ashamed,' said Jo. 'Is my theory, anyway.'

'Of what?'

'Of Len. She found out what he's been saying about me.'

'So she stops talking to you? That's stupid.'

Jo shrugged. 'I kind of understand her. It's the sort of thing my mother would do. Too bloody proud. She'll get over it.' Jo's face was drawn, the whites of her eyes laced with broken blood vessels. Noticing Beth's scrutiny, she turned away.

She's been crying, Beth thought.

———

The school bus trundled along Dairy Road, then turned left onto Fivepence Lane, passing Dr Graydon's laboratory. Hemming Heights receded and the Jugamai hills grew larger, rougher, higher. The bus shifted down a few gears, engine labouring around a succession of hairpin bends.

One too many bends for Natasha Stotte, who noisily threw up on her seat. Two other girls in her clique followed suit. Irritated, the bus driver pulled over at a scenic viewpoint and ordered everyone to disembark while he cleaned up.

Conformists,' said Jo, watching students milling about.

Eventually the trip resumed. Soon they were in the boulder-littered highlands.

Ooralloo village was small and half hidden by trees. The houses were mostly weatherboard, and freshly painted. An old and straight-backed man with a white beard walked onto the road and waved to them.

'That's Jack Netcher,' said Mr Flack. 'Our guide for the day.'

The class piled out and stood self-consciously in the street. Mr Netcher ambled across to them, grinning.

'Where are the kids?' said Irene loudly.

Jack laughed. 'At school! We have our own school. European stuff and our ways as well.'

He took them on a tour. At each stop, an elder would come out and explain another aspect of local aboriginal culture to them. Beth wondered how much of the culture still lived, and how much was just memory, or memories of memories.

After lunch on an expanse of lawn, young men acted out several of the Gugamai people's legends, involving wars, frogs, seduction and, to Beth's disappointment, no dragons.

Jack was proudest of the Ooralloo Art College, an airy wooden building with vast windows. 'This is the college of arts. Notice, no dot paintings. My people never painted in that way. That's the fellas up north. We paint all different styles anyhow.

And sculptures. You know what the worst thing about bein' first peoples these days is?'

A few kids shook their heads.

'People expect us to only do tribal stuff. Carve boomerangs, skin possums, all that type of thing. If I said, 'I'm writing a book, most people think it would be about my people. But maybe it'd be about dance, or business. This is our world, too.'

Jack was an accomplished showman. Two hours had passed and few of the students were showing any signs of restlessness. On one occasion Beth realised she hadn't thought of the dragon for over half an hour.

Sarah remained distant, avoiding both Beth and Jo. By contrast, Jo was almost excessively chatty, as if trying to distract herself.

'Questions?' Jack asked.

Irene's hand shot up. 'Do you have television?'

'Oh yeah,' Jack drawled, 'I'm a *South Park* guy, myself.'

Beth coughed and raised her hand.

'Mr Netcher. What did your people eat before Europeans got here?'

He smiled and held up a hand. 'Good question. But if I told you that, I'd be doin' Mara's job for her.'

Mara was a large and loud woman with wild black hair, spinning jokes and tales so fast that Beth heard only one word in three. 'Well then,' she stated. 'I don't s'pose you know much about bush tucker. 'Cept the stuff you pop with your cap opener.'

She launched into a long discussion of the food gathering knowledge possessed by traditional aboriginal women. 'That's the supermarket,' she said, waving at the bush, 'and I'm goin' to take you down a few of the aisles.'

Mr Flack stayed behind to yarn with Jack. Mara took the class into the forest, stopping frequently, explaining the way her people used the forest.

'This is woman's work,' she said, 'collectin' the roots, plants, most of the food.'

'Sexists here, too,' Jo muttered.

Mara shook her head and smiled. 'Can't judge the old time life by modern standards, you know. It's not so bad, eh? There's power in this job, right. Knowledge. We know what cures, and what poisons. Good tastin' stuff, and bad. How to stop babies, how to make babies. Not that I'm gonna tell you young people about that kinda stuff.' She cackled lewdly. 'Not that I need to nowadays.'

A few metres on they halted before a stand of tree ferns. 'Good tucker,' Mara said, patting a trunk. 'Take out the centre and bake it. Like potatoes, really.'

Or bad turnips, thought Beth, with a jolt. She felt as if the dragon was right behind her.

Mara talked for another half-hour, drawing a surprising number of questions from the boys in the class. All the while Beth thought about the ferns, and pondered how to broach the topic with Mara or any of the other locals.

Time up, they walked back to the bus, chattering loudly. Mr Flack began to thank the elders, and the students actually applauded, a first in Beth's experience.

Time to do some research, she thought, and struck away from her fellows. She saw Mara standing alone, and walked over to her, feeling nervous. Her palms were sweaty. 'Excuse me.'

'Yes, girl? You want to know where the dunnies are?'

'Uh, no. I'm sorry.' *Don't apologise.* 'My name's Beth.' She felt unsure of what she was about to say. 'I would like to do a project on your people for school,' she improvised. 'Would you mind if I came up here and talked with you some time next week? Asked some questions?'

Mara looked at her for a few seconds, eyes searching Beth's face as if looking for minute character flaws. 'We're living, don't forget,' said Mara with some force. 'Don't think we're some dead thing from the past, you know. This place is not a museum.'

'Of course,' said Beth quickly. 'But I want to ask about your history too. It's very interesting.'

Mara smiled, her inquisitorial expression gone. The abrupt transition startled Beth. 'Oh, sure. You seem like a nice kid. Call me and make an appointment. Bus comes up here from Goolgoorook twice a day.' She handed Beth a card with phone, email address and a web address. Beth examined it, noting a border of animal shapes that ran around the business name: *Ooralloo Native Fine Foods Pty. Ltd.*

'You're wanted,' said Mara, pointing back towards the bus. Sure enough, expectant faces were turned her way. Mr Flack had a very odd expression on his normally placid face — almost angry, but also curious. *He wants to know what Mara was telling me*, Beth realised. *Why?*

'I'll see you then,' said Beth to Mara, wishing she could have all her questions answered now.

—•—

Jo's conversation dried up on the way back to Goolgoorook. As the town drew closer she became agitated.

'What's wrong?' asked Beth.

No reply. Jo angled her face away until it was mashed up against the bus window.

'So … I'm getting the silent treatment now.'

Jo turned back to her. 'You are the most impatient person I know.' She put a hand on Beth's arm and began to cry silently. 'I should tell you something before you come around for dinner.'

'Is it your Dad?'

A fresh surge of tears dripping on to Jo's jumper. 'He's in jail.'

'What!?' Heads turned along the length of the bus. Gossip was the only thing in Goolgoorook that travelled faster than the speed of light.

'Shhh. Big ears everywhere. He was arrested in Fiji.'

'What for? A mistake?'

Jo shook her head.

'They found drugs in his luggage. Lots of them.'

Beth gasped. 'What sort?'

'Amphetamines, I think. It doesn't matter. He wants Mum to go to Fiji and bring some money for bail. Probably to bribe people with too.'

'Will she? Bribe people?'

'She's so mad at him, Beth. She always thought he was honest. But she didn't know much about his business.'

'Why hasn't this been in the news yet?'

'No charges yet. Waiting to see how much he can pay.'

'God, how awful. Should I come tonight?'

'Of course! Mum's already neurotic. She thinks people in town will avoid her if they hear of this. She's right, you know. She's tried so hard to be accepted, but she's an outsider.'

'I'll come straight home with you after school,' said Beth. 'Mum knows I'm going already.'

29

Mrs Aarons gave no sign of her problems. Her face serene and long dark hair tied back, she greeted them at the door wearing an embroidered cornflower blue sari.

'Park your bikes down the side, girls. Come in, Beth. How's things? You're looking tall. Pretty, too,' she laughed. 'Almost a grown woman.'

'Still working on that,' said Beth, embarrassed.

She liked the interior of the Aarons house — simple timber furniture, white walls, a courtyard with a small fountain and enough indoor pot plants to make the place feel like a jungle.

Sitting in the lounge, they dipped pappadums into cucumber and yoghurt. 'Your mother says you've had some tremors,' said Sylvia. 'Your house, I mean.'

Beth started a little. She was now so inured to secrecy on the subject that she forgot that other people knew anything about it.

'Sort of. Dad thinks the ground is settling under the house. They can't agree on it.' *I'll have to talk this down, now. Don't want people getting too interested.*

Gradually Jo cheered up a little, and began to join the conversation. After a few minutes, dinner was ready, and they went into the dining room. The chairs were so heavy Beth had trouble pulling hers back. They ate large portions of chilli prawns, curried lamb, creamed spinach and rice.

'I'm as fat as a puppy,' said Beth. 'Really outstanding.'

'My cooking is not so bad, eh?' Sylvia smiled and raised her eyebrows at Jo. 'That is not what my daughter says sometimes.'

'That's only when you try to blow my head off with chilies,' said Jo. She put a hand on her mother's arm.

'It is good for your digestion.'

———

Afterwards, they played twenty one and poker for Monopoly money. Sylvia distracted them with small talk and consequently won most hands.

'This Lenny Crappit ...'

'Cra*bb*it,' Jo corrected her mother.

'He is bad news, no? Spits on Josie. Disrespects everyone.'

'Everyone at school hates him,' said Beth. 'Jo's popular with all the nice kids.'

Jo rolled her eyes.

'And he hates them,' said Sylvia. 'When I was growing up in Fiji, I saw bad things between Fijians and Indians. Bigots on both sides. But most people got along.'

'Lenny's sister is nice,' said Beth.

'Ah yes. True. My goodness, that poor girl. Such a brother! I must invite her to dinner too, one night. Maybe I'll need to go away for a while before that, though.'

Jo took Beth to see her latest paintings, the ones she didn't bring to school. Some were small and detailed, others large and gestural. All were vividly coloured.

'You could make a living now,' said Beth, impressed.

'Artists don't make a living,' said Jo scornfully. 'They scrape by. Who wants to starve?'

'Me.'

'Oh, bollocks,' said Jo. 'Would you like to stay over?' she asked, 'Mum can let your parents know. The lounge folds out. We can watch a DVD. Got a few new ones. You can borrow a set of Mum's pyjamas.'

'No thanks' left Beth's brain but never arrived at her mouth. Jo needed at least one reliable friend. *But I need to go and talk to a creature in my cellar. Who is certainly hungry and probably angry with me. I'd better bring him ten bags of food tomorrow night.*

'That'd be great.'

The movie — involving time travel, the search for the Holy Grail and a shootout in an abandoned warehouse — was entertaining. Sylvia served them ice cream as the credits rolled.

'Do you think Sar will get back to normal?' Beth asked.

'Probably,' said Jo. 'Don't set a deadline.'

Beth didn't enjoy sleeping away from home. Her bedroom was a familiar place, while her friends' houses had odd shadows and unexpected noises. Other families had different rules, and she was afraid of breaking them. Still, it was nice to fall asleep without fear of waking under the house. She slept well, and her dreams evaporated without trace on waking.

Up early, Beth made herself toast and a cup of black tea. She stood in the lounge, studying a photograph of Jo with her mother and father. Mr Aarons was tall and handsome, with silvered hair at the temples and a broad bandit-style moustache. *Like a young Omar Sharif,* she thought. Footsteps crossed the floor behind her.

'Bastard,' said Jo, on her way to the bathroom. 'He could sell anyone anything.'

'What's your mum doing today?'

'Going to the bank. They had a joint account, you see — it might be seized. Proceeds of crime and all that. She wants it all in cash before that happens.'

School was only a short ride from Jo's home. They played computer games until ten to nine and were five minutes late to their first class.

Tuesday 14 March

30

Sarah greeted them. 'Sorry about the excursion,' she managed. 'Bit off-colour from the drive.'

'I hope you took some notes from yesterday,' Beth said. 'I didn't write anything down.'

'I was hanging with the jocks,' said Sarah. 'But I have all the photocopies. I thought classrooms were meant to be paperless.'

Flack glimpsed Beth in four places around the school during the long, hot day, but she quickly slipped away each time. She hid during lunch time, avoiding her usual haunts and friends, creeping around like a wraith. Finally, just as she felt confident that he had given up on his quest for the day, he sneaked up on her as she tried to leave early during the last free study period. They stood alone on an uninhabited expanse of shadeless concrete.

'You're trying to avoid me,' he accused her, but without any heat. 'That golden … *thing* is driving me to distraction.' She became very still. *God, he knows about it as well. What was I thinking when I gave him the scale?*

'What do you mean?'

'I'm *certain* it's real. It comes from something genuine — organic. Some sort of animal. I know that from just the way it smells. I've been through all the books, checked the Internet, rung the state museum — nothing. They think I'm batty. *I* feel like I'm batty.' He looked at her expectantly. 'I know you've got at least one more of these, Beth. Otherwise you'd want this back, no? You haven't asked once.'

'I trust you, Mr Flack,' she said. She shifted from one foot to another. *What kind of fool am I? Why not just tell him?* 'I just found it.' She shrugged. 'I know what you mean about the smell, though. It's something.'

'You're lying,' he said. 'I thought I could trust you. That you wanted my assistance.'

'I did … I *do*. But *you* haven't given me anything useful. I *need* answers.' Beth tried for anger and it felt half genuine. 'I haven't done anything wrong, Mr Flack. This is nothing to do with school,' she said. 'It's not really your business.'

'I know that,' he said, 'but the dreams … maybe they have changed me somehow … I can't put my finger on it.'

'Look, if I find anything else like that,' she said, seeing his anguish, 'I'll bring it to you.'

He looked at her. 'I almost wish you'd never showed me. It's all I can think of.'

———

Final bell sounded and students sprinted for home. Jo was staying behind for violin lessons.

'See you soon,' she said. 'Mum enjoyed having you over. She could pretend everything's alright.'

'But everything *is* going to be alright.'

'Yeah, right. Even if he skips jail,' Jo said, 'Things will have changed. For good. And if he gets sentenced …'

'Are there any local politicians we can write to?' Beth asked and Jo's mouth quirked momentarily.

'Australians aren't exactly popular in Fiji, Beth. I'll see you tomorrow, eh?'

Beth nodded and walked away.

—•—

'You out of here?' Sarah asked. 'Me too. Hey, race?'

Beth bolted, catching Sarah by surprise. Sarah quickly drew level and then sprinted ahead. Beth jogged the last few metres. She stood to catch her breath, surveyed the dust and bike racks ahead.

'Hey, my bike is gone.'

Searching up and down each row, she still couldn't see it.

'I locked it, Sar. I *know* I did. Shit! Bastards!' She kicked at a signpost.

'Look!!' said Sarah, and pointed to the Moreton Bay fig that shaded the racks. Beth's bike was hanging by a frayed length of rope from a low-hanging branch.

'Wha—'

The bike was badly damaged. Most of the spokes had been ripped from their sockets and twisted into a spaghetti of wire. The seat was broken and scratches scored into the bike's paintwork.

'It's wrecked,' said Sarah wonderingly.

'Hey, bitch!' Lenny stood by the fence, hair a crazy ruin.

'Bitch!' he repeated. 'Or didn't ya hear me?'

'Lenny,' Sarah said, 'what the hell?'

'Shut up! None of ya business. Go home.'

Beth looked up at the bike, and back at Lenny.

'Did you ...'

He shrugged violently. 'Your best friend is a darkie. You went and visited more of 'em today. And you hang around with my sister.'

'You're a joke,' said Beth. 'You cheap, gutless piece of sh—'.
She stopped herself. He was still Sar's brother. Out of the
corner of her eye, she saw Sarah stoop and pick something up.
A moment later, a lump of dry clay struck Len in the chest. Hard.
He stumbled, grabbing for the fence, but another pelted into
his leg and he fell.

'Wha—? Christ, that hurt! Stop it!'

A hard and accurate rain fell on Len, propelled by Sarah's
javelin-honed arm. Beth bent and grabbed a clod, heaving it
with less effect than Sarah. Their target was running hard, then
stopped abruptly, holding his ear. He screamed something that
might have been a threat had distance not made it unintelligible.
They stood and watched him disappear.

'All guts when he's on his own,' said Sarah.

Mr Flack, Mrs Dowling, and Mr Singh arrived on the scene
five minutes late. 'Is that your bike?' asked Singh. Flack was
out of breath.

Beth nodded hesitantly, glancing at Sarah for guidance and
not receiving any.

'From what Mr Flack has passed on to me,' observed Mrs
Dowling, 'I don't think we need to ask who did this. We'll give
the two of you a lift home. We'll write this up tomorrow.'

Mr Singh pulled the bike down, then placed the wreckage in
the boot of Flack's car. They all got in and drove away.

'I hate him,' Sarah ground out, almost under her breath. She
couldn't look at Beth.

To think I thought my life was boring, thought Beth. *Now I've
got a psycho neo-Nazi after me and a fire-breathing dream-beast
under the cellar. Oh, and my best friend's dad trafficks in narcotics.
How am I supposed to get the ferns now — or the dog food?*

Mr Flack helped her carry her bike onto the lawn. 'I'm very sorry about all of this, Beth. Come and see me tomorrow. Tell Nick I'll be in touch as soon as possible.' Beth nodded and glanced at the bike.

Nick met her at the front door, hugged her hard. 'Noelene Crabbit was on the phone. About her son and your bike. Where is it?'

She gestured.

He released her, whistled. 'You alright?'

'Yep.' Beth suddenly felt close to tears — the sympathy of others always had that effect on her.

'Noelene apologised. Said she'd foot the bill. I heard Jacob Crabbit in the background telling her not to give us a cent. Said you made Sarah cry.'

'Jacob and Len are completely insane,' Beth said, then described the incident. All the while she was thinking of Len's face and the set of his features.

'I'm driving you to school tomorrow,' Nick said.

'Dad …'

'This is going to be a police matter, Beth.'

'But Sarah … I can't tell them *everything*. Sarah's my friend.'

'I know you want to protect her,' Nick said firmly, 'but what about Jo? Think about her safety. This guy's capable of violence.' He gave her another hug and straightened up. 'Tone this down a bit for Abbie, will you? She's, uh, fragile at the moment.'

Who isn't? Beth thought, but she nodded.

Nick phoned for pizza, saying he wasn't in the mood to master the kitchen. This excuse had always served him well. Soon enough the delivery boy arrived and Beth discovered she was very hungry, as well as shaky.

'Some girl on the phone!' shouted Sam, 'she sounds a bit simple.'

Beth gulped another mouthful of pizza and aimed a rough karate kick at her brother. He blocked the blow and delivered a playful punch to her side.

'Ooof. Piss off, Sam.' Into the phone: 'Jo? You heard the little maniac? Of course he knew it was you. How's your mum?' She fell onto the couch.

Jo's voice was low and guarded. 'She's fine. Tougher than I thought. Can't say much — she might hear me. Hey, I heard about Len. Mr Singh told Mum about it. Crazy shite.'

'There was more to it than Singh knew. You should have seen Len's face. Spacko.'

'He's a car without brakes,' Jo mused, 'going down a very steep hill.'

'And full of explosives.'

31

Abbie arrived home very late, looking worn. Nick kneaded her shoulders as she sipped a cup of tea. Beth lay on a beanbag in the corner of the lounge, staring at the roof. She listened to her mother complain about her current job and worry about future moves.

Beth sat up, hoping to steal away quietly, but her mother looked over.

'Good day, Beth?'

'Like sand through the hourglass,' she said. She began to speak, stopped, started again. 'Mum, can I borrow thirty dollars?'

'What for? No, don't answer that. We said we'd trust you. Take it out of my purse — you know where it is. Pay me back later.'

'Thanks a lot.' Beth turned to go, and *knew* they were exchanging knowing glances. The boy thing again, probably.

Sam grabbed her shirt as she started along the corridor to her room.

'Leggo, you little creep.'

'Charming. Guess what?'

She shrugged.

'Uncle Henry's coming around next week! He's back from Siberia or wherever. He called before Mum got home.'

Henry Ormonde spent his life on the road, as far from responsibility and routine as he could manage. Hence he was a natural hero for those imprisoned at school. Beth often found it hard to believe her solid, career-minded father and Henry were brothers.

Despite herself, Beth smiled. That *was* genuinely good news. 'Why didn't they say something about it?'

'Um, hello, Beth. Reality check. Mum's not feeling that great. And Dad's a bit distracted by your Lenny problem.'

'*I'm* doing stuff with Henry this time,' she said, continuing her room-ward journey. 'You're not taking over.'

Sam waited until she was at her door before clearing his throat. She turned to look at him, immediately wary at his mock-concerned expression.

'Would you know where Freddy's bag of biscuits has gone?' he asked.

She shook her head, poker face. He held out his hands to cut off any answer. 'One at a time — no, don't tell me. Don't tell me — I already know! You keep them in a bowl, and eat 'em like crackers.'

'You're talking shite.'

'Didn't you read the pack?' he asked, 'Not for human consumption. Whoops. At least you'll have glossy fur and healthy bones. Arf!' Sam's laughter quickly faded when a dimly heard parent ordered him to bed.

32

Beth waited two long hours, eager to go down into the cellar again. While she waited, she sat at her desk and wrote on a few scraps of paper. *Things I want to ask the dragon.* When she was down in the cellar, her mind seemed somehow less active, less questioning. If she made up a few prompts for herself up here perhaps she could hold onto her wits a little longer down there.

There is another possibility, she thought, twisting her mouth into a crooked smile. *That the tremors have released some kind of gas into the cellar. That I'm imagining the entire thing.* She snorted aloud.

As she wrote, her parents were talking, their voices low and serious. Beth felt sure she was the subject of their conversation. Other noises also made it to her ears: judging from the sounds Beth heard, Sam had escaped the confines of his room, pattering back and forth, doing something obscure, probably spying on her to boot. Finally a door opened, Nick's voice boomed out and instructed his son to stop mucking around and go to sleep, and the house became still.

A bag of dog food cradled in her arms, Beth went past the open padlock, shut the door quietly behind her and stepped into the lair. 'I'm here.' She turned on the light. Her feet crunched on the debris-strewn floor. 'Come on, I'm back.'

Somewhere up above a possum shrieked and hissed. Beth waited. And waited.

'Why am I helping you? Why am I so easily led?'

Nothing.

'I've got a pack of Meaty Bites,' she offered. 'Nice and fresh.'

A huffing, aggrieved gust burst from the hole. Beth sat on the milk crate, suddenly very relieved. 'Sorry I didn't come down here last night. I couldn't.'

'I can be patient,' said the dragon, sounding both distant and disturbingly near. 'I've been down here in the cold and dirt a long time. Dreaming, slowly waking.'

Beth puffed vapour. 'What do you do all day?'

'I remember, a little at a time. It is always like this when I wake. I have many memories to savour.'

'Do you know how old you are, then?'

'I can't explain things the way you would, Beth. What is a year? It means little to me: simply an odd idea. I see larger patterns. Longer patterns.'

Beth reached into her pocket. Her list of questions was crumpled and faint, and she hesitated before reading out the first. What had seemed insightful now felt simple-minded, and that which had appeared clever now struck her as naive.

'Um ... Where do you come from?'

'I think I knew once, but no longer. Such ideas are difficult for my kind. Maybe here, maybe there. No place is home, everywhere is.' Unexpectedly, he chuckled, and the sound was of stone and fire and darkness. Beth's hands clenched tightly. 'I was always capable of thought, but humans taught me to speak,' he said. 'Sorrow came after that.'

Beth nudged the Meaty Bites forward. 'How do you eat this?'

'Inhalation.'

'Like a vacuum cleaner?'

'I've swallowed many other objects with this food. Pieces of metal and wood. Machines. If you prefer I'll wait until you're gone, before I eat this.'

'Could you eat me?' Beth asked, then fell silent. How *stupid* could a person get? Capability was not an issue, just intent. She felt an instant of primal fear.

'My kind long ago learned that humans are better left alive and undigested. If one is struck down, then the others come forth, like wasps.'

For a few minutes he stopped talking. 'Better leave, Beth,' he said abruptly, 'My heart quickens. Muscles stretch — my body stirs. Not something I have full control over.' A low rumble grew, and the much-abused house shook quietly. She was seeing a quake from the underground up. The dragon's scent was full of fire.

'Bring me more food, tomorrow — if you can. As much as possible. More. Always more.'

'Tomorrow,' she whispered. 'I won't forget.'

The dragon's mini-tremor had died down by the time she made it upstairs, and might not have caused any upset if the smoke alarm hadn't begun to sound once more. She bolted to her room, running on tip-toe.

Turning out the light, she lay in bed, straining to hear her father padding around the house. After a while she rose, cracked the door a millimetre or so and listened. 'False alarm,' she heard Nick say to Abbie a few minutes later, 'though there was an odd smell. Reminded me of something. Rotten eggs, perhaps.'

'The house was shaking,' said Abbie, refusing to be diverted from her prime concern. 'You said the subsidence was all finished …'

Wednesday 15 March

33

Nick drove her to school, stopping close to the front gate. He leaned over and kissed her forehead. 'Here's your taxi money. I can't make it in to pick you up this evening.'

'I'll walk, then.'

'No you won't. Not until things are sorted out.'

'Yeah, right. Like *that's* possible. What about the police? You wanted me to report Len.'

'Speak to Mr Flack about it. He'll sort things out. Len's still missing, by the way.'

Nick grasped her arm and gave her a solemn look. 'If there's anything else wrong, you'd let us know … wouldn't you?'

'Yeah …' Beth said, 'but there isn't. Just normal stuff, and you can't help me with that.' Her father released her arm.

'I'm alright, Dad,' she said.'

After science, Beth did as her father directed, and raised the matter of Len with Flack. Bizarrely, Flack made a point of ignoring her, deflecting all her questions with the same suggestion: to go see the principal and stop bothering him. She didn't know which tack to take. She raised her voice. 'How am I supposed to sort out Len?' she asked.

'Ask the principal,' he said. 'Your problem is not my problem. I've got some essays to mark.' While he talked he kept one hand in his jacket pocket, fist bunched as if holding something.

'You're not much bloody use,' said Beth, in an attempt to get some kind of reaction, but Mr Flack gave her a look of such indifference that she went away.

Why on earth would he behave like that? She stood in a deserted section of corridor shaking her head slowly. Mr Flack was one of Len's nemeses at school, and surely wanted to have him expelled or punished.

You're being a fool, she thought. *This is about the scale, not Len. He was holding it while we were talking. It has an effect on him. I did the wrong thing in telling him anything. Now he's going to blunder around looking for answers.*

Beth shuddered and hurried away to class.

—•—

Geography was up next and after making a late entrance, Beth sat with Sarah.

'What happened last night?' Beth whispered.

'Last night?'

'At your place. You know, about Len.'

'I didn't go home, Beth. Aunt Emma put me up.' She turned her head away.

Beth coloured with embarrassment.

'Sarah— '

'Girls!' said Mrs Honeycutt. Heads swivelled like clowns at a sideshow. 'I don't think it's about the third world this time, is it? Conversations are for lunchtime. Outside!'

They stood uncomfortably in the corridor. Two police officers — a young woman and an overweight older man — walked past, leather belts, holsters and shoes creaking.

Sarah became very pale. 'They've reported Len. The school.'

She didn't say 'because of your bike,' but Beth felt guilty all the same. Silence grew again.

When the class finally ended, Sarah walked off, arms tightly folded.

'He's *your* brother,' Beth said in a whisper, 'don't blame me.'

———

Recovered after several days of illness, Mrs Speck finally made it to Maths class, clutching a multicoloured handkerchief and sneezing constantly.

'Well enough to spread the disease,' said Beth, disgusted.

'Ib been sick,' Speck said, sniffing thickly. 'Lebs do integrals today, children.'

Her whiteboard scrawls were less legible than ever.

'The cops came to talk to Len,' said Jo, 'but he left before lunch.'

'I know. Sarah hates me,' said Beth. 'Or something close to that.'

'She'll get over it. We'll invite her to *She's all Over* at the City Twin. Hear it's only moderately crappy.'

'Oh, that'll work!' Beth hissed. 'Len'll probably come along and attack all three of us at once.'

'Quiet, girlbs,' said Speck, half hidden behind foggy glasses, 'you're far too noiby.'

———

During lunch, sitting on a grassy rise on the south side of the school, Jo seemed on the verge of saying something.

'You're gloomier than I am,' said Beth.

'I've got something to ask you.'

'Sure ...'

'If Mum has to go to Fiji after all ... would you be willing to come over for a few nights? Until Uncle Niladri can come up from Sydney, anyway. Otherwise I'll be on my own and if I am, Mum probably won't go.'

Beth hesitated a fatal moment, and Jo's hesitant smile vanished. 'Not if it's *too* much trouble, Beth.'

'Wait, I didn't say *anything*.'

'Sarah was going on about you again the other day.'

'Oh?'

'She thinks that you don't give a shit about us anymore.'

Beth opened her mouth to protest. A little knot of anger began to flare within.

'Nothing matters to you,' Jo said, 'except the things you're interested in.'

'Shove it, Jo!' she snarled. 'You could say that about anyone. I've got my own problems! *You* keep to yourself when it suits you.'

'Does it suit you now?'

'Jo, I want to come over. I will. It's just ... I have to do something every night. I don't have a *choice*,' she said pleadingly.

Her friend's face changed. 'Well. I don't know what it is that you need to *do*. It must be important, hey? I'll see you on Monday.'

34

A light rain drifted in from the Jugamai Hills. Autumn was slowly unfurl itself. Beth slowly and disconsolately wandered home, a heavy shopping bag in each hand. She had spent her taxi money on three packets of Glossy Kote Dog Food, an exercise book and waterproof-ink pen. She wished that Len would appear.

'I would rip your head off,' she whispered. 'Damn Len. Damn Jo. Damn the dragon. Damn everyone.'

Nothing was worth losing friends and feeling so confused. She reached the yard and stowed the bags beneath a dripping banksia.

Her parents were in the city, according to a note on the fridge.

'Probably checking out a new house,' Sam predicted gloomily. 'We'll have to live in some tiny little place when Mum gets the job. Houses cost a lot more in the city, you know.'

Beth slumped into a lounge chair. *Maybe we should leave. Get as far away as possible.* She felt as though her brain was the floor of a stock market, thoughts screaming and jumping for attention. *Stay and finish the thing you have started. You must help those who need it.*

She glanced over at Sam, wondering what had slowed the usual drip of observations and insults that he usually produced. Sitting on the lounge room floor, he was building a landscape with plasticine, using blue for mountains and rivers, green for foothills, yellow to represent pasture land, and black for roads and vehicles. The whole affair rested on a thin piece of craftwood and looked about half finished. He had a large map open on the floor.

'Do you recognise it?' he asked her.

She looked harder at the model. A town sprawled along a winding river, beneath a series of high plateaux. 'It's us,' she realised, impressed. Every little fold of the Jugamai Hills stood out. Sam pointed to a rise just before the town.

'Hemming Heights.'

'Not too shabby,' she was forced to admit. 'Is it a school project, then?'

'Just for me,' said Sam. He glanced at her. 'I know something you don't.'

Beth scowled. 'Spare me.'

'Dad says you keep setting off the smoke detector.'

'Bull.' She felt sick.

'I heard them talking last night, after the alarm went off.' Sam waited, but Beth said nothing. 'Dad said "where's there's fire there must be smoke".'

'I don't get it.'

'Must be *smoke*, Bethy. Think about it.'

They think I smoke?'

'Dad does, anyway. Yep. Puffing away in the laundry.'

'I've never had a cigarette in my life,' she said, amazed.

'Uh. He's not thinking about *cigarettes*. Other stuff.'

'Weed? Oh, God. It gets worse. Dad asked me if I had any problems this morning.'

'That'd be the one, then. That thirty bucks Mum loaned you? They both think you might have used that.'

'And what did *you* say?'

'Nothing. I didn't tell them anything. No, I might have said it wasn't enough to buy much. Not that I would know.' As he spoke he began to tidy up his model, packing away unused plasticine, putting a cloth over the rest and moving it to a half empty shelf along the far wall.

'OK,' Beth said, easing up. 'Even though there *was* nothing *to* tell.'

Sam shook his head slightly. 'You're not smoking. I know that. But you *have* got a secret,' he said. 'I can smell it.'

Beth sighed. She wanted to stop thinking. Stop being. Stop doing. 'Just back off, Sam. For your own good.' She placed a hand on his arm. 'Thanks for putting the olds off the trail. I don't even know *what* to say.'

'You only give away the things that don't really matter to you. I know. I'm selfish, too. It's in our genes.'

There's a thirty year old in his head, Beth thought. 'If I was as clever as you,' she said, 'you'd never even know I had any secrets.'

'Finished tidying up.' he said. 'I'm going to bed.' He placed his index finger and middle finger below his eyes, then pointed both fingers at her. 'Watching you,' he said. His bedroom door closed quietly a few moments later.

Beth waited a very long time until she was sure that Sam *had* to be asleep.

35

Tonight, the dragon sounded much sharper. Last night's food was gone.

'I have more.' Beth dumped the bags on the floor. 'As much as I could carry, anyway. I guess you're so big — I mean, you really *have* to be, and I have no idea how this could be of any use. Wouldn't you need tonnes of the stuff? Not just a bag. Maybe I'm not being all that helpful.'

'The world has changed, hasn't it?' said the dragon. 'More than any other time I've reawakened. There are so many of you now. So little space left for everything else. I've been listening to those devices you have upstairs.'

'The radio? And the television? The television's not just sound, you know. They have moving pictures.'

'No matter. You all talk — talk all the time. Just to hear a voice. Not to be lonely, to know that the world is full of people.'

'There's a girl at school who spends half her life in front of it. The television.'

The dragon laughed, a great gust of hot air. *At least, I think that was a laugh. Or was it some expression of disgust?*

'Once, humans walked everywhere. Or rode horses. Now the engines go everywhere — I feel their hum.'

'We fly, too. And go into space.'

'Your machines burn, yet are not afire. The air is full of their smell. Repulsive. Much I do not understand.'

I can't explain everything to him.

'What is science, Beth? I keep hearing the word on the talking machines. It seems important. A new religion?'

'Not quite. A way of looking at the world, I suppose. No, it's more than that.'

She thought hard about her answer. Science at her school was a tedious wander through textbooks dog-eared by many readers. On the other hand, she had read a fair number of popular science books.

'It's sort of an investigation, where you don't make any unfounded assumptions. Scientists come up with ideas about the world, and test them.'

He needs a genius to fill him in on the modern world, not someone who draws pictures instead of listening in class.

'Look,' Beth said, 'I'm not going to be much help on this sort of thing. I'll bring you some books, if you like, and read them to you. Maybe some of it will be useful. Better than listening to television.'

'Well,' he rumbled, 'come and read to me — that will bring back memories.' *He sounds pleased.*

She felt uncomfortable at craving his approval. 'Dragon. I want something in return.'

'Nothing to offer, down here.'

'I want *your* story.'

'Too many faces, Beth,' he whispered, barely audible, 'too many sorrows. I must go now, sleep opens her wings.'

'But you come from *somewhere*,' she implored. 'You did things, you must remember them. You weren't born down in this hole, you were up the world. All those legends about you and your kind.'

'I'm just an animal who can talk,' whispered the dragon. 'Why would a human be interested?'

'You're the most interesting thing I've ever seen — or found. And when you've woken up and gone, I don't want to have questions I forgot to ask. Maybe I can help you. This world might not be a good place for you.'

'Yet I must sleep. Let me consider ...' said the dragon, voice tailing off into a long declining hiss.

I'll ask you again,' Beth warned, but he failed to reply. She was a little amazed at her own boldness. Until tonight, she had felt constrained, thoughts bottled up inside her head. What *would* he do when he won free? She hadn't really considered how strange the world was going to be for the dragon. Finding food was hard enough, but where was he going to go? There were people *everywhere*. By helping him escape, was she engineering his destruction?

'Goodnight,' she called back down the stairs. *One does not say goodnight to a freaking dragon.* Leaving the cellar, the certainty she felt down slowly dissipated. *Isn't all of reality like that? An event becomes history, history becomes myth. The dragon was real once and now he's turned into a story that no-one believes. When they see he still lives, they'll need to kill him again to protect their myth.* 'Where's this coming from?' she asked herself.

Her door was slightly ajar, and she was sure she had left it closed. *Sam!* For a moment she was angry enough to consider barging into his room, but his light was off and it was late. He was probably just trying to bait her.

Saturday 18 March

36

Saturday was still young when Henry arrived in a gleaming Mustang coupe. Beth was upstairs.

'Sam,' she said, but when she looked out the window again, she saw her brother was already on the front lawn.

'Mum! Dad! Henry's here!' Beth called out as she strode towards the front door.

Abbie slunk out onto the front lawn. She nodded at Henry, clinched briefly, kissed him on the cheek and stood back. Nick was more enthusiastic, dishing out a vigorous handshake. 'Great to have you back, Henry. Felt like you were due here sometime — like smelling rain in the air.'

Sam was already close to Henry, looking up at him with open admiration. Not that Beth was any less free with her affections. 'Uncle Henry!!' she yelled, rushing forward and hugging him.

Henry had changed in the last year — a little more relaxed, a touch of grey at his temples. He was slender, light on his feet, a good looking man with a tendency to smile at private jokes. He took only his own advice and seemed without fear.

'Any new tattoos?' Sam asked.

Henry rolled up his shirtsleeve and showed them a tiny rearing dragon on his right forearm.

Beth stared at it. *Bloody hell.* 'What does that one mean?' she asked, making every effort to appear uninterested.

'It's my year,' explained Henry. 'Chinese, that is. Year of the fire-breathing lizard.'

'I'm a monkey,' said Sam.

'How apposite. Are you still an imp, Sam?'

'I try,' said Sam. 'I *was* in trouble, but Mum's forgotten all about it.'

'Disappointing.'

Henry drove them down to the Colonial Village Shopping Centre.

Sam leaned over from the back seat.

'What were you doing in Siberia?'

'I was spying for Australia,' he told them, 'counting oil wells and gold mines. Funny place. Mosquitoes as big as terriers. Dragonflies with a poisonous spike between their eyes. Spiders with a penchant for nesting in nice warm beds.'

'For real? said Sam.

37

Henry sprawled in the driver's seat, one arm loosely holding the wheel, the other hanging from the window, beating time on the bodywork. His plaid cap flew off and smacked Sam on the nose. Sam promptly tossed it out the window.

'I saw that. Pick it up on the way back, will you?'

'Can't, old tacker,' said Sam. 'You're dropping me off at my friend's place. Ken's.'

'Your oldest friend,' said Henry. 'I remember him. Overhanging brow, crooked teeth.'

The two of them had an insult competition going, a tradition of prankish one-upmanship. Beth felt a little jealous. Insults and teasing were a way of life in her family, and she didn't like being left out.

'Did you really see anything strange in Siberia?' she asked.

'Not unless pollution on a heroic scale qualifies. Russians really know how to despoil a landscape. Anything weird happening here?'

'I doubt it,' she said. 'We had a few earthquakes. That's all.'

'Oh Just a *little* earthquake?'

'No-one else in the street feels *our* earthquakes,' said Sam disappointedly.

They ate at the Tokyo Dragon Inn. The name made Beth smile a little. *Dragons everywhere.*

The tablecloths were checked vinyl, the chopsticks plastic, and each table had a small smudged bottle of soy sauce.

Sam ripped open three sugar sachets and spread them out more or less evenly on the table. 'Draw a map of Siberia.'

Henry moved sugar around. A waiter glanced over, shook his head.

'That's Lake Baikal, the largest freshwater lake in the world, and home of the only freshwater seal. One part in five of the world's fresh water is in that lake, and I sailed across it this summer.'

Many of Henry's stories contained an element of the incredible: that was part of their attraction.

Henry moved on to Siberian highways (potholed), Siberian cities (old and rundown) and the landscape (endless). The locals were mad, broke, drunk, crooked, generous, mixed up and Henry's kind of people.

A waiter arrived with their seaweed and rice. Sam ate so many nori rolls he began to groan.

'I'm such a pig,' he said. 'We going in the car again?'

'Is a one eyed duck in the woods the pope?' Henry asked.

As the trees and hills flickered past, Beth reflected on Sam. Whenever Henry was around she found Sam close to bearable. The eccentricities of his character seemed to match up with those of Henry. *It's all genetic,* she thought.

Presently, they dropped Sam off at Ken Dankovitz's place. Sam waved as the Mustang backed out of the drive. After picking up Henry's mangy, weather-beaten hat from the side of Dairy Road, Beth felt a sense of relief when Henry turned the car away from Goolgoorook.

'Let's go walking,' he suggested, and they drove to the foot of Mount Acute. He parked haphazardly and rummaged around in the glove box, finally extracting an odd-looking hand-woven bag with a long strap.

'Peruvian,' he said. 'For the water bottle.'

After only a few minutes of walking, he called for a rest stop.

'You get fitter …' he puffed, ' … every time … I come back … or I just get … older.'

'You just pretend to be out of shape,' she said, 'to make me feel better.'

During their rest-stops, she told him about Len Crabbit and his antics.

'A drongo,' Henry said mournfully. 'Would have been better if he *had* gone to Ooralloo. Might have shamed him a bit.' He contemplated that thought for a while, then brightened. 'Could try some kind of camp for people like Len. Take 'em out bush and let 'em fend for themselves. Make him learn bushcraft — maybe he'll appreciate the aboriginal side of things. Make a TV show out of it.'

She shook her head. 'Wouldn't work. Len's far gone. He looked like he wanted to kill me the other day.'

They walked upslope for some time, finally stopping at a daisy-speckled meadow.

'Very pretty,' said Henry. 'So report him yourself, then. Tell the police exactly what happened.'

Beth looked at Henry. *It's easy to say that kind of thing,* she thought.

'No-one gains if you stay silent, Beth. Not even him. Certainly not your friend Sarah. Or Jo.'

'Jo hasn't said she wants to do anything about it …'

'Then do it yourself, Beth. Don't wait for her. Morality isn't a product of consensus. It is what it is — you have to make unpalatable decisions.'

A ladder bolted into solid rock formed the final stage in the ascent of Mount Acute. Eventually, they leaned on the summit platform, taking in the all-encompassing view, dominated by the mighty Jugamai Plateau, home of the Gugamai. 'One day, this will all be yours,' said Henry, fanning a hand at the valley below.

Beth laughed, squinting fine patterns formed by roads and glinting lakes. Her home was too small to see, but she could follow the low ridge on which it had been built. Just like Sam's relief map.

'There's our place,' Beth said. 'More or less.'

'Hemming Heights,' said Henry unenthusiastically. 'Not really the scenic high point of the region. Or the cultural. I was rather hoping your parents might have chosen a farm.'

Beth smirked at the idea of Nick feeding cows or Abbie fixing fences. 'I might buy a place like that someday,' she said, 'but not to grow anything — just to look at the sunsets and go fishing along the river. If there's any land left by then.'

Beth tried to imagine the countryside when the dragon first began his sleep. He would have dug his burrow, expecting to emerge safely into a little-changed world.

'Don't tell your parents what I said about Hemming Heights,' said Henry. 'Strictly between you, me and the blue sky.'

After their descent of Mount Acute, Henry helped her to collect half a dozen tree ferns from a quiet dirt track just outside the park and bundle them into the boot.

'For a school project,' Beth said, and Henry nodded.

When Henry stopped to buy a few bottles of beer for Nick, Beth bought a large packet of Ambassador Dog Bikkies.

'If Mum and Dad are out, can you help me put all of this stuff in the cellar?'

'Should I ask what you're going to do with them?'

'No.'

Abbie and Nick were indeed elsewhere and Sam was not in evidence.

Henry followed her through the open cellar doorway and down the stairs, and stood beside her in the half-light.

He shook his head at the rents in the cellar walls. A moment later he whistled, as Sam once had, at the biggest of the apertures — the space through which Beth took her instructions. Henry's gaze strayed to the seat in the middle of the floor facing the crack, then to Beth.

'Strange place to come and think, isn't it? You don't think it could be dangerous?'

'No. It's quiet down here,' said Beth, willing him not to ask any more questions.

They had just finished unloading the ferns and the biscuits, and were leaving the cellar when Nick rounded the corner. He frowned.

'I didn't give you a key.'

'It was already open. Search me. I don't have a key.'

Nick turned to Henry, and smiled a little. 'Beth's a bit of a secretive girl, these days.'

'She was showing me the after-effects of the tremors.'

'Lucky Abbie's not here,' said Nick, putting a hand on Beth's shoulder. 'You'd set her off again if she saw you coming up those stairs.' He glanced at Henry in appeal. 'We were having some small tremors. Subsidence in the hill somewhere. Abbie got spooked. It's quietening down now.'

'Smells amazing down there,' Henry said. 'Hard to describe, though. Spilled wine? You must have kept some great vintages, Nicky.'

Nick shook his head. 'We drink the good stuff as soon as we buy it.'

She watched them walk away and made her own escape. Inviting Henry down into the cellar had been yet another in a long line of bad mistakes. She hadn't liked the way he looked around. For a moment she had felt he was about to guess the whole thing.

38

Beth spent half an hour choosing a suitable book for that night's session in the cellar. *I know a bit. Not much compared to some people, but I must be better than nothing. Catcher in the Rye?* No. What was the point? *Lord of the Rings?* Too long-winded. *Why don't I spell out a modern idea to him? He asked about science the other night.*

She scanned the titles of her pop sci collection. Finally, her finger stuck on the spine of a book she had recently read when she was supposed to be studying biology: *Climbing Mount Improbable,* by Richard Dawkins. *Kind of appropriate, really.*

At midnight, Beth crept forth with unlit torch in hand, slinking along the corridor towards the cellar door. She had Dawkins and a notebook in her other hand.

'Beth!'

She gripped the torch convulsively. 'Who … ?'

'Who? Who? The night owl, of course.' Uncle Henry stood at the edge of the kitchen area, a slice of toast in one hand, smiling. 'Doing the devil's errands?' he asked.

'Watering. I was going to check the ferns.'

'And take notes? Read them a book, too? S'posed to make plants grow faster. Though perhaps not in cellars.'

'I keep records of the cracks down there. How fast they're growing. I want to tell Dr Graydon about them. And sometimes I feel like reading.'

'A true heroine of science. Remember that smell, earlier? From the cellar?'

'The wine?'

'I *thought* it was wine, but no. It's something else. Just can't quite figure out what.'

'I dunno,' said Beth. 'I'd better get back to bed.'

'Without your notes?'

'Tomorrow,' she muttered. 'Don't feel like it anymore.'

39

In bed, she listened for any signs of movement in the cellar, but heard nothing. She imagined Henry going into the dragon's lair in her place and making arrangements to deliver more food than she ever could. He would be a better conversationalist too. Beth fidgeted, dropped into light sleep, woke, drowsed again.

She knuckled her eyes and groaned. Incredibly, daytime had already arrived. Even more improbably, Abbie was sitting at the foot of her bed, wearing her patented Worried Mother Look.

'I'm concerned about you, Beth.'

'Everyone is. You should buy tickets and I'll perform for you all. Sam said you think ...'

'Don't be facetious. It's got nothing to do with Sam.' She patted Beth's leg. 'Dear, your father is worried about you.'

'Him too? Because of Len?' Beth bit her lip.

'That too,' said Abbie. 'But they'll catch him soon enough.'

'Mum, I've got to get up ... I'll be late ...'

'In a moment, dear.'

Abbie shifted uncomfortably. 'Your father thinks you've started smoking.'

'That's rubbish!'

'I know that,' her mother said quickly. 'I'd smell it on your clothes if you did.'

'Well then ...'

'I'm worried about you, too. You're a lot more mature than the other girls in your year.'

Uh oh.

'I'm not more mature,' said Beth. 'Not even close. Hayley Gervin dresses like she's in a lingerie parade. Jill Herford gets called a ho because she's been with guys from Year 11. You want more?'

'Charming. But you're a lot more grown up than either of them. Whatever else they get up to.'

'Mum, what is it that you think I'm doing?'

Abbie shifted on the bed, fiddling with her wedding ring as if it was making her finger itch. Finally she spoke. 'Making a terrible mistake, perhaps. Who is "D", Beth?'

Beth almost jumped out of bed. 'You've been reading my notebook!'

Abbie coloured. 'I didn't set out to ... I found it by accident ... cleaning.'

What if she found a scale? Or the tooth? Do the diary entries give away too much?

A faint rumble went through the house and Abbie started.

'That notebook was private, Mum. I don't go through your stuff.'

Beth slid out of bed and began to dress, dragging on jeans and a shirt.

'Are you sure you know him? This "D"?'

'I've just figured it out,' said Beth. 'It was *you* who went into my room on Friday night. I thought it was Sam. Was going to blast him.' She shook her head. *Where are my shoes?*

She jammed them on without bothering to tie the laces. 'I'll be back later,' she spat.

'I'm not accusing you ...' Abbie began, but Beth ran past, snatching the diary.

'I'll be back later,' she repeated.

Outside, Beth looked around with wild surmise. Serpentine Drive was quiet. Mr Epadomides waved to her, hose in one hand.

'How are you, Beth? You OK?'

'No. Fine. I'm not too bad, Mr E.'

'You know, I smell a strange smell the other day.'

'Oh?' She edged away. Was there an army of people with an interest in her house?

'Yes. It was coming from your block.'

'It must have been Freddy,' she said, stopping. 'He likes to roll in things.'

'No,' he shook his head with an air of quiet certainty. 'It was like the sea. When I was your age, I lived in a little fishing village, in Greece.'

'That would have been nice.'

'No. Well, sometimes, perhaps. But we were very poor. But that smell — it was of the sea. And the fish, and sand.'

People can sense the dragon, Beth thought. *Maybe they smell what they love, or what they miss.*

Beth heard the door behind her open, then close. 'I have to go. Sorry!'

He bowed and waved her off. 'Perhaps there is something strange. We must be careful.'

'Yes, Mr E,' said Beth. 'See you later.'

The front door opened, feet rapidly advancing over gravel.

'Come here *now*,' Abbie yelled, still sounding more irritated than angry. Without looking back, Beth broke into a jog, heading towards Dairy Road. After a breathless few minutes, she throttled back to a steady walk.

The day *was* beautiful. Fields of beaten-gold grass, blade tied to blade by innumerable spider webs, lit by the smoky haze of late summer.

As Beth strode along, she mentally paged through a volume listing alternative courses of action. Option one: stay and argue with her mother. Option two: try and involve her father as a possible ally. Option three: hire her brother to wreak terrible revenge on parents who denied their children the basic right to privacy. Option four: stay and try to explain away 'D' to her mother. The latter course of action might have compelled her to reveal some or all of the truth.

Every time I even think about telling someone about the cellar, I feel like I'm about to go out of my mind. Even if I really wanted to tell someone else, I don't think I'd be able to get the words out.

Sunday 19 March

40

Fivepence Lane beckoned. Beth took the intersection and walked along the gravelled verge. After a few minutes she stopped, crawled beneath a dense row of hawthorne bushes, climbed through a fence and walked through dry grass to a low granite outcrop dotted with shallow pools of water. Lizards scattered and she lay full length on a flat patch of rock.

The sky was a big empty blue bowl. Beth waited. She sat up and read back through her diary, trying to understand her mother's reaction.

February 22: What does D want me to think? He must have experienced a thousand things in his life. He will leave, perhaps soon, and I'll regret it if I haven't asked him enough good questions.

February 23: Does D make up his emotional responses? Sometimes it seems he has learned to feel like a human.

February 24: Why do I believe D? Why don't I ask more questions? Because of him I have lied to my friends and my parents. I can't tell anyone. I know he doesn't want me to.

Beth turned to a blank page and began writing.

No wonder she thinks I'm up to no good. Now that she's read it, anything I say will just convince her the opposite is true. 'D' could be a boy. How could it be anything else?

She put down her pen for a few moments, then began again.

All that world and space, but so few choices. I can't tell my friends, I can't run away. I can't go against D, and I can't let Henry in on the secret, either. Only two choices really: to accept it all and do whatever

comes next, or to be difficult and ask questions. Am I merely D's
servant, or some kind of ally? It usually feels like the former.

A car horn sounded and she jumped. She looked around but
the meadow was empty. A voice in the distance?

'Are you out there, Beth?'

She waited several heartbeats. She slammed her diary shut
and slid it into her backpack.

'Henry?'

'*C'est moi.*' He emerged from the hawthorn hedge and walked
towards her. 'Ah, the sweet air. There was so much coal dust
in Russia.'

'Did you really go there, Henry?'

'My word I did. Flying back and forth like a blue-arsed fly.'

Beth squinted up at Mount Acute. 'Did Mum send you to
look for me?"

'No, not really.'

'Ha. And how did you know to come out here?' Beth asked,
letting her irritation show.

'Your mama again, I'm afraid. She knows you better than
you'd think. Said you'd go bush rather than go to town. And
that you always went in this direction. And I saw footprints
leading away from the roadside …'

'Am I under arrest?' she asked.

'*Mais non*! No arrests on a Sunday.'

They walked back across the paddock.

'Mum thinks I've been seeing a boy. I haven't, Henry, ever.
I've looked and thought a bit, like all the girls, but I haven't done
anything. I'm not ready for that sort of stuff.' She sighed loudly.
'And she shouldn't have read my freaking diary.'

He shrugged. 'I don't bother too much about sordid private

lives ... since my divorce, *I* haven't even had one.' He picked up his mobile and dialled away.

'Mission accomplished,' he said. 'She's fine — thought I might take her for a drive, let things cool down — OK, check in later.' He shut off the phone and stretched. 'You're off the hook, kid. Where do you want to go?'

'Ooralloo,' said Beth, making what felt like the biggest decision of her life. 'Some research for a school report.'

I want to know the truth, she told herself. *And I'm going to fight for it.*

41

Ooralloo township was almost deserted. Birds had picked litter out of an open bin and a few free-range dogs were squabbling in the dust. Two aboriginal men sitting on a verandah glanced over as Henry's car rolled to a halt and disgorged its occupants. The men were watching test cricket on a small portable television.

'That's Mr Netcher,' said Beth, looking at the elder of the two. 'Met him the other day.'

'You were with the tour,' Netcher said, recognising her. 'Didn't ask any stupid questions, far as I can remember. This yer dad?'

'Uncle,' said Beth.

'Meetcha,' said Mr Netcher. 'Name's Jack.'

Henry shook hands, introduced himself.

'Where is everyone, Mr Netcher?' Beth asked.

'At the football, eh!'

'But it's summer!'

'Hey. We practise a lot, have friendly matches even when it's hot. The boys are down at Tarakarak today, and the whole mob's gone down to watch. We won the league last year — aimin' to do it again this time too. Only way to do that is trainin'.'

'Is Mara here? She said she might help me out with a school project.'

Mr Netcher thought about this for a while. 'She might be ... or she might not. Who can say with that one?'

'Can you tell me where she lives, then?'

He thought about this at even greater length, sucking his front teeth. Eventually he relented, and gave Beth walking directions.

'Do you want to come, Henry?'

'Might stay here and watch the cricket. You go, Beth. Haven't watched a game in years.'

Beth picked her way through the quiet streets. Seeing the township for a second time was strange. The houses seemed shabbier, some windows broken, lawns unwatered and weedy, signs of poverty manifested in cheap toys and plastic bags flattened against fences. She had been struck by the novelty of the township when she had visited with the school, but now she was able to see another aspect. The people here were once free to roam, and were now free only to stay. For a moment she sensed the boredom and lack of opportunity that must be part of life in the settlement.

She turned off the footpath and walked towards a turquoise fibro cement shed surrounded by roses. Beth knocked on the half-open door. She waited for almost a minute.

'Who is that? Hello?'

Beth stood facing a dark, fly wire-covered doorway. She felt nervous.

'I visited with a school group last week. My name is Beth. Is that Mara?'

'I remember you. You said you were gonna come up and talk to me.'

'Yes. Well, here I am.'

'Here you are.'

Mara stepped out, shading her eyes. 'You know, I didn't expect you to come back, not on your own, anyway. And without an appointment.'

'My uncle's here. He stopped to watch cricket with Jack.'

'That lazy old bugger!' said Mara. 'The only bit of him that's permanently employed is his bum. Anyways, you're wearing out the welcome mat.'

'Oh!' said Beth, starting.

They went into the house. The first room was an office, spare but functional, featuring a plain wooden desk with a fold-up chair, an antiquated computer and a surprisingly modern laser printer.

'I put all my orders on that computer,' said Mara. 'Have to watch my nephews though, eh? They come and play their games on it.'

Mara took her on a quick tour. Three of the four original bedrooms were now storage areas for her native food business. The place smelled strongly of eucalyptus oil. Mara made two cups of strong white tea and they sat down at a small linoleum-covered table in the kitchen.

'I saw you takin' notes last week,' said Mara. 'Almost like you was interested. No-one else was. Not much, anyway. Just a curiosity for them, going up to see real live aborigines.'

'We all liked it,' said Beth defensively.

Mara raised an eyebrow.

'So, why are *you* in Ooralloo?'

Beth took a very deep breath. She could not disguise her nervousness. 'Um. We have a cellar under our house. My dad built it to store wine.'

'This doesn't sound like a research project,' said Mara.

'Actually — it isn't.' She waited for Mara to object, and when she didn't, went on. 'The cellar has begun to collapse. Every few days the house shakes like crazy.'

Mara smiled, exposing even white teeth. Suddenly, she seemed much younger.

'Sounds like you should be havin' serious words with the builder, not me.'

Beth took another breath. 'It's not just the bricks, Mara. There's a smell. The strangest smell. Everyone in the house notices it.'

'Mildew?'

'No, nothing like that. People say it's a good smell, mostly. My uncle thinks it's grapes, the next-door neighbour said it reminds him of the sea ...'

'What does it mean to you, girl?'

'Everything. All my memories, when I was a little girl.'

Mara gazed at her, cup cradled in her large hands.

'I think people smell the things they love,' Beth went on. She took a noisy swallow of her tea.

'So why tell me?'

'Well, that's it. The smell comes out of the earth. It must have been there a long time, perhaps. I thought your people might have legends about a strange scent. Down at Goolgoorook.'

'That's not our country down there, you know. Another mob. We were the highlanders. Anyway, we don't really have legends, girl. My people tell stories about the dreaming. To us they are true, not just made-up legends.'

'I know that,' Beth said, 'but is there any story ...'

'About your magic scent? I can't recall one.'

'It's not just a smell,' Beth said. 'I found this.'

She placed the scale on the table. Even in the dim kitchen it glowed. Mara looked at it, then tentatively extended a hand.

Her nostrils flared. 'That is the smell?' she asked.

'Yes. It's much stronger in my house.'

'I can smell rock, and taste it too. Crushed ochre, and the stone we use for axe-heads. Seeds, Bunya pine nuts.' She leaned back. 'Put it in your pocket. I mean it. If you had showed that to Jack, he'd hurt you ...'

'He'd what?'

'I have seen one of these things before. One of these golden flakes. Bit more scratched up, a touch duller, but the same thing. For sure.'

Beth's eyes widened.

'That thing is man's business. Top secret — no women allowed.'

'How do you know about it, then?'

'Old Jack, he fancied me when I was young. Showed me secrets. He showed me something just like that flake to impress me. Didn't work too well, eh?'

'Where did he get the ... flake?'

Mara shook her head. 'Stop talking about it. Don't ever bring it back here again. Hide it good. Too dangerous.'

Beth's mind was still aflame with the notion that Jack had a dragon scale. 'I—I'm sorry. Why would Jack go after me?'

'You don't want to know, girl. I don't want to know, either. I'm sayin' this because you seem like a decent type. You've got a bit of respect and all that.'

'He'd come after me?' Beth persisted.

'If you were a Gugamai, certainly.'

Mara stood and guided Beth back out towards the street. The afternoon sun was hot and bright.

Beth shook hands with Mara. 'I'm sorry—'

'Don't be,' Mara said. Her expression softened. 'Look, girl, I'll ask around, on the sly. Can see that this matters to you.'

'It really does,' said Beth. 'It's ruining my life in lots of ways.'

At that moment a bus full of shouting children crossed the intersection at the end of the street.

'Everyone's back,' said Mara.' So much for bloody peace and bloody quiet.'

Tea had been called in the test match and Henry was ready to leave, bidding farewell to the four older men and an assortment of recently returned boys and girls who were looking at him as if he had just landed in a flying saucer.

Henry played a Purple Haze CD on the way back down to Hemming Heights. He knew Beth had a bit of a thing for music from the '60s and '70s.

'Jack's an interesting bloke,' said Henry. He was a boxer way back when, did you know? Lightweight champion of the state. Went to the Nationals, but lost on points. Says he was robbed.'

'Um,' said Beth, absently. 'That's interesting.'

'Did you get what you were after?'

'Sort of.'

On the way back, and after tapping Henry for a non-refundable loan, Beth bought four more bags of dog food.

Henry gave her one of his more speculative looks. 'That hound of yours goes through this stuff like nobody's business.'

42

Dinner was already on the table.

Sam listened to Henry's description of Ooralloo village.

'Why didn't you take me?' he asked.

'Spur of the moment,' said Henry.

Abbie ate quietly, passing food to Beth, but not otherwise acknowledging her. Nick said little, examining his glass of white wine.

Eventually Henry excused himself, taking a glass with him. Beth caved in.

'I'm sorry, Mum. I didn't mean to say anything unkind.'

'We give you a lot of freedom,' said Abbie. Nick nodded.

'I know. But there is *no* boy,' she said, as calmly as possible. 'My diary is like a story. Some things are true and some aren't. Some of it's kind of … metaphorical. Not literal.'

'How would we know one way or the other if there is a boy? That diary, Beth, is the only glimpse we've had of the real you for a very long time,' she said.

Beth began to cry. Rarely used, but a sneaky, low-down and very effective trick. 'It's hard at school,' she sobbed, 'thinking about Len … and Jo's mum.'

'What's wrong with Sylvia?' asked Nick, alarmed.

'Ah — Mr Aarons is in jail in Fiji. For carrying drugs. Mrs Aarons has to help him. I thought you knew already.'

Her parents exchanged looks, and Beth knew she had distracted them.

After a barrage of questions about Jo and her mother, Beth began a retreat to her room.

—•—

This time, she waited until she was sure Henry was asleep. Down into the cellar she went, dragging a bag of Alpo in each hand. The hole was now the height of a man, running from the floor to the roof.

'I'm almost there,' the dragon said, 'almost alive. 'I'd forgotten what life feels like, Beth. Now, I dream of looking at the moon.'

The cellar was warmer.

'This kindred of yours ...' he hissed.

'Henry? My uncle.'

'Uncle, mmm. He. is unusual ... knows something is happening. Something beyond his experience. It amuses him, interests him. He craves novelty.'

'How could he know?'

'Think, Beth. He sees it in *you*. You've changed. You have knowledge now.'

Wind eddied around her, damp and gritty, smelling like fresh-pulled potatoes.

'He is dangerous,' said the dragon. 'If he found me, perhaps he would not sympathise.' Beth took a breath to defend Henry. *Perhaps he is right. Henry might do something to spoil all of this.*

'Do everything you can to distract him,' the dragon urged her. 'It is vital. This may be my last awakening. There is so little space in the world for me.'

'No,' said Beth, her emotions bleeding, mingling. 'There must be other people like me — who can help. I'm *sure* of it.'

'Precious few. I know what humans can do. And there are so *many* of you now. I doubt there is any part of the world free of your kind.'

'Some places are still empty.'

'Aye. The dry and the cold places. Empty for a good reason. Unlivable.'

'Can you not live with people? Co-exist?'

'That is *all* I can do, Beth. Persuading people they need me is my calling. But now: wherever I go, everyone will know of me, with your television. I cannot convince a whole planet. I have not the strength or cunning. People will fear me, and lash out.

'We're not *all* like that.'

'Yet I have heard of terrible weapons — able to destroy entire cities. If humans are able to use them against each other, do you think they would hesitate to do the same to me?'

'I don't know,' Beth said, but she knew in her gut there would be little hesitation. She felt shame at belonging to a species to which death and destruction came so easily.

Beth sighed. 'We're not good,' she said after a long pause. 'We're small and weak, we have to overcompensate.' She fiddled with the top button of her shirt. 'I'm just crapping on, you know. Would you ask one bee what the purpose of the hive was?'

'I suppose not. Thank you for your honesty.'

'I'll try and think of something,' Beth said. 'You need some kind of public relations person, I think.' She laughed aloud at the thought. She felt giddy and strange.

It's the scent — don't forget the scent. Beth tried holding her breath, to hold out the dragon's aroma for just a moment. No use; the smell was all over her, a thick coating distorting her senses.

'I've got that book for you,' she ground out. 'It's called *Climbing Mount Improbable*. Sums up how scientists see life, I guess. Perhaps it would be a good distraction.'

In the teeth of a long silence, she cleared her throat and picked up the book.

As an introduction, she told him about the great Charles Darwin and Alfred Russell Wallace, the men who first guessed why and how living things change in form and function over time. She was fairly good on evolutionary theory — it was her favourite topic at school.

'Most mutations are useless or harmful, but a few will give a particular organism a small advantage, allowing it multiply faster and create viable copies of itself. Better adapted creatures were able to produce more offspring, and their offspring in turn were often successful.' She stopped and took a breath. *This is pretty freaking absurd*, she told herself. *Pity Dawkins is not here to talk to him.*

'New species arise through natural selection, and many older species die out. Nature is always changing — an endless competition for light, space and food.

She went on at some length, gesturing, regurgitating everything she had read on the topic, until she felt like a Christian televangelist preaching the word of the Lawd.

Then she began reading Dawkins' essays. Her mouth was dry by the end of the first chapter, but in some way she couldn't quite put her finger on, she was proud of her effort.

'More, tomorrow night. About genetics.' Beth looked at the dark hole and wondered if the dragon had genes, or even DNA. Was he a part of life, or something different?

'Oh,' the dragon said, voice muffled. 'There is no more?'

'Not tonight. What did you think?'

'Time stopped ... do you believe this, Beth? It's not just a story?'

'No. It is real.'

'I do not want to believe,' said the dragon. 'Yet there is something in it that I cannot deny.'

'Don't expect you to just *believe* this,' said Beth. 'It's not a religion. You have to think about it yourself.'

'That I will do. Be assured. We dragons have never seen life in such a light. I find it disturbing.'

Beth's sense of euphoria faded. *Now, I'm affecting him — it's not just one way traffic. Enough for now.*

She stood to leave.

'Good night.'

'Wait ... a moment. Was this a test, Beth? Have I used you unfairly?'

'No.' Beth stopped. 'Not at all.'

An odd sound rose, then fell, as if the dragon was talking to himself. 'What is it? What *is* it ... ?'

Beth took the stairs two at a time and was back in her room and in bed in record time, Henry unseen and the house empty and quiet in the night. She drew down sleep like a blanket and snuggled into its folds.

Monday 20 March

43

Monday was already upon her and she felt as if she had hardly slept. *A lot of knots to untie this week*, she thought. *Len, and Sarah. Jo. Henry and Mum, Mum and me, Mum and her job. Mr Flack. Me and the dragon, the dragon and me.*

Abbie caught Beth just as she was walking out the front door.

'I accept you lied in your diary. I don't know why you'd do that, though.'

'Oh, Mum. This is crazy stuff.'

'I'm not crazy, Beth.'

Nick waited in the driveway.

'I didn't say *you* were crazy. Mum …'

'Tell Jo that we'll help out any way we can.'

'Mum …'

Abbie clenched her teeth.

'Look, Beth. It's bad enough having a selfish daughter who hardly ever communicates with her family … !'

'That's *not* fair! Why do you always have to *twist* things?'.

'Not *fair*? No? What's Sam doing? What's happening with my job? Do you think that's fair?

'*Nothing's* happening with your job!' Beth yelled. 'What about *my* life?'

Nick came back up the drive. He looked at them and shook his head. 'Thunderbirds are go. Come on Beth, you'll be late.'

Abbie said nothing, turning her back on the two of them.

Presently they could hear dishes being returned to cupboards with some violence. Beth flinched at the clatter.

'Thunderbirds *are* go,' she agreed, and headed for the car. Sam trailed along, forgoing his usual patter.

Nick drove to the end of the street before releasing a huge sigh.

'That was an awesome reconciliation you guys put on back there. Must have lasted five point two seconds. Beth, can you try to play diplomat? Go for the Nobel?'

'Mum's overreacting! It's her favourite sport.'

'Same old combative Beth. But have a think. Your mum might be moved, or have to get a new job. She wants home life to be predictable, for the moment.'

'She shouldn't spy on me, Dad. Spies always find things they don't like. That's what they do.'

'Leave out a second diary,' Nick suggested. '"Went to meadows, picked flowers. Studied all night, patted dog. Helped Sam with his homework." That sort of thing.'

Sam remained uncharacteristically silent. Beth asked to be let out several blocks from school and walked the rest of the way through quiet back streets.

—•—

I despise fantasy, Beth thought. *I hate goblins and elves and freaking fairies. I would blow up every school of magic. Harry Potter would end up in leg irons. And teen vampires would be hunted down by werewolves and torn apart by zombies.*

She picked up a pebble and threw it at a bush, flushing a red robin. *I hate him for being impossible. I suppose he's real and* not-real at the same time, until he comes out of his underground lair and decides the matter one way or the other.

Ooralloo Secondary loomed through a bank of early morning fog. Students wandered like shades in the underworld. The air was cold and sluggish, out of character for late summer.

Beth paused at the gate, readjusting her books. As she walked through the main gates, she glanced down Tappet Street. An indistinct figure stood in a curl of mist. A boy. With a certain profile and a distinctive way of walking. Then he was gone again and she relaxed. Moments later, a stab of apprehension made her look back, but he was gone.

Jo was waiting inside the gate. She looked as if she had been there for some time. 'Help you?'

Beth thought about it for a moment, then tilted her books into her friend's arms.

'I'm sorry, Beth. I was like *way* harsh on you.'

Beth laughed. 'Way, dude. It was me that harshed *you* first.'

'Harshed? Come *on*.'

'Like, hello. Of course it can be a verb.'

'Oh. So the Grammar Queen says.'

Beth's spirits lifted.

Jo pretended to light a cigarette and struck a cinematic pose. 'I get to thinking I'm the only one with problems, sometimes.'

'No. Jo—'

'Beth, you're the only girl here who doesn't give a fig where I come from.'

'You're from Balmain.'

'You know what I mean. Colour, ethnic background, et cetera.'

Beth shrugged.

'You look tired,' Jo said, dropping her imaginary cigarette and grinding it out with her heel. 'You need to get a bit more shuteye.'

'Can't do it. I hardly sleep at all at night.'

Is telling part of the truth the same as telling part of a lie? Do things left out count as much as things made up?

44

Mr Flack had invited a parks officer, a Mr Wayne Garvey, to speak about Ooralloo National Park. He was wearing dull green shorts, a stiffly ironed khaki shirt and a battered object that appeared to be a slouch hat.

'An overgrown boy scout,' Jo said, nudging Beth.

'Not a good look,' Beth agreed. She slumped into her chair, ready for a doze.

'Good morning, everyone.'

'Go-od morn-ning Mr Garv-vey,' said Simon Dodds, and was immediately ejected.

'Twit,' said Flack. 'Anyone else who wants to play silly buggers is welcome to try. You'll be out before you can draw your next breath.'

Mr Garvey's speech began again. 'Jugamai Plateau is home to a an atypical range of animals. Curiously, there are few large mammals — koalas, kangaroos or wombats — even though the habitat is well suited to those animals. We believe this situation pre-dates the arrival of European settlers.'

No large animals. God. I bet the dragon ate them all, Beth thought, finally tuning into the discussion. She suddenly sat straight, startling Jo. *That proves that he was up there.* She wanted to scream out her discovery, to besiege Garvey with questions, to get out of the school and into action.

If she was right about the dragon, then at least some of his stories were true. She wondered if Mara would call soon.

When the end-of-lesson bell sounded. Garvey packed and left with such speed that Beth could only gaze at his departing back through the open door of the room.

Jo and Beth sat alone at lunch, most of the other Year 9 students compelled to watch a performance of *Othello* put on by a travelling theatrical troupe in the Recreation Hall. Sarah was present, but ignored Jo and Beth, instead speaking to Fiona Atherton, a popular senior whose academic talents were modest at best.

'Sar looks *sooo* comfortable hanging around with Fi Fi,' Beth observed. 'So much in common.'

Sarah must have sensed their attention, because she got up and stalked off towards the canteen. Beth stood, intending to follow, but Jo caught her sleeve.

'Let her go.'

'I want to talk to her!'

'Later. This too shall pass. Once Len is sorted out ...'

'It'll be all right?' Beth said sceptically, resuming her seat. 'Ooh, yeah. Gotta love those happy endings.'

Beth and Jo parted ways after lunch, and Beth endured an interminable afternoon. Her mind buzzed around the dragon. Everything was guesses and supposition. One piece of firm information and perhaps the rest would begin to take shape. After the final bell, she packed her books into her bag.

Flack cornered her just as she was about to walk out the gates. He looked out of breath and unhappy.

'People are going to talk,' Beth said. 'All these meetings.'

'Is that supposed to be a joke?' Flack asked. 'It's in pretty bad taste.'

Oh, Beth thought. *That hit a nerve. Maybe those rumours aren't so fanciful after all.*

'Sorry,' she said. 'Anyway, I don't *know* any more than when we last spoke, Mr Flack.'

'Don't get irritated, Beth. How do you know what I'm going to ask you?'

'Do you *want* another scal … golden thing?' Beth cursed her wayward tongue.

'A *what*? You called it a scale! How do you know?'

Dumb, Beth. Really dumb.

'I'm just guessing. The shape, you know. Deduction.'

'*Scale* sounds right. You want my opinion, Beth?'

She met his stare.

'I think this *scale* comes from something very odd indeed — an undescribed species. Perhaps a large lizard or a snake. Not extinct. I think you know where it lives. Maybe even have photos. You've seen it.' He punched out each sentence as if firing an artillery piece. 'Somewhere up on the Jugamai Plateau.' His face was alight. 'There's been speculation about this in the past. You heard the ranger. No large mammals up there. That means something else must have filled the evolutionary niche! I'm right, aren't I?'

Beth shook her head. 'Maybe, Mr Flack. I don't know. This *is* why I brought it to you. So *you* could tell *me*!'

'You didn't pick this up in your garden. I know you go walking up on the plateau.'

She crossed her arms. 'No. Haven't been up there for months.'

Flack smiled and held up his hands in surrender. 'OK. You win. I'll do my own research.'

'What's happening with Len Crabbit?' she asked.

Flack blinked. 'He's probably about to burn the school down. That's what they usually do, eh? No-one's seen him since Friday.'

She almost choked.

'I think I saw him. I didn't realise at the time.'

'Where? And when?'

'At the gates, this morning. In the fog. Running away from the school.'

'Whoa.' He ran a hand through his hair. 'And you didn't tell us?'

'I only just figured out who it was.'

'Fine. I'll tell the principal.' Flack exhaled. 'I wish I *had* let Lenny go to Ooralloo.'

'Mr Flack, I've got—'

'Hush. I know you were up there on the weekend, Beth. You spoke to Mara.' He waved the scale at her. 'Your trip up there was something to do with this. My theory looks pretty good.'

How did Flack know? I trusted Mara — though I hardly know her ...

'I've got to go, Mr Flack. I'm sorry. My dad's waiting.'

Flack raised a hand, surrendering for a second time. 'Give him my regards.'

'Bye. Sorry.'

'Don't blame Mara, by the way. I had to twist her arm pretty hard. Figuratively speaking, of course. And I get the feeling she could have told me more.'

45

'What's *that*?' Beth asked.

An ambulance passed at high speed on the way up Dairy Road. Nick was forced into the gutter.

'Idiot!' he yelled.

The ambulance barely made the right turn into Serpentine Drive.

'Anyone we know?' Beth asked, alarmed. 'Hurry, Dad!'

'Look,' Nick said, shouting over engine noise and rushing air, 'Sam's OK. He's at Pete Biscoff's. And your mother wouldn't be home yet. So don't worry.'

'What about *Henry*?' she shrieked, her skin prickling. 'I think it's *our* place, Dad.'

Her father shook his head.

'No way. Oh … you're right. Oh, damn.' He braked heavily and stopped the engine. The ambulance had halted, lights still flashing, without accompanying siren. Two paramedics alighted, and made their way across the street. They moved swiftly, but calmly.

Nick leapt out of the car and began running. In a moment she too was running, following her father.

A tableau revealed itself. A prone figure on the lawn, men in uniform, a paramedic's equipment box. Nick yelled something, almost barrelling into the uniformed men.

In following, Beth tripped on the gutter, rolled onto the dew-wet lawn and grunted as she came to a stop. 'Henry!' she whimpered, raising her head. The body on the lawn was being examined by many people, her father among them. The figure's face was deep in shadow, its build slight.

This is my fault, she thought. *My fault. It's all part of the same thing and nothing would have happened if I hadn't made it all happen.*

'Is Henry alive?' she asked.

'Please stay back,' said an ambulance officer. He stood between her and the body. 'Treatment is in progress. We only arrived a moment ago.'

'But it's my uncle,' she said, getting to her feet.

'I'm afraid not,' said a man to her right, 'he's far too young.'

Beth looked at the figure. She gaped. 'Henry?'

'Rumours of my demise have been greatly exaggerated,' said Henry.

Beth felt it very important to stay cool, to seem collected. 'And who is that?'

'Ah,' said Henry. 'Let's just stand over here, out of people's way.'

They stepped away from the melee, Nick following. Beth sniffed the unmistakable funk of dragon scent, earthy and over-ripe.

Mr Epadomides arrived, breathing heavily.

'Hello, Nicholas,' he said, 'and little Beth. What is this over at your place? Is everything all right? Is there some mistake?'

'A mistake, George? I really don't know. You probably saw more than I did.'

'I'll tell you what I saw,' said Mr Epadomides, 'but we're not about to alarm your kids.' He grabbed Nick by the elbow and drew him away from Beth and Henry.

As he did, Beth glanced across at the body and caught a glimpse of a running shoe, then another, and a bare foot, half obscured by the legs of the paramedics.

One of the paramedics stood up and wiped her forehead. It was Louise Beaucoup, Irene's much older sister. After a few moments, Louise returned to the prone figure.

Henry tried to appear nonchalant, and almost succeeded. 'To think, yesterday I said suburbia was boring.'

Beth edged around, trying to get a better view of the prone figure, but she could see only dirty, torn jeans.

'Who is that?' she hissed.

'I don't know,' said Henry. 'But he started throwing things through your windows. A lot of them. I was reading the paper when a house brick whizzed past my left ear.'

'God! Are you alright?'

'Just surprised. I ducked down — taking more incoming fire. A moment later, he moved on to the next room.' He paused. 'Anyway, after a little while, I snuck out the back, and worked my way around, hoping to scare him off. But by the time I got out here, he was face up and drooling. Rock in one hand, steel bar in the other. Most incriminating pose in the history of vandalism.'

The sun touched the horizon and a cool westerly breeze arose.

Louise Beaucoup ceased her labours once more and walked across to them.

'Hello Beth. Could you look at the patient, please? Your father doesn't know him.'

'Is he alive?'

'Ye. Very unconscious, but otherwise, BP is fine, heart rate a little elevated.'

Beth finally got a good look at the vandal. Recognition was instantaneous.

'Len Crabbit!'

Once the still-catatonic Len was loaded into the ambulance, it quickly departed, though this time without sirens and flashing lights. Henry drove to the hospital a few minutes later, promising to return with a detailed report.

Sam and his trusty BMX hove into view five minutes later, a fine sunset at his back. He cursed when told of the drama.

'I *always* miss the good stuff.'

Beth frowned at him. 'You little ghoul.'

Sam finally noticed the shattered lounge room windows, and moved in for a closer examination. He halted, deep in thought.

Gradually, the small clot of onlookers dispersed, and Nick drove the car into the garage, wheels crunching on broken glass. As he emerged, the driveway bucked and shifted so hard he almost fell.

'Dad?' A smaller tremor forced her to stand with feet splayed. Sam lay on the grass until the movement stopped.

With a loud crunch, the cement beneath Nick cracked and dropped several centimetres. He made a strangled sound, completely lost his footing, and fell heavily.

'You OK?' Beth cried, then tumbled sideways. She felt as if she was riding a badly sprung car along a corrugated road. After an eternity that probably lasted five seconds, ground stopped moving. Beth groaned, resisting a strong urge to throw up. Then she looked to her left.

'What's wrong with Dad?' Sam asked. 'He looks real sick.'

Beth was already at his side. Nick grinned weakly, and opened and closed his mouth a few times. No sound came out. He pointed to his chest.

'A heart attack!' Sam exclaimed, his voice shrill, 'get the ambulance back!'

Beth shook her head. She'd seen this before. 'No. I think he's just winded. He went down pretty hard.'

Beth held her father's shoulder and tried not to let him see the fear in her face. Finally, Nick gasped convulsively, drew a shuddering breath and sat up, rubbing his grazed knees. Sam hugged him.

'Perfectly good pants,' Nick croaked, chest heaving. 'I just ripped my best cords and buggered my knee. And look at the bloody driveway!'

'Are you alright?' Beth demanded.

He stood carefully, then looked at his anxious children. 'If you want to stay in Goolgoorook, then don't tell your mother about this ... yet. The broken windows and Lenny are quite enough, thank you.'

He picked two slivers of glass from his palm, and wiped away droplets of blood with his sleeve.

'What are you going to do?' Beth asked, feeling queasy.

'I'm going to change my clothes. Then, I reckon I'll fill in the cellar. Between your escapades and the tremors, I've lost all affection for it.'

'Do you need to sit down?'

'I'm fine, he said. 'No drama. Just a bit more subsidence.'

Trailed by a clearly worried Sam, he hobbled off. Beth was left to stare at the spider-webbed cracks across the driveway. A few areas of the concrete had crumbled into a kind of powder, and little hillocks and valleys were evident from the road up to the garage door.

'Like Mum's not going to see *that*,' she whispered.

Abbie didn't notice the damage to the driveway — not immediately, at least. The sight of her custom-made drapes billowing
out over the shrubbery through the broken windows was far
too distracting and traumatic.

She pulled up at the kerb and strode towards Beth and Henry,
just returned from hospital.

'What the hell is going on? Is everyone alright?'

Beth sketched the past hour's events as quickly as possible.

Abbie stared fixedly at her. Beth took a step back, more
than ready to start crying in the face of such scrutiny. She felt
exhausted and irritable.

'Why was he just lying there?' Abbie seemed offended. 'On
our property! And the windows!'

'He hadn't eaten in the last three days. Must have gone a bit
mad.'

'And he just collapsed?'

'Lack of food, and sudden exertion. That's what the ambulance people said, anyway.'

Abbie's face abruptly softened, and she embraced Beth and
kissed her on both cheeks. 'I'm so glad you weren't here when
he attacked the place. God knows what he would have done.'

Beth could only shrug.

Abbie turned to Henry. 'I'm so sorry about all of this.'

He smiled. 'I'm afraid I haven't been of much use. I did call
a glazier to repair the windows.'

———

Half an hour later, Constable Helen Darling from Goolgoorook Police Station came to take a statement from Henry. Her uniform was immaculate and she had a sour expression on her narrow face. She took Henry's offer of a cup of tea with ill grace. 'No thanks. We don't have time to waste.'

'Miss …' said Henry, waving his hand airily at her ' … Sergeant …'

'*Constable* Darling,' she said.

'Darling, I've already given this story to about ten people tonight. Do you mind if I drop by the station tomorrow morning?'

'I'd prefer to do it now. Regulations. We need a statement while the event is fresh in your mind.' She smiled. 'The *average* person is quite poor at recalling detail.'

Provoked, Henry re-told the evening's events in every particular. He even remembered the brand of sneakers Len had been wearing, and a bad graze he had glimpsed on Len's upper arm. *Sarah's rock attack*, Beth thought. By the end, even the hyper-thorough Darling was fidgeting. 'Is that everything, sir? Nothing omitted? Thank you for your assistance.'

'It was a singular pleasure.'

As she departed, the window repairman arrived and began work.

46

'We're off to see Sylvia.' Abbie had changed out of her business clothes. 'We're late, but at least we've got an excuse. Henry has kindly agreed to babysit — kidsit, or whatever,' she corrected herself, seeing Sam's thunderous expression.

Showered and much improved, Nick carried Sam out to the car by his feet.

Beth guessed he had said nothing to Abbie about the latest tremor. Abbie still hadn't noticed the driveway — perhaps he would try to get it fixed tomorrow without her noticing.

He was carrying Sam in a fireman's hold and generally horsing around. 'Don't put him down, Nicky!' Abbie hectored, 'there's still glass all over the grass!'

Sam giggled, wriggling out of his father's grasp. He always seemed to regress when playing with Nick. Beth caught herself hoping he would come through this strange time unscathed. *Since when have I worried about Sam?*

Beth caught a whiff of rotten fruit. Her fists clenched.

'Lock the doors as soon as we go!' yelled Abbie.

'*Yes*, Mum!'

'And *what* has happened to this driveway?' Abbie snapped, finally looking down.

Nick affected not to hear, starting the car and reversing slowly. Abbie was forced to jump in.

'Pwauuggh,' Sam grimaced, watching them reverse out of the driveway. 'Cop that stench.'

Beth shrugged as nonchalantly as she was able. She nodded to Henry, went inside and flung herself on a sofa, planning for the silence that followed bedtime.

———

Henry cooked some kind of Italian dish, heavy on mushrooms, parmagiano, pesto and semi-dried tomatoes. Beth enjoyed it in a distracted kind of way. Freed from parental surveillance and determined not to miss *Catastrophe: a history of aviation disasters*, Sam ate his helping slumped on a beanbag in front of the television. Beth sat in the portion of the open living area sometimes referred to as the dining room, and chatted quietly with her uncle.

'Beth,' he said, 'I didn't tell everything to the Constable.'

Beth laid down her fork, and looked at him.

'When I got out there,' he said, 'I saw this character lying flat out, like I told the police. Strange, I thought, but then I fell over, too. Tried to get up, but my legs were boneless. A damned aphid crawled up my nostril and I couldn't even twitch. It was the weirdest sensation. I felt like one of those spiders that gets paralysed by a wasp.'

'The smell ...' she began, but she *knew* the answer.

He smiled at her, tapped the table in agreement. 'It was everywhere. Like half-cured leather, but sharp, charred. After a minute of staring at the sky with my tongue lolling from the corner of my mouth, a little breeze came up, and gradually everything came back. Blew that weird gas away. I must have inhaled a lot less than our man in the hospital.'

'What did you do then?'

'I got up and checked his pulse — saw he was OK. Then I called the ambulance.'

'What are you going to do about it?' she asked.

He looked at her and raised an eyebrow. 'Nothing, I guess. I don't want to tread on your territory.'

'My territory—'

'Uh huh. I'll leave my little insight with you. You'll be able to make more sense of it than I can. Am I right?'

Dry throated, Beth nodded.

Catastrophe went to an ad break. Sam struggled up from his beanbag, and walked across the room to tug at Henry's sleeve. 'Hey, Henry, can you take me fishing soon? I want to find a friend for Horatio.' For once Beth was happy to be interrupted by Sam.

'So Horatio can eat them? He will, you know,' said Henry.

Sam smiled. 'If anything happens, that's nature, anyway. Beth's kind of stuff.' He sniffed. 'Me, I prefer rockets and rock fights.'

Henry laughed and sat on the end of the lounge. 'I've about had it with rocks. Can't help with the fish either. Much as I'd like to. Back to work tomorrow, in Canberra, among the toiling bureaucrats.'

He lifted a cigarette from his breast pocket, fished in his pants pocket for a lighter and held the two up in triumph.

'You quit,' said Sam. 'Didn't last long.'

'Don't be like that. I took time off to see you two. Besides, there's far too much action here,' he said. 'Earthquakes, bigots, feuds ... the whole bloody works.'

'Can't smoke inside, anyway,' Sam said. 'House rules.'

Henry took a long breath, pinched his cigarette in half and dropped it back into his pocket. 'I want you to keep in touch,' he said, glancing at Beth.

47

Worried about paralysis, Beth descended the steps tentatively, lugging three packets of Gourmet Chunky Bites, courtesy of Henry.

'You've been asking questions about me,' the dragon said flatly, its voice filling the cellar.

Why can't anybody hear him? she wondered. *If they can't hear him, I suppose nobody would be able to hear me, either.* She considered dropping the food and running back up the stairs.

'What else would you expect?' she managed.

'I'm not angry. I don't blame you, Beth. I *could* be a liar. You know I exist, but beyond that ... I have to be cautious, you understand. I am vulnerable. As are you.'

'I understand,' said Beth. 'But no-one knows about you.'

'Yes. You have told no-one directly. But you may have aroused suspicions, no? Allowed others to make guesses, develop an interest?'

How does he know any of this, stuck down here? Beth felt for a moment that he must have some ability to see at a distance.

'Do the first people remember me?'

'The first people ... you mean the aborigines?'

'That is what you call them. Did they tell you any stories about me?'

She hesitated a second too long. 'No.'

'Are you sure?' This time she could sense *something* in his tone — but was it disappointment, or a threat? *He doesn't want* the aborigines to know he is awakening. Why would he fear them at all? An armoured flying monster versus men with spears. Doesn't make sense.

'Y—es. Why? Did they know about you? How would that be possible?'

'They are not a people to forget. Stories instead of writing on paper. Lasts *much* longer.'

She found herself nodding. *He's doing it again. Persuading me, stopping me from asking the questions I want to ask. He doesn't lie: he doesn't need to. He just pushes me a little, and I surrender.*

She pinched herself hard. The fog in her mind thinned a fraction. 'What did you do to Len?'

He continued as if she hadn't spoken. 'I have hardly begun to tell you about myself, Beth.'

'Did you try to kill Len? Remember? I could *smell* you up there.'

He didn't reply for several seconds.

'A boy began to damage this house. I defended it for you.'

'For *me*? With *what*?'

'I exhaled, but did not ignite. A hunting trick.'

'You nearly killed him!'

'The gas only stuns, Beth. It seemed the best way.'

You could do that to me!, she thought.

As if anticipating her, a powerful rush of fragrances flooded into her nose, a mixture of freshly primed canvas, aniseed and red wine vinegar.

This time she bit at her lip, almost hard enough to draw blood.

'You accused me of getting careless,' she said, 'Don't you think knocking people out on my front lawn is *risky*?'

No answer. The smells swirled and eddied about her — something sharp and electrical, a hint of cloves, the smell of a crushed leaf, the acrid scent of coffee grounds.

'What are you doing to me?' she asked. 'Stop it.'

'*Doing* to you?'

'The smells. I can't put my thoughts together. Don't know whether I can trust you anymore.'

'It is not an intentional act. As I get stronger, so does the smell. It is a part of what I am, not separate, not an invention.'

Beth thought of Len, pale and twitching, face blank. 'But I feel like it does something ... to me. Makes me slow ...' *Why haven't I asked you about why no-one else can hear you? Or how you plan to get out of the cellar? Or how it is that eating a few bags of dog food and dried up old ferns is enough to revive a monstrous half-dead beast?*

'You speak of trust, Beth. I think you are right.

The time has come for me to be more open with you. If you are willing to take risks for me, then I should do the same for you. Perhaps then you will come to trust me more, and we can progress to the final stages of my liberation.'

Beth searched for a reply, wanting to continue her line of questioning. But a blankness invaded her mind, filling every space.

'Yes,' she said, giving up, disgusted with herself. 'You're right.' Immediately, the pressure in her head eased.

'Very well. I wish to help you get a better sense of what I am, and to speak of my experiences with human beings.'

Yes, and tell me lies.

48

'Once we were many and free, each of us with a realm of our own. We girdled the earth with our flights and lived fully. We knew happiness. By and by we began to encounter an ape that came out of the African plains, but seemed able to live anywhere. It could make for itself the fire that we kept in our bellies, and instead of growing claws made crude weapons from stone and wood. We found the ape and its tools ludicrous, and terrorised it whenever possible. Yet it spread still further, doubled quickly, doubled again. We are slow to increase, and could not keep pace. Like swallows, they learned to make nests of mud and straw. Where they lived, game soon vanished and we were forced to move. All too slowly, we realised these apes were competitors, bloody and remorseless.'

He's talking about us, Beth thought. She felt a perverse thrill of pride in the deeds of those remote ancestors. At the same time, the dragon forced his perspective upon her, and she saw the humans as rats or worse, bent on destroying the fine and beautiful world of the dragonfolk. For a flickering moment, Beth *was* a dragon and she knew their slow demise was a tragedy.

'And our dominion did shrink, until it was a tenth of what it had been, and all the finest land across the globe was under plough and hoof. Too many of us were crammed into this final patch. Beth, when a dragon is forced into the territory of another, bloodshed may occur. Did occur. As the humans built new nests, dragons were dying at each other's claws. We accelerated our own downfall. We became so few that humans turned us into a myth. As if we were a fiction contrived by the human mind.'

'What about hibernation?' Beth heard herself ask. 'Why didn't you just go to sleep for a few hundred years at a time, and try to outlast us? Humans aren't going to go on forever.'

A billow of warm air puffed into the cellar, peppering Beth's face with small particles of grit. 'We have tried that,' the dragon said. 'But each time we awoke the humans were stronger, and we were weaker. This awakening is the worst of all. You have eaten the planet, eaten its future.'

'We've made of lot of things extinct,' Beth, trying to think of something consoling to say. 'We mightn't last much longer.'

'You don't deserve to, said the dragon, 'but you will still be here in another million years. Along with your friends, the rats and the cockroaches.'

Beth thought she heard feet moving on floors above, but the sound was faint and soon faded into inaudibility. She allowed her hands to relax a little, brushed at dust on her knees. She blinked slowly. She struggled to think critically, to question his word. *He wants me to think he is harmless, always the victim. And right now,* she thought, *I believe him. I can't help myself.*

'I was going to warn you about something,' she said.

The dragon was silent.

'Dad's going to fill the cellar. I don't know when.'

'I heard him.'

Beth shook her head. 'We can't keep a thing from you, can we?'

'Your father had a builder down here this morning.'

'He did?!'

'This man cannot start work for another few days. I will be fully awake by then, and gone.'

'And if not?'

He did not reply.

The cellar was a dim cube of silence and dust. Beth shifted in her seat. 'How do you know when you are ready to fly?'

'When there is no choice. My flesh itself sings, calls out for the sky! Even now I despise my imprisonment, this shroud of earth.'

'Can you take me with you?' she burst out. 'Into the air?'

She imagined herself holding thorny scales, leaning low along a winged back. Mount Jugamai would grow small and Goolgoorook would disappear in mist.

'Allow me that domain at least,' the dragon said. 'You may fly with me in dreams only.'

'I woke up yesterday convinced it was *all* a dream,' Beth said. 'But then I felt the scale.'

Beth yawned involuntarily, hand over her mouth, and tried to focus on her watch. *Four a.m.* Suddenly she was exhausted, her legs completely leaden. She wanted out of the cellar.

'Bed,' she said. 'I don't get enough sleep anymore. Be back, I promise.' She fled up the stairs. She plunged into the silent house, and on into her room.

Was the beast offended by her sudden departure?

Sleepless, she jotted a short diary entry. There was no pleasure in keeping a journal any more: Abbie's espionage had spoiled it for her. No longer private, no longer *hers*.

D told me a bit more about himself. It sounded believable, at least while I was down there. I started to ask him questions, but I couldn't go on.

I can't understand how I can be doing these mad things and still leading an ordinary life. I eat toast in the morning, I'd pat the dog if he'd go anywhere near me. Then at night I have these lunatic conversations. It's as if he dampens my fear. He wanted to know if the aborigines at Ooralloo told stories about him. Maybe he did something horrible to them. Or they did to him.

She fell asleep with pencil in hand, a feeling of foreboding seeping into her heart. *Things cannot go on this way for much longer.*

Part Four

Tuesday 21 March

49

Abbie woke her with a shout from the hallway: 'Phone call, honey!'

'It's only seven!' Beth complained, feeling all too human. 'No. Can I call them back?'

'*Beth*! I told her you were awake.'

'OK, OK.'

She stumbled down the corridor. Her? Not a friend, or her mother would have used a name.

'Mara here,' a faint voice told her, 'Is that you girl? Thought I'd call you early.'

Beth tried to remain lucid. Her mouth tasted of acid.

'I've heard some interesting stories,' Mara said, 'very interesting.'

Despite Mara's boast, Beth could hear something else in her tone, an overtone of anxiety, or even fear.

'What stories?'

'About your scent. The little golden scale.'

Beth remembered that the dragon might be listening to her side of the conversation.

'I can't come out there, Mara. School today.'

'I know that, girl. I'll meet you in town, this afternoon. I'm coming in to do some shopping.'

'Mara ...'

'I'll pick you up from school. Four o'clock.' Click.

'Who was that, dear?'

'A lady I met at Ooralloo. She's helping me with an assignment.'

'She sounded a bit abrupt.'

Beth laughed. 'That's what I thought, too. But she's kind. Do you mind if I meet her in town after school?'

'No, that's fine,' said Abbie after a long absent-minded pause. 'Just give the taxi money back to your father if you do.'

'She *can* walk,' said Sam, 'now that big bad Len's in the clink.'

'Suits me,' snapped Beth. 'Do I still have to see the police?'

'Mr Flack can tell you about that,' Nick called from the bathroom. 'He's handling the matter for the school.'

In the end, Henry drove them both to school.

Sam quietly sang, and one of the verses seemed to involve her and a series of grisly incidents.

'That's sweet,' she said over her shoulder, 'may you suffer a similar fate.'

'One day you'll be best friends,' said Henry.

'We already are,' said Sam, 'like Huck and Jim on their raft.'

I'm already on a river, thought Beth. *And it's a barbed wire canoe, not a raft.*

'I'll be back this winter,' said Henry. 'Take you skiing, I will.' Sam stopped singing the next verse of his song long enough to voice his approval of this plan.

They drew up by the school fence and stopped.

'Be careful in Patagonia,' said Beth.

As Sam climbed out, Henry leaned over and whispered in her ear. 'I bought two dozen tree ferns for you and some dry biscuits. Under a sheet of black plastic in the garage. Kind of hidden up the back. Would have put them in the cellar, but Nick might have thought it a bit strange ...'

Beth stared at him.

'Tell me your secret when I get back. I'm sure it's a good one.'

She nodded, not trusting herself to speak.

Henry watched them both until they rounded the corner.

'He's as bad as Dad,' Beth observed. 'Always waits until you're out of sight.'

———

Beth found Jo sitting under a forlorn-looking Canary Island palm. To Beth's relief, she smiled and waved.

'Your mum and my mum, you should have seen it. It was completely sad.' Jo mimed the pouring of wine and slurred her voice. 'They started complaining about their kids. Beth this, Jo that. Blah, blah. Then about their husbands. Pretty soon it would have been about the pets. It was like some kind of therapy session.'

'What was my dad doing?'

'Watching a day-night cricket match in the family room. They excused him. I think he was relieved.'

'Yep. Dad loves boy stuff.'

'Don't we all,' said Jo. 'What did you get up to? And don't say homework.'

'Just read a bit,' said Beth. 'Wrote some stuff in my journal. Dazed and confused, basically.'

'And you're feeling better? You seem a bit better. More here than there, anyway.'

'That's the bell,' said Beth, getting to her feet. 'I feel OK. Sometimes I get ... I dunno. I feel like I'm finished with high school. But there's all those years to go.'

'We're all over it,' said Jo.

Sometimes, I think my friends know all about what I am doing, and then they go and act as if everything's normal. I have to remember: to everyone else, the world is still normal.

50

Len Crabbit's arrest/detention was announced at a special assembly. Naturally, everyone already knew about it. A camera crew from the local television station attended. Principal Betts primped for the camera and put on his best Leadership act.

'The behaviour of this lad has been shameful. Leonard Crabbit is currently facing vandalism charges, and has of course been suspended from Ooralloo Secondary College. We wish to assure parents and the local community that we will not tolerate racist attacks and the denigration of minority communities.'

'Bullshit,' Jo said loudly, causing heads to turn, 'you let Len get away with it for three years. It's a disgrace.'

Betts carried on with a vague account of Len's misdeeds and wrapped it up with a less than stirring exhortation to maintain harmony and diversity.

'He's just worried about the school being sued,' said Beth. She was privately grateful that she had not been publicly named as a participant in the whole affair.

Crabbit's small band of sympathisers were quiet now, possibly wondering whether this turn of events marked him as a hero or a failure. The assembly swiftly came to an end and students slouched off to their classes, dissecting the news in a hundred different directions.

'Sarah's away today,' said Irene, semi-professional gossip-monger, 'Must be *ashamed.*'

'Put yourself in her position,' Jo whispered to Beth, 'the humiliation of it all. It's not her fault.'

'I know!' Beth said. 'Nothing is anyone's fault. Even mine.'

'Good. That's the spirit. We'll write her a note. We'll say all is forgotten, and come out with us.'

By the last class of the day, they had almost finished. Beth was yawning so often her ears started to ring. Too many late nights and strange dreams. They found Skye Hicks, who lived near Sarah's aunt, and she promised to deliver the envelope.

Jo went to meet her mother, in town for a final consultation with someone from Legal Aid before leaving for Fiji.

Beth waited at the school gates. And waited. No Mara, just a dwindling flow of swearing, jostling students. Could she be waiting at the wrong school … ? Beth chewed at her nails and wished she had a book to read. Anything to distract herself.

Suddenly a dusty Toyota four wheel drive squealed out of Tappet Street, and almost went sideways before skidding to a stop. The passenger door flew open.

'Get in!'

Mara was dressed like a Chicago gangster: dark glasses, black suit with charcoal pinstripes, white shirt, black tie and a trilby. An unlit cigarette dangled from her mouth.

Beth smiled broadly, all her stress released in one moment. Mara was an out-there kind of woman. 'What're you *doing*, Mara? And what are you *wearing*?'

'Hop in!' Mara barked. 'Double bloody quick. Old Jack's in town today. Don't want the nosey old bugger to see me or the vehicle.'

Beth ran around to the passenger seat, climbed in and the vehicle shot forward like a fighter jet from an aircraft-carrier's catapult. Mara took the Toyota along a zigzag route through Goolgoorook's back streets, braking very late when gaining on other vehicles or swinging out into the opposing lane to overtake. Fortunately, the town's cops seemed to be elsewhere. Dust swirled through the cabin, mixing with the strong fug of diesel. Finally, Mara skidded to a halt on a wide stretch of dirt road down by the edge of Redgum Swamp, and switched off the engine.

Beth wrenched open the door, alighted, and stood a safe distance away. 'I think I'll walk home, Mara,' she said shakily. *Craziest driver I've ever seen!*

'Been a while since I've driven that much,' said Mara, oblivious to Beth's shaking hands. 'This'll do, but.' She wiped her brow. 'It's hot down here in the lowlands. Never did like it. My folk are mountain people, you know?'

Beth nodded.

'Let's walk back, shall we?' said Mara. 'I just needed to find a place to hide the Toyota.'

They walked back into the centre of Goolgoorook, a distance of around one kilometre. Beth imagined she could feel the dragon pulling at her mind, trying to draw her back home.

'I'm not going,' said Beth.

Mara looked over at her, curious.

'Just thinking aloud,' said Beth, and Mara nodded.

'I get the feeling you're a bit jumpy, girl.'

51

The only half-decent café in Goolgoorook nestled between a boarded-up Masonic Lodge and Kurt's Krazy Cutz Hairdressers. According to Mara, Jack preferred the local pub to any other place in town, and would not be seen dead sipping a latte.

A line high up on one wall of the café showed the level of the 1957 floods. Mara and Beth took a seat in front of a clumsy painting of a dead gum tree.

'Herbert Thepping,' said Beth, deciphering the signature.

'That fella's not fit to wash the paintbrushes of an Ooralloo artist,' Mara said.

'Welcome to Jugamai Café,' chirped a teenage waitress, 'can I help you?'

Orders were made and soon afterwards coffees appeared.

Mara sipped at her drink cautiously. 'I said a short white, eh! This is just plain garden variety coffee.'

The waitress looked sideways at Mara and then went back into the kitchen area.

'Should have a 'No Abos' sign up front,' Mara said loudly, 'then I'd have known to expect crap service. Or no service.'

'Do you think they really ...'

Some of the other patrons *were* staring at Mara. *That's just because she's noisy,* Beth tried to convince herself.

'Maybe it's just unusual. To see ...'

'A black woman drinking coffee? I forgot, blackfellas are only good for pickin' the stuff.'

'To see you in town, I was going to say,' said Beth, her face reddening. 'I mean, you don't come down here much.'

'Spare me, girl,' said Mara, but her expression softened. 'I've copped a lot of crap in my time,' she said. 'You've got no idea.'

The waitress eventually returned with the correct drink.

'What I'm going to tell you, ain't supposed to ever leave my people. Like I said before, if Jack ever finds out …'

Beth tugged at her ear, then rested her hands in her lap. She tried to stay calm. Henry always said calm people got to put their argument across. 'That's not what I want. I don't want you to get hurt, Mara.'

Mara smiled and shook her head. 'I'm not gettin' hurt. What you asked me the other day made me curious. When that happens — watch out, eh!'

'OK,' Beth said. 'What did you find out?'

'If I go around my village askin' about this story of yours, I'll get speared, if Jack and the other elders come to hear of it. No joke. Ain't no real secrets in Ooralloo.' She jabbed a biscuit with a teaspoon.

'But there's ways, my girl. Jack, he's a real vain man. Nothin' he likes better than a mirror. He likes to boast of his boxing career and other stuff. Mostly about the ladies.'

Ceiling fans were barely moving the tepid air but Beth felt completely awake for the first time that day.

'Anyway, this was my plan, girl. Invited the old bugger over. Bought him some good beer. I made up a crazy tale about a magic scent. Somethin' in the Dreamtime, with snakes and big feller frogs. I'm pretty good at that, what with all the bus tours and such. "Jack," I said. "I read some book by a white fella anthropologist, 'bout the legends of our people. Real secret, special legend. Something about a real good smell that came out of the ground. Makes people change How come I never heard of such a thing?"

'Now, that got his attention. He says: "Just tell me what the book has in it," because he doesn't read too well. I told him my made-up story.

When I finished, he got real angry. He walked up and down. "That's rubbish. The white fella invented all of this. Not a word is true. Don't know what rubbish dump he picked that up on. He's tellin' lies about us."

"'Are you sure, Jack?" I said, real innocent. "It sounded like proper stuff."

"Of course I'm sure, woman!!" he shouted, full of pride and stupidity, "you think I'm a stupid old bastard, don't you? I'll prove it if you promise to keep your dumb face shut." Then he told me the *real* story just to prove how stupid he is.' She smiled mischievously. 'I'm going to trust you, Beth.' Mara lowered her voice. 'Because I think you're a good girl down deep. Anyhow, this is what Jack Netcher told me, more or less:

———

'A long time ago, before the white man came, the Gumagai lived high in the Jugamai Hills, just as they always had. Each year they climbed down from their home country and traded with the lowland Bidgee people. They swapped spear-heads, ochre and held a corroboree or two. Most of the time, there was peace, so long as the elders kept the young hotheads in their place.

'Nearly all of the year the Gugamai lived in the open, sleeping on grass, making small campfires. They wore possum skin coats and their feet were tough as stone. In the winter, they had to find shelter, so they lived under big rock overhangs near Mount Acute. They called it Narringa — place out of the wind.

'The head warrior was called Woolgangie, and he was the first to see the strange thing that came to the Jugamai Hills that winter long ago.

'He was out searching for yabbies, his favourite food, when a shadow crossed the sun. Now Woolgangie was a brave man, so he looked up instead of running away. In the sky he saw something that should not have been there. A great scaly lizard, like a frill-neck, but with wings.'

Beth's arm spasmed and she spilled her tea. She muttered an apology and swiped it away with a serviette.

'Woolgangie waved his spear, hoping to frighten away the bad spirit, but instead it came down toward him, and landed on the ground.

"Go away," said Woolgangie. "We have done no wrong. Our ancestors are at peace. We show respect to the world."

'The creature had teeth sharp as splintered stone and eyes brighter than the setting sun. "If you listen to me, I will not harm you," it said, speaking in an odd but recognisable dialect, "but you must assist me before I can leave."

'The great beast made the elder take him back to the Gugamai camp. When his people saw the beast coming through the trees, they ran away into the bush, shrieking. "All is lost! A goanna spirit. It has bewitched Woolgangie!"

"Come back," Woolgangie cried. "It will spare us if we give it what it wants."

Gradually, reassured by his example, the women and men returned to camp. They crouched as far away from the monster as possible, babies crying and brave warriors hiding. With a voice more terrible than a valley-full of fire, the lizard spoke.

"Indeed, tremble before me. I have come to your lands, hill-people, and I can find nothing to eat."

Despite their fear, the Gugamai sneered a little at his ignorance, for the plateau was rich with food.

"I have not yet learned to catch the kangaroos, and I do not know which plants are nutritious. Once I have enough of them, I will leave."

The only person among the Gugamai who was brave enough to stand before the lizard was the wife of Jurambai.

"My name is Norna. Can you follow me?"

She led the lizard to the bushes that store nectar. The beast snatched up a plant and gobbled it down whole. Then she showed it some mushrooms, and it ate them all, dirt and everything. "This is a tree-fern," she told the lizard, "eat only the middle." Soon, it had consumed more ferns than the Gugamai ate in a year.

After that, the goanna spirit appeared satisfied, and thanked her.

"That is enough for today." It promptly dropped to the ground and went to sleep. The weird smells that came from the lizard's mouth both intrigued and terrified the Gugamai.

"I don't think it will harm us," said Norna, yet she felt very strange.

"The elder spirits have sent it from the dreaming," said Woolgangie. "Perhaps it was once a mighty warrior. We may be judged on the hospitality we show."

"Whatever it is," Norna said practically, "I think it will eat all the food in these hills. Who knows when it will leave, if ever?"

'Over the next few moons the lizard became a familiar sight, tearing out food trees, digging up bulbs and even eating koalas. In addition, it learned to hunt kangaroos very effectively. Wombats and koalas soon followed. After a while, all the tribe's favourite food animals in the Jugamai Hills were gone.

"We are becoming hungry," said Narrapin, Woolgangie's wife. "And none of us dare ask the creature to go away. Whenever I go near him, my objections seem to stay in my mouth, unable to emerge ... "

'By winter the Gugamai were desperate. The Bidgee people would not help them, and feeding the goanna beast took up all their time. Whenever they slackened in their efforts the goanna would become angry and make terrible threats.

'Norna thought about their problem for a long time, then suggested a solution. "We will feed him a special medicine. But we must be careful to do this in secret, or he will stop us."

'The women gathered and pounded ingredients for several days, until they were soft and frothy. They then poured the juice into a huge bowl, and took it to the lizard. "This is our favourite drink. For strength and endurance. Will you try it?"

'With a great gulp the lizard did so, cracking the bowl in two with its strong jaws.

'After a day, it began to stagger a little, and went to sleep early.

'Norna awoke the next morning to find the great goanna staring at her.

"What have you done to me, woman?"

"You must be allergic to the special drink," she said, terrified inside. "There is a plant which might cure you. But you must make haste, or your life will be lost."

'She led the groggy creature to the top of Mount Jugamai, and pointed to a little patch of forest down on the Bul Bul Plains. "Down there. Look for a small tree with blue leaves and yellow branches."

'The goanna leaped into the air, but not for long. Such was the power of the medicine, it could not flap its wings properly, and tumbled from the sky. Norna watched it until it struck the ground, and a tremendous cloud of dust rose into the air. She felt great sorrow at tricking such a magnificent creature, but joy at rescuing her people from starvation.

'The Gugamai celebrated, though it was many years before food was as plentiful as before. The next summer, they climbed down to see the body of the lizard, half buried in a small rise, near where Goolgoorook town is now. Over many weeks they worked to cover it in earth so that it might not wake again. Finally, a warrior walked up the hill and put his ear to the ground.

"The goanna is not dead," he said, "but let us hope he will sleep for a long time."

'Woolgangie and his men covered the creature with dirt to protect it from the sun. Then they went home to their mountain fastness and never went to the lowlands again.'

———◆———

'It fits,' Beth said. 'Every bit.'

She gripped the table's edge tightly.

Mara's smile faltered. 'It's a good story, girl, and very unusual. Is it the one you wanted?'

'Of *course* it is, Mara,' Beth said in a whisper. 'I owe you so much!'

'You and I are the only women who know this secret.' *And please keep me out of this, now,* her expression said. Passing on secrets could cost her any position among her people.

They both stood.

'Be very careful, Beth. When I came down here today, I said to myself: this story is rubbish. Just some nonsense dreamed up by some fool man long ago. Now I see from your face that it is the truth. And they were happy to be rid of it, and so should you.'

'I'm glad I met you,' said Beth. 'It was pretty lucky.'

'Maybe not luck,' said Mara. She paid the bill.

'Uh,' said Beth.

'*Beth.* This *thing* in the story is not anyone's friend. It is old and very dangerous. Do you think that fooling a child would come hard for it?'

Beth shook her head and slipped past Mara. She turned back at the door.

'Thanks,' she said. 'I'll careful.'

At Mara's shrug, Beth turned and left. She stepped out into the warm late afternoon sun. She was tried to commit to memory every detail of Mara's tale.

She waited at a crossing light, arms crossed.

A short, balding man stopped beside her.

'Is that you, Beth?'

She came out of her reverie, puzzled for a moment. 'Oh. Dr Graydon.'

They stepped out onto the pedestrian crossing.

'How are your "quakes" getting along?'

'We're still having them,' she said warily.

'Oh. I assumed they had stopped, because we haven't seen you in a few days.'

'I'm sorry. Assignments … you know. Dad thinks they're just subsidence.'

'No,' the doctor shook his head decisively, 'Subsidence? No way. Not right on *top* of the hill. That kind of thing should only happen on the slopes.'

'OK. Right. Anyway, don't worry about it. We're kind of used to them by now.'

'Look,' he said, 'No insult, but that's just silly. I've got some time free later this week. I'll call your parents and arrange a visit. Action is required.'

'But you thought it was all a joke,' said Beth.

But Graydon was already charging across the road, leaving her shaking her head. *The dragon won't like him poking around.*

On her way home, she walked through the war memorial park, scooting along between an avenue of yew trees. Gazing between their scabbed, spider-webbed trunks, she could see most of Hemming Heights. A low rise started near the memorial, rising towards her home, before falling again in a series of small, steep slopes towards East Goolgoorook and the golf course. A deceptively normal hill, she thought, and the dragon in there, right at the top, where he fell. Just how much earth would the aborigines have heaped over him? She knew they did it out of apprehension, but also, she suspected, with some kind of respect.

'No,' she said beneath her breath. 'They just deferred the problem for someone else to handle, at some other time.'

52

Sam was home, but their parents weren't. The windows were all fixed, and in the twilight the lawns appeared to be free of fragments of glass. Horatio hovered in front of her, pumping his gills. He was quite a handsome fish when viewed in the right light.

'You got rhythm, baby.'

'Dad says he's going to put in more fish. Make a bigger tank,' said Sam, sprawled on a couch reading a comic.

'Which will fall through the floor when the cellar collapses.'

Sam smiled. 'Something strange, Beth. The meaner you are to me, the more I love you.'

Beth scowled. 'That's just weird, Sam. And I'm not mean. It's just called self-defence.'

'Yeah. That's right. You never start anything, do you?'

'I have to live with you. That's my defence.'

'I want to stop,' he said, assuming the angel's face that he normally saved for Abbie or Nick. 'I don't want us to end up hating each other.'

'Look,' said Beth, 'I don't hate you. I'm like that saint or whatever — love the sinner, hate the sin.'

'St Augustine,' said Sam.

'How the hell did you know that?'

He shrugged. 'I've been getting a bad feeling. Something's going wrong, with this house, with Mum and Dad.'

'So you *want* us to move to the city?'

'If it makes us safer. We're almost there anyway.'

'Bull,' Beth said. 'I'm fine. Everyone's fine. Don't be such a dramatist.'

She walked out into the hall. *He's right.* She checked the answering machine; no messages. 'I thought the floor wasn't strong enough.'

'When the cellar's filled, he'll put more supports in. That's what he told me,' said Sam, following her.

'Leave me be, Sam.'

Beth didn't feel like doing homework, she hadn't done a scrap for two weeks. Three assignments were overdue, two essays and a report.

In her mind, playing over and over, was a vision of the dragon plunging from Mount Jugamai, smashing into the soft earth of Hemming Heights. The force of the impact would have half-buried him — in that case, perhaps covering him up would have been relatively easy.

No wonder he didn't tell me how he ended up in Hemming Heights. Tricked by puny little humans. But what strength he must have, to survive a fall of a thousand metres. I wonder if he suffered.

'I've got something for you,' Sam said, rummaging in his school bag. 'Getting into the fairy tales, are we?' He handed her a heavy, sauce-stained book. *Dragons in Literature and History — A Complete Survey.*

'Ms Davis gave it to you?'

'How I can I tell one old fossil from another? I was going to the bus, and she saw me. Said you'd want it.'

'Well, thanks,' said Beth. 'A project, you know.'

'I prefer dinosaurs,' said Sam. 'At least they were real once.' His face brightened. 'Chinese people might have seen dinosaur skeletons. That's where the myth comes from.'

'Oh,' said Beth. 'That would make sense, I guess.' She patted him on the shoulder. 'I'll go read it.'

She sat at her desk and opened the hard-back book. Dragons cropped up in many mythologies over thousands of years. If they disappeared in one place they'd soon crop up somewhere else. *Dragons in History* contained a little on Ancient China, but European and Egyptian dragons were covered in some detail. Dragons could be bad or good; it depended on the circumstances. In Western Europe, they were mostly bad, slithering and flying around the countryside eating sheep and terrorising villagers. After a lot of mayhem and upset a knight errant generally showed up on a mission of decapitation. End of story.

'But what did they *look* like?'

She discovered a series of coloured plates at the back of the book. She leafed through them, stopping occasionally.

The majority of the dragons depicted were not the resplendent and glossy creatures featured on the covers of fantasy novels, but glorified worms, low-slung and malevolent. In fact, one of the most evil was simply called the 'Lampton Wurm' and left a slug-like slime trail. Also known as: Wyvern, Guivre, Lindworm — all ugly critters with too few legs and tiny, useless wings. None of them meshed with her mental image of the creature beneath the cellar. *He cannot be like these things. These are just medieval fantasies.*

The last plate depicted something called a Heraldic Dragon. Beth sighed with something approaching relief. 'That's got to be closer.'

It had a long jaw, sharp horns, a wide snout, paws tipped with what looked like serrated kitchen knives, and a tail perfect for stabilisation while flying. All over, large interlocking scales, and eyes the size of hubcaps. *Is that you?*

'Is that what you read to get away from reality?'

Beth flinched, reflexively closed the book.

'God, Dad. I didn't even hear you come in.' She stood and stretched. 'You're home early.'

'Your door was open,' he said apologetically. 'I'm glad you were reading, anyway.'

'I'll have nightmares,' said Beth, truthfully. Already she could see the last dragon in the book floating before her mind's eye. Was it really him? Or was he just a low legless worm, able only to wriggle forth and eat the local livestock?

53

I'm the chef tonight,' said Nick, putting on a tattered apron. 'Asparagus and chicken in red vino. Mushrooms simmered in olive oil plus a nice bruschetta with roughly torn basil leaves. Not bad, eh?'

Beth watched as he chopped, fried and diced and the house filled with cooking smells. He seemed relaxed. Yet all was not well, with the house, his kids or his marriage. Maybe part of him sensed impending disaster, but another part was able to go on unhindered. People just blundered on, trusting to chance, lying to themselves about reality.

By the time Abbie walked in, she had only to put her bag down and pick up her cutlery. She managed a smile. 'Any news on our Len?' she asked Beth.

'No. I don't think so. Mr Flack didn't say anything to me. But I didn't have him in any of my classes.'

'Well. I've got some news for you,' said Abbie. 'Our branch is going to stay open. We finally convinced management that Goolgoorook has a future.'

Sam cheered, but Beth noticed her mother's smile was forced. 'Is there something else, Mum?'

Abbie hesitated. 'We're going to move house.'

'Why?' gasped Sam. 'This is the best place in the town.'

You just wanted to move, you contrary little beast.

'You may not have noticed, but it's falling down.'

'But there haven't been any tremors for a week!' Sam protested.

'That's not true, darling. I saw the cracks in the driveway!'

'We could fill the cellar.' Beth wanted to join his protest, but for some reason she remained silent.

'I'm sorry, honey, but no. Too dangerous. If either of you was hurt ...'

'We won't go down there. I don't go ...'

'It's not just the cellar,' said Nick with a palpable air of reluctance. 'It's the whole thing. Too risky.' Beth knew her father regarded their home with affection. Her parents had taken out a monster mortgage to get the place built. If he was willing to walk away, Beth realised, he would only be doing so to keep his marriage intact and the family together.

'But you'll never get rid of the house,' said Beth finally, 'if it's got these problems.'

'This is a popular area,' said Abbie. 'We've got a huge block, and it can be subdivided. And we can get a better house.'

'I don't want to hear anymore,' said Sam. 'The new house is going to suck. Some crap place with fake pillars and no yard.'

'You're being very unfair,' said Abbie. 'If this was another family in another house, you'd think they were insane not to move.'

'This is our *home*,' said Sam.

'I'll be in my room,' Beth said and got up to leave the dinner table. Crushed, yet deep down, where dragons affixed their subtle claws, she felt a traitorous sense of relief. Any damage the dragon made to their yard in digging clear would no longer matter. If the house collapsed, no-one would be hurt. She could sneak back into the deserted building to speak with him.

'Dad, you can't do it.' Sam began to cry. 'This will ruin everything.' Beth stopped and stared at him.

Nick held up a weary hand. 'Let's leave it for a bit. Talk about it tomorrow.'

He lifted his plate, and carried it out to the kitchen, where he could be heard scraping it into Freddy's bowl. Abbie shook her head and walked away from her unfinished meal.

'Mum.'

Abbie rounded the corner, heading bedroom-ward. She did not look back.

Sam sniffled once, patted Beth's arm and departed.

Beth headed straight for her room. Read more about the dragon. Waited.

After midnight, she sneaked out to the garage and grabbed some of the ferns and biscuits left by Henry, returning to sweep away evidence of her passing. Each time she slipped through the back door, she held her breath, but no-one stirred. She had no plausible excuse for being found with such items in her possession. Perhaps sleepwalking, or just plain old insanity.

54

'Are you there?'

'Are you?'

'Not for long. You've heard we're leaving, I suppose?'

'It won't affect my escape.'

'Forget your escape, just for once. It means that because of you, we're leaving the place where Sam and I grew up.'

'I didn't choose to be here,' said the dragon, so quietly that his words seemed to evaporate before they could be properly heard. 'Nor did I nominate the day of my reawakening.'

'I know,' said Beth.

Time to read the second chapter of *Climbing Mount Improbable* to the dragon. Every few lines, she was forced to try and explain aspects of genetic theory, and she hoped her memory was serving her well. She spoke of a tiny spiral-shaped chemical found in every cell, containing a very long list of instructions that enabled a whole complex creature to be built. 'They don't spell everything out — just manage the composition and nature of growth. Until they make up a functioning creature.' *Whatever that means*, she thought.

'What about me?' the dragon finally rumbled. 'My kind, that is.'

'You must have evolved, too.'

'Of course I did not,' the dragon said. 'My flesh is of an entirely different sort.'

'Oh. Where did you come from, then?'

'Not from an invisible speck of matter, I can assure you.'

'But everything on earth is related,' Beth argued, feeling combative. 'All life came from the one source. There's no such thing as magic. Science can explain almost everything.'

'Nonsense. Just a trick you play with all of your words. Humans love words — they think that giving something a name somehow explains it.'

Dark, humid scents laced the air. Beth tried to breathe slowly, worried that he was once more attempting to control her mood and thoughts.

'Did the woman of the first peoples speak to you again?'

Oh God. Mara again.

'Not since the other day.'

He can't make me say things, only stop me, and even then, not all of the time. I don't think he knows when I lie.

'Are you sure? I thought I could smell some of the plants favoured by the first people when you came in. I would like to know if she does.'

Beth said nothing. *Perhaps you can force me to tell you, but not willingly.*

'I think we are finished for today,' said the dragon. 'I thank you for the food. A little of it has far more effect than you might imagine.'

Beth mopped at her forehead. *It's hot down here.*

'Soon I will be gone. Not long to wait,' he called after her, as she climbed the stairs.

In bed, she listened for him, but heard only the usual house noises. After a while, she took out her diary and jotted down her latest notions: *He's some kind of freakish holdover from the age of the dinosaurs. They evolved a way of controlling their prey with a flammable gas. They could ignite the vapour if the animal struggled. If they ran out of food, they'd burrow down and sleep until things changed. Then the humans came and their long reign was suddenly over.*

Was it possible that such a thing could evolve? Why did it not appear in the fossil record? Why didn't the dragons band together and eradicate the humans while they could?

What if he doesn't know much about himself? Maybe all he knows is how to live, and nothing about what he really is. After all, humans have only known their true origins for a little while.

A few minutes later and her pen slipped from her hands. Later, she dreamed the dragon had shrunk to the size of a gecko, his wings too weak for flight.

Wednesday 22 March

55

At breakfast, Beth kept her eyes on her cereal. Sam was so downcast and inattentive that Freddy, seeing an opportunity, put his paws up on the table and stole a mouthful of scrambled eggs.

'You were right. Dogs *are* in charge,' Beth said. No response. 'You need more sleep,' she said. 'It's just a house.'

Sam snorted. 'Don't bother, Beth. I don't need you in my head.'

Beth finished her food, and picked up her schoolbag. On her way out she saw her father. He stood with his hand on the cellar door. As if testing its temperature.

She raised an eyebrow.

'Warm to the touch,' he said. 'The boiler might be playing up — pipes run above this door. Something to do with the tremors.' He sniffed. 'And what's that bloody stench?'

Beth made her way to the front door. Let the dragon do whatever it was that he was doing.

'I'm getting Barry Stanford in tomorrow to fix all of this stuff,' he called to her.

'What's the point, Dad, if we're going to be moving anyway?'

'Because we're not leaving *tomorrow*. It'll take a while to find a new place. And we need the place looking good before we can sell it.'

Walking down Dairy Road towards school, Beth attempted to consider her situation calmly. If Barry the handyman arrived on Thursday, he probably wouldn't start work until Friday. If he showed up on Friday, he'd work slowly, or not at all. She remembered how long he had taken to renovate the decking in the back yard. With luck, the dragon would burrow out before the cellar was filled in.

She had been useful to the dragon. Perhaps he was grateful, but she had no way of knowing. If the dragon was able to fly free, she would count herself satisfied. He would go away into the wilderness, the hole in the yard would be filled in, the tremors would cease and they could shelve their moving plans. Not only that, but Flack would give up on his obsession with the scale, she would become supremely popular at school, Jo's father would be acquitted and Lenny would ...

'Hello there, Beth.'

Flack was waiting by the school gate, grim faced.

'Beth. The police are here. They want to talk to you.'

She was ushered through into the principal's office. Her first time on the Captain's Bridge. Tacky, she thought — the usual cheap potted palm, a fingerprint spotted glass-topped table and a photograph of the education minister. Two officers rose from a cracked vinyl lounge, one of them familiar.

'Constable Darling.'

The constable smiled, but without warmth. 'Hello Beth. How's that eccentric uncle of yours?'

'He's left the country.'

'This is Inspector Craig, up from Marshalton.'

Craig was freckled and red-skinned, face bisected by a clipped ginger moustache. They shook hands.

'You know why we're here?' He gestured at Principal Betts. 'Mr Crabbit. We understand you've had encounters with him.'

Beth almost felt sorry for Lenny Crabbit. A mongrel dad and pokie-addicted mother, and probably beaten regularly for no reason at all. Convinced of the cruelty of life, full of hateful ideas and terrorised at school until he was big enough to turn the tables. *He never had a chance. Especially not now.* 'It's his dad who gave him all these stupid ideas. Why not go after him?'

Betts glared at her. 'Don't you worry about Len's family. Leave that to the police.'

After that, there were many questions about Len and his various outbursts. Beth answered most without elaboration, just wanting to be far away. Principal Betts was obviously glad to see her gone, and could be heard apologising for her as she walked out through the secretary's office. *What did I do wrong? So I couldn't remember everything — who can?* She got to thinking about the dragon and his memory. If he really was as old as he claimed, perhaps he could only remember small portions of his own life, or hardly anything at all.

The lunch bell had obviously sounded without her noticing, for the quadrangle was filled with students playing handball. Jo had one end of a slatted bench, and was eating nori rolls with soy sauce while reading a paperback. She looked up and smiled.

'Warm, ain't it? I hear you were being interrogated?'

'The Lenny saga goes on. *Inspector* Craig from somewhere, and that maggot Betts.'

'Aha. And what did you tell them?'

'About the bike, mainly. And some of Len's little jibes in class. I ended up feeling sorry for him.'

'I *knew* you'd get soft on him.' Jo's voice rose. 'Len isn't going to thank you for ignoring what he did. No-one is. Betts wants him gone, save the school from any more stuff-ups. I know exactly what he wants to say: there's no race problem — just one nutcase, et cetera.'

'I don't care about Betts. I'm just trying to be fair.'

'Why be fair? You know what he called me. Was that fair?'

'I *do* remember. It's just ...'

'Forget it, OK?' said Jo, 'I hope you never have to do jury duty. Have to wait a month to get a verdict.' She returned to her novel. Beth waited for the bell, watching students move around the schoolyard. Sarah could be seen in the middle distance, conversing with her supposed friends. Every now and then she glanced surreptitiously towards Jo and Beth.

A shadow fell across Beth.

'Hi!'

'Hi, Hanford.'

She hadn't really thought of him for days. *You're just too wholesome*, she mused, looking up at him.

'All my friends call me Hans. What're you two up to?'

'Melting,' said Jo, finally looking up from her book. 'Too hot for much else.'

'Not for completely everything,' he said, sitting down beside Jo. 'A few of us are going swimming by the railway bridge this evening. We've all got our gear. You guys have got swimming this afternoon, don't you? Well, did you want to come down with us?'

Beth nodded. 'Jo's not much of a swimmer ... ow!'

Beth received another elbow in the ribs, harder than the first.

'I've got my bathers,' said Jo, 'just forgot my towel. But I don't need it.'

'Cool. What about you, Beth?'

She nodded, amused. 'I'm in.'

When he'd gone, Beth turned to her friend. 'I thought you said he had a *silly* name. And *clumsy,* you said.'

'I like clumsy. It's sweet.'

'*Sweet?*'

'And you're not snippy with me?' Jo asked. 'For liking him?'

'No. Life's crazy enough.'

56

Walking slowly on the way to the waterhole, they took off their leather shoes and bathed their feet in roadside dust. 'Mum had to delay her flight,' said Jo. 'The trial was put back another two days, because the case before it went too long.'

'What do you think will happen? At the trial, I mean.'

'Who knows? If he's bought a good lawyer, maybe he'll be back. Maybe it's corrupt. Mum always says that you have to know who to pay. And the sooner you pay, the lower the price. That's just the way it is in poor countries.'

'I hope she knows, then. The right guy.'

'Yep. And I hope she doesn't find about me coming down here,' Jo said. 'Boys and girls swimming together — it's a catastrophe!'

They changed into their one piece swimsuits behind an overgrown willow tree.

They ran the last few metres, throwing their gear under a tree by the bank. Beth was determined to forget the dragon, if only for an afternoon.

'Where are they?' asked Jo.

'Who cares?' Beth shouted, wading straight in and striking out for the opposite bank. The water was cool and deep, the current strong. Hanford and his mates arrived a few seconds later, and within minutes Jo was making a fool of herself for him (*let it be me*, a part of Beth cried). She swam and dived with the rest of them, trying to become a part of the moment and admit no speculation or troublesome thoughts.

Clown prince of the year, Damian Ibbot, made Beth try a precarious-looking rope swing. She arced through space, let go and flew, exulting at the sting of water against her body. For a few minutes she was only aware of the blue sky, the current, and pebbles beneath her feet. There was real pleasure in forgetting everything.

The boys decided to climb the railway bridge. One by one they reached the top, launched themselves and slapped back into the water.

'They're doing it for us,' said Beth in mock admiration. 'All at once. Who'd have thought sheep could climb a bridge?'

They goggled when Steven Facey hung upside down from a girder over the railway line.

'I've seen him do that when a train was passing underneath,' said Hanford, 'nearly smeared from Melbourne to Sydney.'

When the others had gathered up their towels and left, he walked them back into town.

'I'll bring a few lilos — we can go rafting. Can you come next week?'

Jo nodded emphatically.

Hanford halted at the turn-off to his street. 'Well then,' he said, 'this is going to be a good summer. I can tell.'

'I know you saw him first,' Jo said as soon as he was out of earshot. 'But do you think he likes me?'

'Does a one-legged Catholic duck swim in the woods? Stop worrying, Aarons. You're well suited to him. He's pretty cheesy, though. He's all Mormon wholesome.'

Jo flicked her damp hair back and smiled. 'Cheesy beats selfish arsehole.' In the waning evening light she looked much older. Beth envied her.

'You know, it's strange, but I can't help thinking you've already got someone, Beth. You certainly act that way.'

Beth laughed at that comment long after Jo had rounded the corner and vanished from sight. 'Have I ever,' she said, cutting through a small park. 'He's out of sight a lot of time, hot-headed, likes to sleep in, and a bit of a control freak. But I think he'll dig himself out of his rut and soon he'll be up in the air.'

Sam came into the kitchen in time to witness Beth wolfing down cold leftovers from the fridge. Her afternoon's activities had left her ravenous.

'You'll never guess who's down in the cellar!' Sam said.

She almost lost bit her tongue. '*What*? No-one's allowed down there!' She brushed at her mouth, trying to steady her hand and appear casual.

'It's Dr Graydon. He says *you* invited him.'

'Graydon is in the *cellar*? *Now*?' She ran down into that hot, dry room and smacked into her father.

'Oof. Signal before overtaking.'

'Hi Dad. Sam said ...'

'Have you met Dr Graydon?'

'Of course she has,' Graydon said, his voice muffled. He was working in shorts and a T-shirt, sweating in the heat and his head was halfway into the hole.

Get back! He could kill you in a second!

'I don't think that's a very good idea,' she said.

'Half a mo',' came the doctor's muffled voice. 'I'm getting sulphur readings, and traces of a lot of other things. Methane, carbon dioxide, hydrogen disulphide ... extraordinary.'

He stood up, beaming and brushing dirt from his hair.

'Welcome, Beth. There's regular venting of gases, though this area isn't supposed to have any geothermal activity. Unless there's a burning coal seam somewhere down there. But there are no known coal deposits in this valley.'

'Is that possible?' Nick asked. He seemed to be enjoying himself. 'Or maybe a break in the local sewer? Part of a cave system?'

'All possible,' said Graydon, looking like he hoped all options were true at once.

'It's dangerous,' Beth broke in. 'the gas, I mean. Knocks people out. Remember Len?'

'Maybe. We don't have enough data.' Graydon started to pack away his equipment. Sam bumped into Beth, trying to get a better view.

'I'll be back in tomorrow,' Graydon said briskly. 'I'll bring a little fibre camera to poke down into the hole. See how far it goes. Might shed some light on this, ha ha.'

'Are the vapours dangerous?' Sam asked.

'Not yet. Just smelly. They won't build up too much — it's fairly well ventilated down here. You children should stay out, though.'

They trooped upstairs and lingered while Dr Graydon washed his hands in the laundry tub. Nick offered him coffee.

Sam sat and made a show of surfing on his iPad, but Beth could tell he was listening not playing.

'Just glad Beth mentioned this to me.'

What would poking the camera down there reveal? His eye? His teeth? 'No,' she muttered fiercely and the others looked at her. 'Freddy,' she said, 'he wanted to go outside.' The camera wouldn't matter — for surely the dragon would melt it before it came anywhere near him.

'I'm ringing Barry and delaying him for a day or two,' said her father. 'This is worth finalising now.'

When Graydon had gone, Nick walked back up the drive with Beth, scratching his head.

'Pinch me! Volcanic gases in the cellar? I think I preferred subsidence.'

'Graydon's not such an expert, you know,' Beth said. 'Or why would he be working in Goolgoorook?

Nick laughed. 'That applies to me too, you know.'

'I didn't mea—'

'I know. You just want to keep the cellar for yourself. For ages I thought it was Sam going down there. He's got form. But now I think it's you.' He bent to pull a weed from the side of the driveway. 'I'm not upset. You like to figure things out.'

'I don't want to move, Dad,' said Beth

'Even I know that,' he said. 'But I'm afraid that the secret of marriage lies in compromise.'

'What if we could prove that there would be no more earthquakes? And no more fumes?'

Nick shrugged. 'Maybe.' He smiled. But I have no idea at all how you are going to do that. Unless the non-expert Dr Graydon comes up with something.'

Beth made a face.

They took seats on the wicker lounge by the front door.

'Guess I'll have to explain Graydon's visit to your mum, too. Any suggestions?'

———

Abbie was surprisingly calm at the news, relayed to her in the lounge. 'I don't care anymore,' she said, taking Nick's hand. 'We're selling.'

'We *can't* go!' Sam insisted, 'not from our home!'

'We can be at home somewhere else, darling. In a lovely house.'

Beth frowned. 'But this is the only place he's ever lived in.'

'For heaven's sake, Beth! Grow up! We're even staying in Goolgoorook. In the area, at least.'

'*If* we can afford it,' Beth shot back. 'But I don't think that's the issue for Sam.'

'What issue? He's had a good childhood!' Abbie snapped. 'You both have. People move houses all the time!'

'I'm going to bed, Mum. 'Night, Sam.'

He mumbled something to her, but didn't raise his head.

Nick caught up with her on the stairs. 'I'm the other half of this decision, OK?'

'I've got to do an assignment, Dad.'

'Right. You don't seem too committed in that department recently.'

'Flack said something to you,' said Beth. Trying to get at her through her parents. 'I have to go, Dad.'

'OK,' he said. 'Be unfair. Go hide in your burrow.'

She slammed her door and leaned on the other side. Opening a textbook and starting an assignment was unthinkable. She paced for a few moments, fell onto her bed.

When very small, she would lie quietly on her bed, pretending to float. The pale white ceiling would become a cloud filled sky, or a galaxy thronged with stars bright as cracked quartz. Tonight, the roof was just plaster and paint.

57

She woke without needing an alarm, as if part of her mind had been counting the hours. On her way through the house, Beth collected a bottle of chilled water from the fridge. The cellar was even hotter than it had been in the afternoon. The dragon started talking the instant she descended the cellar stairs.

'Your science is coming for me, Beth.'

'Dr Graydon, you mean?'

'He was down here, too near. His machines smell me.'

She frowned. 'You're wrong. He thinks the tremors are natural. He has absolutely no idea that you are down here.'

'Yes, yes. Am I *not* natural, Beth? That is what you said the other day. Do you think I am a machine, a piece of metal like his cold little tools? Do you think he will not smell me?'

'Of course he won't. He was only measuring the air.'

'He smelled with a thing that is not a nose. Perhaps it can see me, know me ...'

'No. Machines are not intelligent.' she said. 'Not very, anyway.'

'He will be coming back, no? You must stop him.'

'Come off it, will you?' She forced her voice down. 'I have no control in my own life, let alone over anyone else. He's an adult, and I'm just a useless kid.'

'Not useless. But if you cannot stop him, I will hurt him.'

She hesitated. 'We only have to wait two days, and you will be free.'

'I do not want your science to see me. Bringer of death, singer of oblivion.'

'It's not *my* science. It's just a way of looking at things.'

'Then *don't* look at me!' he growled, his voice filling the space until she felt she was swimming in sound. 'Look elsewhere and let me go free.'

'I *want* you to be free. To fly. You know that.'

He quietened. 'I know. You are an honest creature.'

She looked down.

'I want to *see* you fly,' she said quietly.

'Indeed. When I am abroad, perhaps I shall fly past. Let you see the wings of the dragon. In payment for what you have done. The difficulties I have created for you.'

'I'll stand on Mount Jugamai at midnight,' she said, 'on the next full moon. And wait for you.'

'Yes. I will be there.'

Right.

'These men,' said Beth, 'want to help my father. That's all. If you leave them alone, your moment will come.' She felt a fraud. 'Just trust me, can you?'

He was silent now. 'Dragon?'

She could hear the house ticking as the gutters contracted in the cool of the night.

'Yes, Beth?'

'What is it like to live forever?'

'I haven't lived forever. Nothing is eternal.'

'You know what I mean. Not to become old.'

'Each cycle, my body wears out. When I return, I am reborn.'

'Like a phoenix,' Beth mused. 'It's still the same you, though. Same memories.'

'In a way, yes. But I feel just as precarious as any other living thing. The future is as uncertain for my kind as for you. We are almost all gone now, whereas you are so many. Perhaps it is you who will prove immortal. As a group, if not individually.'

Beth made a noncommittal noise. 'That's not very comforting for me. I'm frightened of dying.' She smiled. 'Can I tell you a joke?'

'That is one thing dragons and humans have in common.'

'It's not really a joke,' said Beth, 'it's just something someone wrote. He said that rather than achieve immortality through his work, he'd prefer to do so by not dying.'

'I think I understand,' said the dragon, after some hesitation. 'He sees through the lies humans tell themselves to make death seem less final. That somehow achievements during life will give you an presence beyond it.'

'Something like that,' Beth said.

You are a very strange creature, Beth. Like a child in some ways, but sophisticated. How odd to think you have only seen ten and four summers.'

'But there aren't so many more summers than that for *any* human,' Beth said. 'Doesn't it seem pointless working with us? We're gone in an eye blink.' Beth took another sip from her bottle.

'A life's worth is not based on its length, Beth. As long as I live, I'll remember a girl with courage enough to face the unknown.'

'Aw shucks,' said Beth, but she blushed anyway.

Once more the cellar filled with a million scents, and Beth knew that those she was able to detect were vastly outnumbered by those she could not. *It is his song, and I can only hear the odd note.*

'So when does this new life begin?'

'Perhaps two nights? It is already happening. I am not in full control of the process. But I will warn you, I know what I owe.' The house groaned overhead as if it was a ship slowly scraping past an iceberg. Beth suddenly felt a chill radiate out from her core, as if her heart had begun to pump liquid helium in place of blood.

'I thank you for that, Beth. I hope to see you tomorrow night.'

Friday night. *God, so soon!* Her family would be out for dinner, out of town, out of danger — if she had an ounce of cunning in her body.

Thursday 23 March

58

In the morning, Beth packed her swimsuit, anticipating another hot day. Never a particularly sociable student, the previous evening's outing to the waterhole had made an impression on her. Perhaps things *would* change during her later years at high school, a bigger circle of friends, parties, boys ... Or perhaps Jo and Sarah were her friends for the duration, and in not trusting them with the dragon, she'd betrayed their friendship. *Yeah, and why would they have believed me anyway?*

My real problem, she thought, *is that I don't completely believe that any of what is happening is real. That I am in the throes of a delusion. But what about the scales and the tooth? What about the hole in the cellar, and Graydon and Flack?*

Perhaps she was able to pass her own madness on to others.

Life seemed to fall into partitions: to go to school, and appear relatively normal, then to dabble with ideas and actions which contradicted all reason — worlds where walls spoke, and issued forth fumes that smelled of things she would never encounter.

A warm breeze followed her to school, birds riding it from telephone line to rooftop. *During the day, the dragon's just an idea. When night falls, the idea fades and he becomes real.*

———

She met Jo a block away from school. Jo seemed happy enough, invoking Hanford's name at least three times in five minutes.

'What's up with your brother?' Jo asked, finally changing the subject.

'What do you mean?'

'Look,' Jo said, pointing.

The lad in question was trudging past on his way to school.

'He's usually atomic powered, Bee. It's like someone took out the reactor.'

'Closer than you think,' said Beth. 'He's not very happy with our parents at the moment. Mum thinks the house is unsafe. So they're talking about selling it.'

'And leaving Goolgoorook?'

'Something like that. Or maybe just moving somewhere else in town.'

'He'll adapt,' said Jo. 'Smart kids do.'

Beth wasn't sure. Undoubtedly, Sam was smart, but his was a strange kind of intelligence, often focused on things that interested few other children — tropical beetles, the surface of Mars, insects in amber, carpets from Central Asia. Once or twice she'd wondered whether he might be autistic, having read that autistic kids were often very good looking. But gradually Sam formed friendships with a few of the quicker kids in his year and developed his ongoing feud with his big sister — and he began to seem a lot more normal. Now, brat of the century that he was, he needed her help. Yet all she had done so far was to ignore him.

———

Ms Davis stopped them as they passed the chemistry labs in B Block.

'Oh, Beth. My quest endeth. Did that brother of yours hand the book on to you?'

'What book, Miss?'

'The book about dragons you had on reserve. Funny, wasn't it?'

'What was funny? I think I'm missing something.'

'That you reserved it, and it was Sam who had it out before you.'

Beth shook her head. 'He didn't tell me that. I didn't know the primary kids could borrow from our library.'

'All on the same database, Beth. I told him to hand it on to you when he finished. And to return all his other overdues. He's been obsessed with mythical creatures lately.' She sighed. 'He's such an advanced reader — I wish we had more like him to cater to.'

'Weird,' said Jo as Ms Davis strode away. 'Sam gets personal service.'

'Um,' said Beth, distracted.

A moment later, Sarah appeared. 'I've been looking for you two.'

Beth looked around for escape, then guiltily realised what she was doing. Jo stood and looked levelly at Sarah, expression neutral.

Sarah raised a hand, and Beth involuntarily flinched. 'If you're going to hit me, just do it.'

'Hit you? Jeez. What've you been smoking?' There was a scrap of paper in Sarah's hand, much folded and tattered. 'I got your note, Beth. Read it twice.' She returned it to her pocket and laughed. 'Life's too short.'

'I thought you must have thrown it away …'

'No. Almost. I had a good think about it instead. While I was playing a game of tennis.'

'As you do,' said Jo.

Sarah nodded at Jo. 'Sorry about all the crap, guys.'

'Don't,' said Beth. 'an exciting week, it was. People say things.'

'Yep.'

'We can't pick our own family, can we?'

Beth glanced at Jo. She smiled and shrugged. 'No. That's the shame of it.'

The first period bell sounded, and Jo shouldered her bag. 'Off, then. See you at lunch, crew.'

Sarah watched her go, then turned to Beth.

'Let's be a bit late to class. Come outside — we'll talk down by the front gate.'

———

They walked between flower beds and over prickle-infested grass. As they moved around, Beth tried to recall what she had wanted to ask Sam — something that had disturbed her, but the moment swept these memory queries away.

'Let me guess, Beth. Jo thought I hated you and her because of Len. Well, it wasn't like that,' she said. 'When Len smashed up your house, I was ashamed. I knew he had it in for you, but I didn't do anything. I thought you despised me. Or that you should. Wasn't everything my fault, in some weird way?'

'I'm not being a smartarse,' said Beth, 'but I thought it might be something like that.'

Sarah nodded. 'When you're inside something, you can't really see it for what it is.'

They reached the far end of the schoolyard and turned back.

I feel guilty too, Beth thought, *even though I'm not.* The truth was that the dragon had distracted her from her other problems, and that, at the moment, she was more concerned for a monster than her friends.

'Jack Netcher suggested Len go and stay at Ooralloo for a month,' said Sarah. 'He's already there, in fact. If he stays, all charges will be dropped. And he can go back to school.'

'God,' said Beth, nonplussed. 'That's mad. Why would they want him up there?'

'Flack said it's like the martial arts moves — you know, where you use your opponent's strength against them. It's going to be pretty intense for Len. All that non-white skin.'

'Jo's going to *love* that,' Beth said, seeing the humour of it. 'I wish it was a reality show.'

'Maybe they'll initiate him,' Sarah suggested. 'Without anaesthetic.'

Beth smiled. As they turned back, she saw Sam — *on the loose during school hours!* — sidling towards her, hiding himself behind the shrubs that lined A Block. He raised his hand, then saw she was with Sarah. Before she could return his wave, he darted back behind a bush and vanished. Beth shook her head. *Does he want some money?* she wondered.

59

During study period and on her own for a while, Beth gave in to an inner prompting and dragged *Dragons in History* from her bag. She began to read.

A previous reader had underlined many passages in pencil, scribbling accompanying notes in the margin in an irregular childish scrawl. Obviously Ms Davis had not gotten to leafing through the book recently. Beth tried to read the scrawls, but a letter or two aside, they were basically illegible. Between pages 172 and 173, she discovered a loose sheet of sketching paper. Beth picked it up, inspected it closely. Nothing. She turned it over. She took in a beautifully drawn sketch stretching from one side of the scrap of paper to the other. There, coiled, scaled and clawed and convincingly sinuous, was a sleeping dragon.

The dragon was not a direct copy of any illustrated in the book. Rather, it took the eyes of the Wyvern, the snout of the Guivre, the thick legs of the Heraldic dragon and mixed them together. The result was inspired — perfect. Without any doubt, or any rational reason for her certainty, she knew this form belonged to the voice in the cellar. *It is him.* Her mouth went dry. She forced herself to keep thinking.

This is right, Beth scribbled in her notepad. *Everything is in proportion, all the parts look like they have a use.* She could visualise the creature flying, leaping and sleeping. Her neck prickled. *Someone else knows more about the dragon than I do.*

Another cryptic scribble marked the base of the illustration, in the same hand as the annotations scattered through the book. She traced the mark with her finger, trying to riddle out letters. This time she was determined to make a full translation.

An eight? B? No, she realised, *it's an S. Followed by … A zero? If so, maybe the S really is an eight. That would make it 80. No. The second mark has to be an O. SO. So what? No, it's really S dot O dot. S.O. Like initials — the artist's signature.*

Initials. Had to be.

She closed one eye and rubbed at the other.

S.J.O. Samuel Julius Ormonde.

'Holy crap,' she whispered.

Part Five

60

Sam was nowhere to be found on the school grounds, and she gave up looking when she saw Flack regarding her from the other side of the quadrangle. Beth considered running out the school gates, but hesitated.

She passed through the afternoon's remaining two classes in a strange kind of daze.

Computer Skills was the last lesson of the day and probably the most useless of the week, which was saying something. When Ms Gare let them out early, Beth departed the school grounds at great speed without waiting for Jo or Sarah. Gradually she calmed as she warmed up. She had to think things through and come up with a plan. To give herself time for this, she walked the long way home, turning east on Golf Links Road, then north across the Goolgoorook Golf Course.

I haven't been this way for a while.

Hemming Heights looked quite different from this angle. The hill on which the suburb perched rose steeply from Circular Avenue to her house, then fell away, rose again, finally declined more gradually to the west. Two hills, really, one smaller one on top of the other.

Exercise wasn't really helping; her mind remained muddled. The dragon wanted her to help defend him, but from which direction would danger arrive? Via Mr Flack and his conjectures, or Dr Graydon's fibre-optic camera? Or something completely unexpected? And strangest of all: where did *Sam* fit in?

She walked up the drive and let herself in the front door.

'Anyone home? Hello?'

She ended up in the lounge.

Abbie glanced up from her paper. She looked tired.

'Hi Mum. Sam?'

'At Ken's place for the night. Keen to go, of course. Last minute thing. Your father's at a farewell dinner. Can't remember who for.'

'Oh. Thanks.'

'Are you feeling well?' Abbie asked, folding the paper and putting it aside. 'Tell me if you need to. About anything.'

'Do you have the Dankowitzes' number?'

'Whiteboard. Next to the fridge. Why do you ask?'

'Just in case I need to find something.'

'Sam's been taking some of my stuff.'

'Maybe things are falling down the side of your bed.'

'He's a different person for you, Mum.' *And a different person for everyone else as well, perhaps.*

She moved through the house, wondering why it felt so alien, as if she was visiting it for the first time. The cellar door now had *two* padlocks, the second even bulkier than the first. She hoped the dragon would be up to opening both of them for her.

Abbie found her gazing along the corridor to Sam's room. Beth had reached a kind of impasse. She didn't know what she was doing or what to think or which action to take next.

'Your father found this in the cellar this morning,' Abbie said, proffering a tattered notebook.

'That's mine!' exclaimed Beth, scandalised, grabbing it.

'Before you go berko, Beth, I haven't looked inside it. Didn't even crack a single page. I wouldn't make *that* mistake twice!'

She stood with hands on hips. 'I don't know why you go down there, young lady. Perhaps I don't care.'

'But ... ?'

'*But* you can't do it anymore. Doctor's orders.'

'Graydon?'

'He says the gases down there might be dangerous. Very dangerous, he said.'

Beth puffed out a gust of air, her shoulders dropping.

———

Nick arrived home at eleven, talking a little too loudly, his voice waking Beth from a doze. She sat up, and took a sip of water from a glass by her bed.

He's had a beer, she thought and almost smiled. One glass and he was half sloshed.

'Would you believe,' Nick said, voice carrying clearly, 'Jim Risdon — from 'cross the road ... funny old bloke ...'

'Yes?'

' ... is worried about his *property* values? He's heard about our tremors. Says we should *do* something about it. *Do something for the sake of the neighborhood* — that's what he said.'

Abbie made a disgusted sound. 'Greedy. Christ, he'll probably background people who come to check out the property. Not good.' 'Damned property parasites,' said Nick. Real estate agents and their tactics were among his pet dislikes.

They moved away, voices tailing into inaudibility.

Beth lay still in bed. She felt lonely. Eventually she got up, put on her shoes and took the dragon's scales from their hiding place. They were much warmer now. She slipped them into her jeans pocket.

At the foot of the stairs, Beth paused and wished Henry was there to surprise her. At that moment, she knew she should have told him everything.

One padlock was already open but the other lock had disappeared. Stooping, she saw it on the floor, bar bent back like a green twig. 'Damn.' She went on.

Stairs number three and seven were buckled, and looked as if they might soon collapse. The floor of the cellar was worse, concrete humped up in waves, fragments canted at random angles. A light coating of cement dust lay over everything. crackling, sharp electrical stench.

'Oh my *God*. This is not supposed to happen today.' How could she have presumed to understand something powerful enough to do this?

'Beth—'

She jumped, skin prickling. *I should have stayed frightened. Instead, I let him lull me, with his scents. Fool.*

'Scales are hot. Hotter all the time,' she said, balancing both of them on her fingertips. Everything was baking down here — heat was pouring from the hole in great shimmering waves. Beth knelt and let the scales rest on the floor.

'The warmth will take me from this cold place, Beth. Away from the long death of sleep. I burn my own flesh to rise.'

Beth felt sweat trickle down her spine and her legs prickled. 'How did you bend the padlock? Why?'

'Dragons know metal, think the way it thinks.'

He'd only bothered to answer the first part of her question. 'I can ask Dr Graydon,' she said, trying to wrench her mind back towards independence. 'Maybe he can explain it. Magnetism or something ... quantum mechanics, maybe ...'

At the mention of Graydon's name, the floor began to shake. Instinct and fear told her to move away to the side — quickly. Two steps and a sprawling leap over an undulating segment of the floor took her back to the foot of the staircase.

Searing air poured from the hole, fiery and desert dry. A cloud of opaque, lung-searing particles obscured the whole room. Beth coughed as if her lungs were being scoured by a coarse bristle brush. Her feet were bolted down, eyes watering and heart hammering hard enough to shake her whole body.

'What're you doing? You promised to wait—'

'No, Beth. I was wrong to promise you that. There can be no Gray-don. Never again. I do not want to kill. Do what you have to. Keep him away. You are able to fit me into your world, but he is fixed, blind to me — he cannot be allowed to continue. People destroy what they cannot accommodate. This is my warning, not a threat.'

Beth staggered, ears ringing.

I can't hold my head up. The room is turning, I think. My skin is full of sand.

Silently, dry lips parted and eyes closed, she slid towards the floor.

Friday 24 March

61

Diary: I woke up in my bed this morning. Nothing unusual about that, except I can't remember getting there. The cellar door to my room memories are gone — I hope I didn't drop anything out there. I have a big bruise on my left hip and three small cuts across the upper part of my right arm. My shoulders and ankles are bright red and itch like fire. Some kind of allergic reaction?

I had another nightmare. This time D was some type of judge, wearing a coat of golden scales. When he tried to sentence me, flames shot from his mouth. D is somehow alive, in a faint kind of way, in my dreams. Pulling strings, twitching me this way and that. I think the longer things go on, the weaker his control becomes. But I would be very wrong to think I am now running things. Sometimes along the way I thought I was in control, or equal, but really, I knew nothing. At least I've woken up, I think.

What if he hurts me, or someone else? Dr Graydon will be here this afternoon, and no-one is going to listen to little Bethy and her freaky warnings. What to do, if anything at all is to be done?

One little idea occurred to me — when I was thinking over the story of Woolgangie. Too crazy to write down. Some things that feel true don't look true in print. Maybe later I'll try to figure it out and put it down here. Maybe.

———

Breakfast was a strange affair. Beth did her best to act as if all was normal, but felt her true state of mind must be obvious. Sam's absence made her uneasy, though she knew he would go straight to school from Ken's place She kept wishing he'd walk through the door.

Her father stood before her, and raised his eyebrows.

'Well? What do you think of the suit?' Nick raised an arm, turned, slung his coat over his shoulder.

'Very nice,' she told him, deciding not to comment on his creased coat, and the dog hairs on his trousers. Rare was the day a tie could be seen around Nick's neck, so she considered his get-up a great achievement. 'Sharp, almost.'

'Almost is good enough,' he said. 'Have to squire around a few visitors from Sydney today. Come to see the local infrastructure. Such as it is.'

'Congratulations,' said Beth.

'Need a lift?'

'No thanks, Dad. Len's out of town now, so you don't have to worry. I'm meeting Jo.'

Liar, liar!

'Okey dokey. Your mother and I are catching some opera tonight.' He rolled his eyes. 'I'll catch up on some sleep. You kids can buy pizza. A *healthy* one. If that's possible.'

As soon as he was out the door, Beth limped down the street, leg aching. The sun was already warm and steady. At the corner of Serpentine and Topaz, she entered a graffiti-covered phone booth, and dialled. *The dragon flies tonight. He flies he flies, someone dies, he flies ... we all die ...*

One ring. Two ... three ... twelve. She fidgeted. The distant phone chirped away. 'What?!!' The voice was loud and gruff.

'Who's that?' she asked, quailing.

'Who's askin'? Whatterya want!!??'

Beth flinched away from the earpiece.

'I'm looking for …'

'Ya better look somewhere else!'

' … Mara! Is she—'

'Yer want her? Not me then?' He seemed vaguely disap-pointed. 'Graannnnn!! Phone! How should I know? Get stuffed you old bag!'

A minute passed, a TV blaring, dogs barking. 'Hello?'

'Is that you Mara?'

'Hello? Who's that?' The old woman sounded unwelcoming. 'Shut up, Marky!'

'It's Beth. From Goolgoorook.'

Mara took her mouth away from the receiver for a few moments, busy reprimanding the child who had answered the phone.

'What's the matter, girl?'

'Things are going wrong, Mara. I thought I knew what was happening. I'm frightened.'

'That old fella's real bad news, girl. Why do you think my people got rid a' him, eh? Pity you didn't ask my advice earlier. You wouldn'ta gone nowhere near him.'

'That's a bit bloody hard when he's camped right under our house!' Beth shouted. '*Help me.* Without you, there's no-one. I'm out here in a phone booth so he doesn't hear me. So he can't look into my mind and take what he wants.'

The ensuing silence was so long Beth thought the line had gone dead.

'We can talk. That's *all*, though. Just talk.'

'Thank you. Can I meet you?'

'Yes. Try to be calm. I'll get you from your school, at one. Too late to worry about old Jack. But maybe it's not too late to fix this thing.'

When Beth put down the phone, her knees were weak.

She'll probably just tell me to run away, and that's the one thing I can't do.

62

Beth looked around the quadrangle, trying not to seem too wild and unsettled.

People darted this way and that, laughing, joking, talking about things from another world. *Sam!* She had to speak to him, but about what? *What am I doing here? Why couldn't Mara come at once?*

Finally, Beth saw Jo and Sarah with a group of other students under a large elm. *They look complete without me,* she thought. She sidled off before they saw her, and frittered away time by sitting in a quiet corner of the quadrangle and reading more about dragons on her tablet. *These legends don't reveal hidden knowledge,* she thought, *they're an admission of ignorance. The dragon is just a memory of a memory. Once our only rival for dominion over the earth, and now almost completely forgotten.*

At a specially convened recess assembly, Principal Betts put in another award-winning performance. 'The scourge ... of racism ... shall be ... overcome!!'

'Thinks he's bleedin' Martin Luther King,' whispered Mr Singh loudly, to the amusement of nearby students and more than a few teachers.

'Racism ... has been eradicated ... from this school ...' Betts let the words hang for a few moments, and looked grandly out over his captive audience, ' ... thanks to innovative policies ... and fast work by school administration.'

They applauded dutifully, and they were finally dismissed.

Beth trudged towards class, unable to focus on anything but the ground beneath her feet.

'What a freak,' said Jo, falling in beside her. 'Are we supposed to respect him?'

'I don't know,' said Beth.

'It's a power thing,' said Jo. 'Or an ego thing. I'm not sure which.'

'Both, maybe?' Beth decided at that moment to put her energies into pretending to be her ordinary self. The task seemed insurmountable, but wasn't making an effort everything in life?

Jo inadvertently bumped into her, and Beth nearly collapsed, clutching her hip.

'Sorry. Christ, Bee, what's wrong?'

'Sore leg. Nothing much. Came off my bike last night.'

Sam burst through a clump of students and stood between them.

'Gotta see you, Beth!' Sam was pale and breathless. His expression wasn't the usual mixture of mania and sardonic amusement, but something far stranger. He looked frightened, almost anguished.

'I tried to find you yesterday,' he said, staring around. 'To tell you something.'

'No,' said Beth. 'I can't just …'

'Please … come …'

'God, Sam.' Beth tried to think herself into a state of clarity and calm, but it didn't work. 'I'll be back in a sec, Jo.'

'I've got to tell you something,' Sam repeated.

Seeing her brother so serious and yet unsure of himself was a novelty. She glanced over at the gates. Still hours before Mara was supposed to arrive. Suddenly she noticed that Mr Flack was watching them intently from several metres away, his face unreadable.

'It's important, Beth,' Sam said urgently, grabbing at her hand. 'I'm not joking.'

'Then tell me,' she demanded, turning her back to Flack, in case he was somehow able to read lips. 'What do you *want*?'

'I can't say anything here.' He jerked his chin in the direction of Mr Flack.

'Don't bring him into it.'

'Why not? He asked *me* to *spy* on you!'

Sam now had her complete attention. He tugged at her sleeve again. 'Beth, he wanted me to look for things your room. Said I could have a voucher for computer stuff. *Freak.* There's more, but I have to show you.'

The final bell for first period rang, and Flack walked off to his class with obvious reluctance, looking back over his shoulder until he rounded a corner. Eventually, Sam and Beth stood alone on the assembly area, Jo and Sarah lingering on the A Block verandah.

This is a day for being reckless. Act and damn the consequences.

'All right. You win. Where are we heading?' she asked, already knowing the answer.

'Hemming Heights.'

'OK. But wait — I have to tell the girls.'

She walked across to Sarah and Jo.

'Sam needs me. I have to go.'

'What is it? Is he in trouble? Do you want us to come, too?' Jo asked.

'And get you suspended?'

Sarah's eyes were bright. 'As if we care. Tell us!'

Jo put a restraining hand on Sarah's shoulder.

'Look, guys,' said Beth. Stuff's been happening at my house. It's too freaky to put into words. First you wouldn't believe me, then you'd think I was crazy, then I'd have to show you stuff you should never see ... look, it's much better not to be anywhere near me for the rest of today.'

Jo and Sarah looked at her as if she had just sprouted a pair of antennae and was waving her gleaming mandibles in the air.

'You what?' Jo asked.

'I have to sort out some stuff.'

'And you want us to go to class?'

'Yes,' said Beth. 'If you came with me, your lives could be in danger.'

'Oh,' said Sarah. 'This doesn't have anything to do with Len, does it?'

'Not a thing,' said Beth, relieved at being able to tell the truth for one moment.

'You're pretty weird sometimes,' said Jo. 'Whatever you're doing, I would have thought it would be better to have some help doing it.' She held up her hands. 'But what would I know?'

'Can you tell Speck I'm sick, please?'

'If I do,' said Jo, staring very hard at Beth, 'you have to tell us everything. Start to finish. And if you're doing something rash, and we could have helped, I'll never forgive you.'

'I'll tell all,' Beth agreed. 'But only afterwards. And you'll think I'm insane. And stupid.'

'We *have* to go!' hissed Sam, close behind Beth.

'Later, guys' said Beth.

Jo nodded curtly. 'Go, then. Try to stay alive.' She turned and walked away, Sarah a pace behind.

63

They moved fast, Sam running, stopping, then waiting for Beth to catch up. She half expected Flack to come running down the street with a two metre wide dog-catcher's net, and drag them back to class. They said little, Sam full of purpose, Beth out of breath.

'Slow down ...' she puffed.

'*Hurry.*'

'I've got a sore leg,' she said, but he did not relent.

Sam led her to Cowan Court, a short cul-de-sac near their home.

'There's no way through here.'

'We're here already,' said Sam. He pointed at the pavement, then at the roadway.

'What? What am I looking at?' Then she saw it. A maze-like pattern of cracks ran in a broad band from one side of the road to the other. A few metres on, the same thing, with wider gaps and more buckling. Beyond that, more cracks, and so on right up to the end of the court.

'That wasn't there a week ago.' he said. 'But it is now. And in most of the other streets in this area.'

Beth sat on the nature strip, trying to hide her shivering. 'You dragged me up here to look at cracked bitumen?'

He gave her an odd, knowing glance. 'There are patches like this all over the suburb.'

'What about Flack?' she persisted. 'The bribe?'

'I told you about that.'

'What did he ask you to do?'

'To tell him where you went, and make a list of the things in your room. And to bring him any diary that you might have.'

'Did you?'

'No. I didn't. It was too weird.'

'You could have told me this at school.'

'I know. But Flack is only a bit of the story. It's the cracks. It's just—' He broke off and stood up. Tapped his thighs and cracked his knuckles. 'I know that you—' He circled around. She'd never seen him like this. 'Beth, will you listen to me?' He glared at her.

'I am,' she protested. 'I'm not saying a thing.'

'I know what's causing the cracks, and the tremors. And so do you.' He pointed jerkily in the general direction of their house, of which only a portion of the roof was visible. Then he pointed downwards, into the earth beneath their feet. '*Under* the house,' he hissed. 'Under.'

If she hadn't already been sitting, she would have fallen. 'Sam—' she breathed, trying to draw in air. Panic settled on her like a thick cloak. She knew he knew — had known since yesterday, she realised.

Cars trundled past, heedless.

'No, she said. 'You can't possibly know!'

'I've been watching you, Beth. You're not very good at keeping secrets. I really *did* read your diary. Put it right back where you had it hidden.'

'But he only spoke to me,' she said plaintively. *I was the only special one.*

Sam shook his head. 'No. He talks to anyone who he thinks

he can use. You changed. So did I, but I guess it wasn't so obvious. I'm a much better liar than you. More practice.'

Beth had no rejoinder.

'I saw your drawing in the dragon book,' said Beth, 'but I still didn't ...'

'So *that's* where I left it!' Sam exclaimed. 'I couldn't find it anywhere. But it was just a guess.'

'It's *right*,' said Beth. She breathed deeply. 'This has been driving me mad, Sam. Knowing, and not saying anything.' She began to search her bag. Pricking her finger on the tooth, she held the gleaming thing out to Sam.

He held out a hand, took it. 'He gave you *that*? All I got were stories.'

'I needed something real. Otherwise I wouldn't have believed. So he gave me that. And two scales.'

'It's horrible,' said Sam, handing the tooth back to her. 'And awesome at the same time. Everything is like that with him.'

'If we both know, what do we do about it?'

Sam shrugged. 'I have something else to show you.'

They began to walk around the edge of Hemming Heights towards Goolgoorook, stopping to look up and talk. Beth kept shaking her head, unable to believe that she was sharing this experience. Something that had been so solitary and mad should have stayed in the shadows.

'A few days ago,' said Sam, 'I was in heaven, taking orders from a hidden monster. It was *my* big adventure, creeping down at dawn, stealing meat, telling him about the world. Then I saw *you* with that dog food. And I *knew*.'

'I must've gone through forty bags of it.'

'He was running the two of us all over the place, getting

exactly what he wanted. I was jealous. I wanted you to stay away. But there was nothing I could do.'

Beth grasped the tooth until it cut into her palm. 'He gets in my head. That's how he convinces people to help him.' She coughed. 'Do you think we should stop him?'

Sam looked at her sharply, then began to laugh. She reddened.

'Can we stop the sun from rising?' he asked, 'I don't think so. Beth, we've played our part. Once this has started, no one can stop it.'

'There's more to it than you know, Sam.' Beth told him of her own dealings with Flack and the scales, and then about her meeting with Mara, finishing with the story of Woolgangie.

Sam stared at her. He laughed.

'I can't believe you know how he *really* got here. Tricked? Poisoned? *Awesome!*'

She blushed. 'Mara will be in town soon, to meet me.'

Bark clattered down from gum trees, and the day grew ever hotter. They stopped walking and stood beneath a tree, glad for the shade.

'The reason I feel so hopeless,' Sam said, 'doesn't make much sense. Or maybe it does.' Crouching, he reached for a twig. 'Yesterday, when I was cycling back from Ken's, I looked up at our place.' He sketched a profile of their portion of Hemming Heights in the dirt. 'Steep at the top, then it flattens out, rises a bit — then falls away towards Mannering Court.'

Beth tilted her head, felt a glimmering of recognition.

'What does that line remind you of?' *I can't see a thing.* Sam poked at the diagram with his toe. 'Head.' The rise on which their house stood. 'Body.' Serpentine Drive. 'Tail.' Lower Hemming Heights. 'That's over two hundred metres.'

Beth's flesh prickled.

Sam scuffed over the drawing. 'I know. Stupid.'

A low grumble came up through their soles, and the earth shook, first gently, then with some violence. They both looked up at Hemming Heights. Telephone poles were swaying and windows shattering. A geyser of water erupted from a drain, and poured off down the street. All around them alarms sounded, car and house. With a wet slapping sound, great swathes of roadway began to crack.

'It's started early,' Sam said, crawling over to her. His face had lost all colour.

'He's coming out?'

'Surely not in daylight. He's afraid of being seen. But soon. Maybe tonight.'

The larger tremors gradually died away, replaced by a low bass vibration.

'It's us,' said Beth with morbid certainty. 'We're a threat, now. He knows I've been to visit Mara. He doesn't want us to go back to the house.'

She held out the tooth in the flat of her hand. 'Can you smell it? Somehow he can sense us through these parts of himself. But perhaps the effect fades.' She swallowed on a dry throat.

A fine cloud of reddish dust rose from the heights, fanning into the sky as a vast, obscuring veil. Cars began to hurtle down Dairy Road, horns beeping and glancing back at their damaged homes.

'Christ, Sam. What about Freddy?'

'Outside. Don't worry. Let him out before I went to school. He'll run away.'

'Are you sure?'

'He's road-smart,' said Sam defensively. 'Better than being up there at the moment.'

A police car slammed past, wheels thumping hard on new bumps and ridges, skidded to a halt at the entrance to Serpentine Drive, and disgorged three officers. One of their number began to stop people attempting to drive into Hemming Heights, and the other two waved fire engines through.

'Let's go before they see us,' Sam said.

Beth followed Sam haltingly, grimacing. 'They're only setting up a roadblock. Slow down!'

'I can't help it. If we don't hurry ... I don't know ...'

'We have to find Mara,' Beth said with sudden certainty. 'That's our only chance.'

Sam thought for a few heartbeats, then nodded.

They worked their way along one badly damaged street, took a pathway through into another, crossed their own avenue then turned back towards the town. Here the bitumen was broken into tiny fragments as if it had been chewed up and sprayed out.

A sizzling noise split the air like a whip crack, and Beth turned to see a high tension powerline snap and fall to the ground opposite the Saraband River chicken farm. Blue gouts of current sparked into the air, then circuit breakers cut in and the flashes of light ceased. More work for Nick. Serpentine Drive and North West Arterial traffic lights winked out. Several houses seemed to be on fire, fingers of smoke poking up towards the sky.

'Holy hell,' said Sam.

Beth's hip was sore now, and only bloody determination kept her from sitting down and resting it. Sam finally slowed and walked beside her.

'S'all right, Bethy. We'll make it.'

'God, Sam. It's half past twelve already. What if Mara leaves? What if we don't make it back in time?'

'She's not even here yet.'

64

They turned towards the school, trotting past the war memorial. Simpson and his donkey were now tilted, staring straight up at the dust-reddened sun. A First World War artillery piece had rolled off its pedestal and into a tree. In the middle distance, Goolgoorook itself seemed undamaged — for the moment, just far enough away from Hemming Heights.

Beth could see small knots of people, all of them with eyes and hands oriented in the direction of Hemming Heights.

'It's ten to one,' Beth shouted at Sam, indicating Captain Chicken's temperature n' time readout, 'Come on!'

They lurched on, Sam frantically trying to assist her. About a hundred metres short of the school, he abruptly turned and pushed her off the footpath into a shrub. Caught off-balance, she hit at him but fell anyway, woody fingers scratching her skin and catching at her clothes.

'What is it?' They were screened from the school by the shrub and a row of paperbark trees.

'Flack's at the entrance,' he said, 'and he's looking for us.' They fought their way through the undergrowth and after emerging, tried to peer through the foliage. Beth could see Flack, scanning the street. Beyond him, teachers were herding children indoors, though most wanted to stay and watch.

'Why did I agree to meet Mara here?' Beth said. 'Stupid. I never think things through.'

Sam brushed away chips of bark and shook his head.

'The dragon *makes* us stupid,' he said.

'We've got *no* plan,' she said. *How many times did you speak to him, you little ...*

Beth pinched her own arm hard. She drew closer to her brother, and gripped his shoulder.

'I don't *want* a plan, Sam. If we have a plan, I'll have to think, and I don't want to do that. We have to do what we feel will work.'

'Oh? Whatever you say. That her?' asked Sam, pointing at a distant vehicle.

Beth blinked a few times. 'Umm ... I'm not sure ... . Yes! It's Mara!' she cried, ready to jump up, feeling a twinge from her hip.

'Stay down, Beth!'

'But we have to let her know we're here!'

Mara came to a halt opposite the school. Flack recognised her and began to cross the street. As his left foot hit the bitumen, a crimson line of fire engines turned out of Newbegin Road, flicked their sirens on and headed towards Dairy Road.

Recognising opportunity, Beth grabbed Sam's collar and heaved him up.

'Move,' she screamed, 'Quick, this is it!'

The din was terrible. Shopkeepers and shoppers alike came out into the street, faces caught between wonder and alarm. Flack's face flickered and contorted, peering between the trucks as they passed.

Mara looked up and saw Sam and Beth sprinting towards her. The last truck honked and was gone. Realising what was happening, Flack shouted and plunged onto the road.

'Beth! I want to see you now ...'

'Mara, go! Go now … He's crazy!'

Impassive, Mara merely raised an eyebrow. Sam and Beth scrambled and fell onto the tray, and the Toyota began to accelerate. A large hand gripped the tailgate and Beth cringed, pushing herself against the cab. Flack's face was red and shone with perspiration.

'Get back to class!' He tried to pull himself up, but years of long lunches and short walks proved his undoing.

'We can't, sir' said Sam, slipping on an oil-soaked rope coiled at his feet.

'Let me know, then!' Flack hissed, then lost his grip on the vehicle.

He almost fell, but recovered himself, staring after them.

Beth leaned over the driver's side window.

'Mara! Turn down Fivepence. Flack might come after us!'

Part Six

65

Wind thrashed their hair. Over the Bul Bul Plains, a thunderstorm was sliding in from the sea and darkening the sky.

'This is crazy,' Sam screamed, 'We should keep driving.' He gripped the side of the Toyota's tray.

Beth knew then that the earthquake had terrified him more than he would ever admit. Here was the dragon's power made manifest, an undeniable physical statement.

Mara drove along Fivepence Lane for another two or three kilometres, then skidded sideways into a farm access road. She turned the engine off, then stepped out and stared at them. She bent to pick up a handful of dust, then scattered it to the winds.

'One of ya was bad enough, but now there's two. Bloody hell. He's only a little kid.'

'Not that little,' Sam protested.

'Sam knows all about it. He's my brother, Mara.'

'Oh?' she said, slapping the tray and making Sam jump. 'I'd never have guessed.'

Behind them, black plumes, the dusty sky and the wail of sirens. Beth felt a stab of guilt that such devastation was being wrought with her connivance. 'We need to stop this,' she pleaded.

'Ah well,' said Mara. 'Maybe some things can't be stopped. And some can.'

A vehicle burned past on Fivepence Lane, barely under control, spitting gravel and revving loudly. Beth though it might have been Flack's wreck of a car, but she wasn't sure.

'That it?' Mara enquired. 'Cos we gotta get going.'

Sam and Beth both nodded. Their reluctant rescuer sighed ponderously, leaning against the Toyota. She was wearing more casual attire today — a loud red checked shirt, and blue jeans hacked off just below the knee. Her feet were bare, hardened by long days of bush food collecting. Her polished brass belt buckle sported a large bucking rodeo horse.

'My people are finished with this thing,' Mara said. 'Long ago. We made our mistake and learned.'

'But it's your fault!' Beth said in a rush. 'He doesn't hurt people! If Woolgangie hadn't tricked him, he'd be gone long ago! Now he feels trapped, surrounded by hostile people.'

Mara slapped the tray with a large hand, and Beth jumped.

'Look, girl. *You* allowed yourself to be deceived. You don't know what he's like or what he wants. Or even if *he* is a male at all.'

Their argument was interrupted by a sound like a rifle shot. The earth jumped once, rattling the Toyota. Birds shrieked.

'What was that?' Sam asked, head swivelling back and forth.

'You're safe here,' said Mara, without much conviction, 'and I gotta go home. The elders have called a meeting. You just walk into town, get help. Stay away from your home.'

'We can't walk away!' Beth yelled, losing all self-control. 'We just can't!'

A car blurred past in the other direction. Flack again?

'Go then!' said Beth, seeking a knife to twist. 'Jump to Jack Netcher's tune!'

Mara's face set hard, and she turned to climb into the Toyota.

'You *know* what we want, Mara. The only reason I asked you to come.'

Mara stopped, face impassive. 'A miracle?'

'It is the *only* way we can stop this happening.'

'Don't be smart, girl. The *only* way to stop something like this is not to start it.'

Sam hollowed his cheeks, looked pensive. 'Will someone explain this cryptic crap to me?'

'Mara is the plant lady!' Beth said in a rush. 'She does the medicine. Just like Norna. Things get handed down, from mother to daughter. You have Norna's secrets — don't you?'

Mara looked away. 'You don't trample over me, girl.'

'Save lives, Mara,' Beth hectored, unable to stop herself. 'Help me! Do as Norna did. Stop this before it goes completely crazy.'

'I must respect my ancestors,' Mara said. 'I've taken enough forbidden knowledge already.'

'People might die, Mara. Show us where to look and what to do,' Beth hissed, 'We won't ever tell anyone.'

Mara fiddled with her belt buckle then twisted strands of her hair between her fingers. 'There's only one place,' she finally said, after a long hesitation. 'Once I've showed you, forget where it is. And never tell anyone else. If you can't promise that, forget it.'

Beth swore oaths until Mara seemed mollified.

Beth and Sam climbed back into the tray of the Toyota, then settled down among greasy tools. Sam remained silent, lips moving occasionally as if to follow some confused thought.

He's lost faith in words, or himself. I know exactly what he's feeling.

66

After turning left from Fivepence Lane onto Dairy Road, Mara and her passengers rolled through the tiny hamlet of East Goolgoorook (a town hall, pub, war memorial and an antique shop). Two more fire engines barrelled past towards Hemming Heights.

The Toyota noisily climbed up to Malcolm Pass, a low saddle in the range that separated Goolgoorook and its hilly surrounds from the narrow coastal plains. Looking west towards Goolgoorook, Beth now counted twelve plumes of smoke.

A blue line in the distance was the ocean, bordered by white beaches and ti-tree scrub. Two large, eucalypt covered granite domes rose from farmland. *Malleson's Peaks.*

Mara ploughed along a confusing network of bumpy little roads, gradually trending closer to the larger of the two domes. Finally the Toyota slowed, deep in shadow beneath a stand of ironwood trees. Beth alighted. She helped Sam down — something he would never have allowed her to do in normal circumstances.

'This way,' Mara said. 'No stuffing around.'

Mara powered her way across rocky scree to the base of the dome.

'Wait,' whispered Sam, looking up apprehensively, chewing at his fingernails. 'I'll stay.'

'No,' said Beth decisively. 'I'll carry you. I'm not leaving you alone.'

Sam's sense of pride abruptly rekindled, and he pushed away her hand.

'I'll be alright.'

'Norna-gul, we call this hill,' said Mara. 'The spirit-home of Norna.'

The first few metres of the trail wound through heavy ti-tree scrub, which soon gave way to a confusing maze of enormous granite boulders. Mara led through the apparent chaos with assurance, turning this way and then another, and soon they were gaining altitude. Suddenly they emerged at the edge of a cliff.

'No more clumsy feet,' Mara said sternly. 'Careful with each step and you'll go well.'

Inching around a ledge towards a rock overhang, Beth was determined not to look down. Following close behind, Sam flattened himself against the stone. Eventually the ledge widened and they walked into a smooth sandy floored space with a stone roof eroded into a complex honeycomb of ridges and voids.

The far end of the cave was covered with white areas of ... something.

A powerful ammonia stench filled the space.

'What's that gunk?' Sam asked.

'Gunk?' Mara laughed. 'Close. Some call it guano. And we gotta get up close and personal.'

Beth looked up, and the stone ceiling quivered, rippled, and shook. Abruptly, a patch of the roof fell, opened many pairs of felty wings, shrieked and flew roofward once more. 'Bats!' Sam said, showing signs of animation. 'Their forefinger runs along the whole wing. The wing is a membrane of skin.'

'It certainly ain't feathers,' Mara agreed.

In seconds the air above them was thick with noise and movement. Mara signalled Beth back, and gradually things settled down again.

'Upset 'em. Not used to people. Harmless, though. They usually live in trees, but this cave is good. Whitefellas chopped down the big trees, eh?'

Mara crept over to the bat guano. She began to dig into the reeking white mound, coughing quietly at the dust and acrid smells.

Beth spent her time looking up. The bats were large and rather handsome, their pointy muzzles reminding her of Jack Russell terriers. Patches of golden fur contrasted with the black of their wings. Beth noticed they were watching the humans below, and chattering softly. 'Look, the humans are digging up our crap.' 'Haven't they enough of their own?' 'Revolting, parasitic creatures, wouldn't you agree?'

Mara whistled with satisfaction. Using a sturdy branch she had broken from a tree on the walk in, she had excavated a grey, fan-shaped object the size of a softball. She wrapped it in a piece of cloth, and immediately started back to the Toyota.

'What was that thing?' Sam asked, struggling to keep up in Mara's wake. He had grown oddly listless. Beth wondered if the dragon was somehow responsible for the way Sam was behaving.

'A fungus, I think,' Beth said, 'living amongst all that bat crap.'

They soon reached the Toyota. Mara rummaged under a tarpaulin and dragged out a grinding stone and bowl. She lowered the tailgate, covered it with two hessian sacks and used it for a table. 'Beth, girl, come help me.' Mara brought forth the weird grey fungus she had excavated from the guano and placed it on the table.

'Flatten the bugger,' Mara ordered. 'But don't lose a single bit. We need it all.'

Pounding and scraping the fungus to pulp, Beth saw a thin clear fluid collecting at the base of the bowl.

'Don't spill that, girl — it's what we want! And don't lick your fingers or rub your eyes! Bad news if you do!'

Sam wandered around, following Mara's directions, collecting fern fronds and grass, sluggishly matting them together into a large ball.

Mara slowly poured the liquid over the ferns. The juice of the fungus smelled of crushed ants. *Formic acid*, Beth remembered.

'He'll smell this,' Beth said, 'it's dreadful. He won't let me anywhere near him.'

Mara silenced her with a frown, unscrewed a jar of strongly perfumed reddish fluid and poured it liberally over the fern ball. 'Honey. Everyone likes sugar.'

Then she wove more ferns over the honey and wiped her hands on one of the hessian bags. 'It's a pill, don't you see. Takes care of your headache.'

'Hurry up,' Sam urged, looking out to the road along which they had driven. 'I heard something!'

'Don't be such a doofus,' Beth said. 'Flack was on his way to Jugamai. He's got no idea where we are.'

Mara slid the fern ball into a plastic bag. A distant noise brought their heads up.

'A car?' Mara guessed.

'It's Flack!' screamed Sam. 'I know it is. The sound.'

'You're panicking,' said Mara. 'How would he know where we are?'

'Mara, Sam's usually right about that kind of stuff,' Beth said.

'Then we go,' said Mara. Moving quickly, she flung her gear onto the Toyota and slammed the tailgate. 'Get in!' she screamed and Sam and Beth climbed aboard just as Mara brought the vehicle to life and caromed off down the road. Springs bounced and branches slashed at them.

Sam grimaced. He shouted to be heard. 'I saw him when we were coming down from Malcolm Pass. I think he saw us turn off the main road.'

'And you didn't say anything?' Beth was incredulous. 'How come you suddenly got worried?'

'He hadn't seen us when I saw him first off. But then I started thinking. He *really* wants to find us. He'll try every side road, one by one.'

She almost kicked him, but remembered how tired he was.

Mara hit an unmarked intersection and turned to the west. Moments later Flack's car flew through the same crossroads, heading south. A second later he skidded, then sprayed gravel in a frantic turn.

Beth slapped the roof of the Toyota's cab. 'Go! He's *right behind us!*'

And right behind them he was, hunched over his steering wheel to get a better look at them, slipping in and out of visibility in the cloud of dust streaming out behind the Toyota.

67

Flack's maniacal determination terrified Beth. The dragon's suspicion of humans was well founded, she thought. *Either they hunger for him, or long to destroy.*

Flack stayed close no matter how Mara jinked and skidded around corners or tried to outrun him. They were almost out of the forest. The track swooped through steep little gullies like a fun park ride. Pursuer and pursued, they flew through more corners, more intersections, until Beth was no longer sure if they were heading inland or coastward.

Although Flack's car would have easily outpaced the Toyota on a surfaced road, in the rough it struggled, the chassis striking rocks and bottoming out.

'Mara's going north!' Sam yelled. 'I'm sure!' Towards Ooralloo National Park.

Metal struck metal, Mara slewed for a few sickening seconds, then regained control. Flack shouted in triumph, head poking out the side window. He yelled something, then snatched his head back in as the vehicles bumped across a dry creek bed. After that, he fell back a few hundred metres. A series of sharp turns allowed him to creep up again. Fortunately, high embankments on either side temporarily prevented him from passing, and he hammered his dashboard in frustration. Beth smiled.

Mara braked abruptly, drifting towards the left gutter, reducing forward progress to a crawl. Flack's face lost its intensity, rearranging into a broad smile.

'What's she doing?' Sam asked, agonised, drumming his hands on the side of the tray. 'Why so slow?'

The light in this gully was dim, tree ferns and giant gums crowding out the sun. The air was noticeably cooler. Looking sideways over the tray, Beth blanched.

'We're on some sort of bridge,' she said loudly, 'I think.'

The 'bridge' was a brace of long, half-rotten logs held together in the middle by a heavily rusted steel cable. In places large portions of the logs had fallen away, leaving holes easily large enough to trap a wheel. Below ran a fast-flowing stream. Timber warped and sagged as the vehicle lurched forward, wheels slipping, biting, slipping again. Sam was flung to the right and vaulted half out. Beth shouted out and grabbed for his hand. A sharp jolt brought her jaws together hard, and her teeth bit into her tongue. She cried out at the pain.

'Beth! What's wrong?'

'Jub my 'ongue. Bib ib off, almobt. Sabing you, you bugger.'

She could taste blood in her mouth, and she spat it into the river in a red arc.

Mara reached the other end of the bridge, clashed a few gears and accelerated wildly.

Flack was in the process of turning, having obviously recognised that the bridge was impossible for a two-wheel drive car to cross.

'Are you alright?' Sam asked.

'Ibt's still on,' Beth mumbled. She poked her tongue out for him to inspect.

'Cuts,' said Sam. 'I don't think they're real bad. Can you put stitches in someone's tongue?'

'How long hab we been gone?' Beth asked.

'About an hour and a half. Maybe two.'

Beth slumped back, tasting more blood in her mouth. The trip to the forest seemed like it had taken an entire day. Now the only thing keeping her on the move was her desire to get back to Hemming Heights and to save the house. *And to save everyone,* a quiet voice announced.

Finally, they turned on to the Ooralloo to Goolgoorook Road, following it until it once more became Fivepence Lane. Lying down in the greasy and leaf-strewn tray and staring up at the sky, Beth hoped Jo and Sarah were safe, *their* adventure for the day restricted to staring up at the chaos sweeping through Hemming Heights. She half sat, suddenly alarmed.

'Oh, shit. G'abon! I forgot! In all the rush.' Her tongue did not want to touch the roof of her mouth at all. 'He'b comib over! To the house.'

'Who? Did you say *Graydon*?'

'Yeb. Bragon's frighted ob him.'

She tried desperately to speak clearly.

'He ... wants to measure the gases in be basement. 'ragon will kill 'im if he does that. We've got to get there before he does!'

'But the police won't let him in.'

Beth snorted. She knew that nothing would be allowed to come between Graydon and the cellar.

68

Once more, Hemming Heights came into view. Deep blue-grey thunderclouds formed a cap over the plumes of smoke that poured from dozens of houses. She remembered reading somewhere that fires could bring rain. Beth saw a helicopter spin overhead, television station logo prominent. TV interest in Goolgoorook — that made this a genuine disaster, she realised. *If it bleeds, it leads.*

Mara slowed, leaned out and yelled. 'Get under the tarpaulin now!'

Unfolding a grimy canvas tarp, Beth slid under, helping Sam do the same. They lay in dirt and greenish darkness between two large toolboxes. Beth prayed that no part of her foot or head was visible.

'I can't breathe,' Sam said, voice muffled by their heavy shroud.

A moment later the Toyota came to a sudden halt. Feet crunched past, and stopped at the driver's window.

'Oh, g'day Mara. Fancy meeting you down here. Strange weather, eh?'

Mara laughed, but her tone was forced. 'Hey, Frank. Not just weather, eh? Shit hit the fan down here, eh?'

'Yep. Hit*ting*, I'm afraid. At great velocity. Christ knows what's *really* going on.' 'Look, Mara, you're going to have to turn here and go back. We've sealed off the town. Too bloody dangerous.'

'But I don't have enough fuel to get home,' Mara protested. 'Just let me go to the fuel depot first.'

'Oh, I dunno about that. Let me check. A radio crackled. 'Mate, I've got Mara here. From up at Ooralloo. Dunno ... low on fuel. Wants to come through. Ta, mate. Over.'

'OK. Off you go. Through to the fuel depot on the old Western Highway. Then come back here fast as you can.'

Instead, Mara pulled off the road less than two minutes later. She let down the back of the tray with a clatter of steel. Beth and Sam climbed out gingerly, brushing at their filthy clothes and taking gulps of clean air.

'This is it, kids,' Mara said. 'You're almost home.' She handed Beth the plastic bag containing the ball of fungus, ferns and honey. It was unexpectedly heavy.

'Come with us!' Sam pleaded.

Mara shook her head. 'This is going to sound mean, but it's really your problem, now.'

Beth stared straight at Mara.

'Look, girl,' said Mara. 'Do you think that old beast's going to want *me* near him? He'll sense me from a mile away. If he's frightened of other people, how do you think he'd go with a Koori?'

She's right. The dragon would fear the Gugamai. More than anyone else.

'Your brother can stay with me, if you like. I'll look after him.'

'No,' Sam said instantly. 'I'm going with Beth.' His face was a uniform white; even his lips were pale.

Mara nodded. 'You're gutsy enough. Be bloody careful, eh? Don't take any more risks than you have to. When this is finished, we'll make you honorary Gugamai.'

She hopped into the cabin, swung the vehicle across the road and accelerated towards her home.

69

Downdrafts from the coming storm pushed smoke everywhere.

A fat raindrop hit her forehead. Others splashed into the dust as Sam and Beth began to climb the hill towards Hemming Heights. The suburb was coming apart in slow motion.

'If we don't do this soon,' Beth shouted, 'there will be nothing left to save.'

Except for the howl of emergency vehicles, the hill seemed lifeless. Beth vowed to at least rescue Horatio, *if* his tank was intact. She hefted the bag over one shoulder, then after a minute or so, shifted it to the other shoulder.

As they picked their way along Logos Circle, marvelling at tilted slabs of bitumen and downed telephone lines, an exodus of fire engines began. Dozens of red trucks and CFA water tankers filed back down Serpentine Drive, and out past the roadblock. Beth huddled behind a parked car, afraid someone might see and 'rescue' them.

'Too dangerous,' Sam said in a subdued voice. 'Even the firemen can't stay any more.'

The ground trembled and wobbled. Day was halfway to night, clouds so dark that streetlights flickered on.

Someone reconnected the power, Beth noted. *Go, Dad.*

'Xavier's place!' Sam looked dumbstruck as they rounded a corner and stared straight at a glowing ruin, the only remnants a pair of white pillars topped with cement lions stained with smoke. Sam took a step forward, as if to look for his friend.

'He'll be at school,' Beth said. 'Anyway. The fireys wouldn't go unless they have everyone.'

Occasionally she spat a streak of blood onto the footpath, but her tongue was beginning to feel like an instrument of speech again.

A few metres on, a telephone pole had crushed a car like an empty soft drink can. They looked away, both unwilling to check for occupants. *Get to the house. Give him the medicine. Wonder why I let this happen. Why I was so weak…* The one thing she had done right was not to involve her friends. *My selfishness kept them safe. I didn't want to share the dragon with anyone.*

'He *made* us do it, Beth,' said Sam, evidently guessing her thoughts, 'we had no choice.'

'He didn't *make* me do anything,' she said slowly. 'I did what I wanted, and damn anyone else.'

'Then I did the same,' declared Sam.

70

The signpost for Serpentine Drive dipped over and kissed the road with a metallic clink, its concrete base having vibrated free of the soil. More rain fell, and steamy wisps of vapour rose from lawns. Beth smelled smoke and dirt and concrete dust.

A late model, dark blue car sat in the driveway of 17 Serpentine Drive.

'Graydon,' Beth said. She had *known* he would show up.

She pointed to his parking permits: CSIRO Researcher — 2003/4. A smaller sticker invited the world to *Rock your world with a Geologist*.

'Maybe our street will be the last to go,' said Beth.

Beth's head was abruptly invaded by dragonscent. No doubt seeping into her brain, seeking to commandeer her will.

The front door of the house was ajar.

'Kids,' said Graydon, peering out and causing Beth to come within an ace of wetting herself. 'I didn't expect anyone. You probably shouldn't be here. Can you come in and help me?'

'Hell, why not,' said Beth. Graydon no longer scared her. 'Our house, ain't it?'

Sam muttered something, but he followed her in.

Inside, the house was sweltering. A deep, itchy flush crept down Beth's arms, and the swollen cuts on her tongue stung.

'How did you get up here?' Graydon asked. His sweaty face was flecked with dirt.

'Shank's pony. What about you?'

Graydon pointed. 'Drove in before the road blocks. I *knew* something would happen today."

The doctor looked much less arrogant than usual, and very tired. He was wearing a stained yellow T-shirt.

'You've got blood on your face,' said Graydon.

'It's just a flesh wound.'

'Huh. I've been trying to get into your cellar. No luck at all. Smell that vapour!'

'We're in great danger, Dr Graydon,' said Beth with sudden urgency. 'More than you know. You should leave.'

'No!' he said urgently. 'That would be foolish indeed. I've still got time.'

'No, you don't,' she said. His gaze slid away, unwilling to be confronted. He hesitated for a second, then shrugged, and turned back to the cellar door. 'You look after yourselves then. I will go on, like Pliny the Elder,' he said.

'The elder who?' Sam asked.

'No idea,' said Beth. She looked at Graydon's back as he struggled with the cellar door. She wondered if anyone was looking for herself or Sam yet. Flack wouldn't have reported them as absent.

'Where's the key for this damn door?' he asked, turning his head to glare at them.

'On Dad's keyring,' said Beth. Her hand flew to her mouth. 'God! The fish, Sam. I forgot about him.'

Sam ran through the lounge to check Horatio's tank. He returned a moment later with welcome news. 'He's still alive!'

Graydon began jemmying the cellar door again. 'Lock ... looks new ... but it's seized up. Melted, almost.' He fell back.

Quietly, Beth led Sam back towards Horatio's tank. On a scrap of paper by the phone she scrawled a note: *D is listening — don't say anything important. We have to stop Graydon before he gets into the cellar.*

Sam nodded, and added his own note, penned in a jittery and barely readable scrawl: *D can't make Graydon leave, however much he tries. He wants to stay too much.*

Behind them, Graydon growled, and began thumping at the door. Rushing back, they found he had emptied a terracotta plant pot and was about to bring it crashing down on the door handle. Beth spoke without forethought. 'Dr Graydon! This is our house!'

To her surprise, he stopped.

'The chance of a lifetime,' he said unhappily. 'A volcanic eruption in an area that's never shown any sign of activity. And I'm the only one on the ground.'

He returned the pot to the floor, shaking his head. 'Measurements. A good scientist must measure ... and record. Measure, record and hypothesise ...' With that, he went out to his car.

A moment later Graydon strode through again. He piled his equipment on the floor of the lounge. Then he began waving a probe at the ceiling, and along the floor. Exclamations and curses punctuated his work. He climbed the stairs, and could be heard chattering above their heads. 'Potential for ash flows ... no evidence as yet ... correlate ... compare ...'

Sam's foot came down hard on one of Graydon's black carry cases, and then another, and he began jumping on delicate instrumentation.

'*Stop!*' Beth hissed.

'If he doesn't have any tools,' Sam retorted, 'he can't do a thing.' Small-handed and dexterous, he swiftly removed several batteries, rolling them beneath a lounge chair.

'That's enough, Sam.' The house rocked and swayed as if at sea, and they retreated to the lounge. Horatio did not want to leave his home, either. He outraced Beth's hands and hit the far end of the tank hard.

'Bloody thick-headed idiot. I'm trying to save you!' The groggy fish only submitted when cornered by a spaghetti strainer. Working together, they flipped him his smaller companion into a large water-filled bucket and tied an empty onion sack over the top to prevent them from making any ill-advised leaps.

'They won't last long,' said Sam gloomily. 'We'll have to hurry.'

Working with sign language, they decided to deposit the fish outside and go back inside. Leaving the bucket hanging from a tree, Beth turned to survey the scene from the front door. Orange beams of light streamed through beneath the thunderclouds — the sun making a final rush towards the horizon. Beth saw every house in the street, water gleaming hard and bright on roof tiles. Lightning divided the sky into jagged fragments. Thunderclaps ran together, drumming so hard the air and ground shook in tune.

Tears crossed her face. *I love this house. How can we lose it all?* A shiver went through her. *He was always here — even when we were tiny children — like a bomb on a very long timer. This was always going to happen.*

They went back inside. During a brief lull between thunderclaps, the telephone rang. 'Answer it,' Beth commanded, but Sam shook his head.

'It might be Mum,' Beth said. 'You answer it.' *No, don't. Don't touch it.*

'I don't want to,' Sam said.

'Right now,' Beth predicted, 'Mum and Dad are losing it. They rush back when they hear about the fires and the quakes, but they're not allowed up here. And we're gone from school. All the other kids are safe, and we're gone!!'

'If I answer,' Sam said, 'I won't be able to help you anymore.'

Beth clenched her hands, and eventually the phone stopped ringing.

Don't say anything more! she mouthed. *Let's go and talk to D.*

Just as they went into the corridor, Graydon discovered his ruined gear and groaned in disbelief.

'I'm a fool,' he sobbed, as the telephone began to shrill again. 'So badly prepared. Can't give up now ...' He ran past them and out the front door. They heard his car start and move off.

Beth shook her head. Sam had done exactly what was necessary to get rid of Graydon, for a little while, at least.

If he parks on Circular Ave, Beth printed, *it's only a short walk across a paddock to his labs. He doesn't have to go through the roadblocks. He'll be back — soon.*

71

Picking up Mara's bag of fungus and grass, Beth stumbled towards what was probably certain incineration. She could only continue moving forward if she treated the whole thing as a fever dream. Sam followed.

Wanna go home ... oh. Stay with me, Sam — I can't do this alone.

The cellar door opened without fuss this time, releasing a billow of hot, horribly dry air.

The house stopped shaking, the storm outside seeming to halt for their descent. In its place, a thumping, pulsing noise. Something stung Beth's cheek. She plucked at her face and saw a black smudge across her fingers. Sam did the same, wincing. Small red lights swarmed randomly through the dark air like stars. Several settled on her shirt, and she smelled burning fabric. *Cinders.*

'Firebreath,' said the dragon, making them jump, 'My belly — my guts — one of the things that marks us off from your kind — has awoken with the rest of me. I am full of fire now — it seeps from my very pores.' The rough low tones of his voice seemed to form out of the air itself, coming from all directions.

'You're destroying our town,' Beth whispered. 'Our lives.'

'And it is your kind who have destroyed my kind. Symmetry.' Embers flared and circled in sudden silence, then he spoke again. 'I must live, no? A natural imperative. The blood wants to live. Isn't that a part of *evolution*, Beth? The urge to survive?'

'Something like that,' Beth muttered. She was beginning to forget why she was down in the cellar. Some kind of mission, but what?

Thud ... thud ... thud — the thumping noise grew ever deeper. Red lights multiplied, until there were millions of tiny embers.

'Why did you come back?' the dragon asked. 'I warned you, but here you are ... '

More lights flowed from the gap in the wall, pooling near the floor.

'We thought you'd kill Graydon.'

'You *have* saved him, by making him leave. He should thank you. Leave now, and save yourselves. I am to be born once more.'

'You can't just use us! We helped you! And you've lied about everything.' Beth shouted.

'So be careful. Sometimes a thing can turn out to have a life of its own.'

'But you tricked us!'

'Bad luck and deceit put me under your house, Beth. Deceit gets me back out. Once more there is a symmetry.'

Thump ... thump ... thump — the noise was oceanic.

Sam hugged her awkwardly, leaning close. 'That's his *heart*!' he hissed. The rhythm slowed, and the dragon spoke again.

'Be honest, child. Has your existence ever been as vivid?'

Beth slumped, on the verge of agreeing with him, and reverting to obedience. 'We ... can't thank you for that. Not if people's lives are being destroyed.'

'Let the sin rest on me. It is I who acts, not you. Actor and acted upon. A rock cannot feel guilty if used as a weapon, and nor should you.'

'When you're gone,' she managed, 'we'll have nothing. No home.'

'Build again,' said the dragon. 'Is it not a human project to build ceaselessly? To turn this planet inside out? I am sorry. But unless you leave now, you will *be* nothing.'

The smell that poured through her was the earth itself, and life as well, and it was a sensation of infinite grace. Beth sighed and sank to her knees. She'd come down here to carry out a task, but couldn't quite remember its nature. Answers darted out of reach. She felt a blankness rising.

Sam released her from his embrace. He tried to snatch something from her hand. 'Don't do that …' but he succeeded and wrenched a plastic bag away from her.

''S mine. Give it back.'

But Sam was much too quick, swinging the bag over his head. 'No. It's *his!*' he screamed, rushing at the hole, now many feet across and widening by the second. The space seemed to broaden, ready to swallow her brother. His small body was surrounded by a galaxy of tiny sparks.

'Get back!' she screamed. Like a javelin thrower, Sam skidded to a halt, flinging the bag away into the dark, smoking chasm. Teetering, he flailed his arms wildly. Beth suddenly found her legs and jumped towards him. The feeling of lassitude and inactivity vanished like a popped soap bubble. *Mara's medicine! He's thrown the medicine!*

Torrents of air rushed past them into the hole

'Fall down!' Sam hollered, arcing back into life. He pushed into her and she collapsed with him. Hurricanes of flame burst over their heads into the cellar, searing her lips and hair and sucking air from her lungs.

Gasping, Beth blindly crawled towards the stairs, pushing Sam ahead. The cellar's timber roof caught fire. A brick shattered and sprayed hot shards down the stairs. The pain in her hip had returned. *We were so very stupid!*

'What have you done?' she thought she heard the dragon roar. Flames and soot flew back into the hole. Beth stood, bellowing. She snatched up Sam, crashing up the stairs and throwing him into the hallway. The door flew back and knocked her into the frame — but she was out of the cellar. Air rushing into the cellar abruptly stilled, and she could hear the roof crackling away, flames eating up into the house. Without a word, she bumped her brother across the living room, picking him up when he fell. She was breathing in short sharp pants, and her lungs were sore.

Throwing Sam out onto the lawn and shouting for him to grab Horatio, she paused for one last glance back from the front door; it almost ended her life. The cellar door bulged and exploded cartoon-style from its hinges. Flames thick as burning mercury flowed towards the front of the house. Only the air pushed ahead of the inferno saved her — smashing her down while fire jetted like a chameleon's tongue into the street.

'Your shirt's burning,' Sam cried, swatting at the flames. Soon the flames were beaten out, converted into curls of acrid smoke. They crawled away towards the gutter, dragging the miraculously intact fish bucket behind them. The ground beneath them heaved wildly.

For a moment the house seemed about to lift off, and then everything exploded. Beams and glass whined past, smashing into the houses across the street. Beth was afraid to lift her head, plugging her ears against the nightmarish noise. Smaller detonations could be heard — exploding paint tins, light fittings, perhaps even bottles of wine.

Gradually the tremors decreased, before fading completely. She huddled against Sam, who was shaking uncontrollably. He had been so sharp, resisting the dragon's mind-warping scent.

We did it. He can't hurt us now.

Gradually, the house was consumed, and she cried. Everything her family owned, all the memories, her whole childhood; in ashes.

72

When a hand grasped her shoulder, she grabbed convulsively at Sam. Dr Graydon's face looked into her own.

'Thank God. You're alive. I saw your house explode.' He helped them to their feet.

Hemming Heights' streetlights were all out, the only light coming from fires burning at various points along Serpentine Drive. Sam's shirtless back was covered with small burns, hair scorched from his arms. 'I gave it to him, didn't I?' he said. 'We almost forgot, eh? Didn't give him the pill. Huh. He almost got me, though.' He laughed, but the sound had a ragged edge.

Graydon guided Sam to his car, carrying the fish-in-a-bucket in his other hand. 'He's not quite right. All those little burns. We need to find a paramedic.'

The doctor's madness seemed to have completely evaporated.

'Is he gone, Beth?' Sam asked, as they drove away, Graydon zigzagging to dodge the many chunks of burning debris strewn across the road. 'He's quiet now. Is he asleep? I want him to go away.'

She nodded her head, and Graydon gave her a strange look. Graydon's car crunched across a drift of debris.

'Is he talking about the earthquakes?'

'I think so. We had to come back for the fish.'

'Ah. Not much of a reason to take such a risk. Oh, hell!' he broke off. Rounding a corner, the street was blocked. Three streetlights had fallen, blocking both lanes.

'We'll have to hoof it,' he said. Rain began to fall again, cold and fine, blowing into their faces, wetting them through. The interrupted storm resumed. They passed dozens of damaged houses and lightning-struck trees. Soon, Graydon picked up Sam and carried him. Sam looked very small in his arms.

Beth's mouth was almost permanently agape. *Big news*, Beth realised. Not just for Goolgoorook, but Australia. Hell, the world? She didn't want to see the ruins of her house on a flat screen.

He's gone, she breathed, hardly daring to hope. The ground beneath her feet was absolutely still. *Gone back to dreams. Gone to sleep for another five hundred years.* In the distance she caught glimpses of the main roadblock on Dairy Road, surrounded by flashing lights and emergency vehicles. Horatio dangled in his bucket. She wondered how long his air would last, and willed him to breathe slowly.

'Almost there,' said Dr Graydon soothingly.

Without warning, a figure rose from behind a wrecked car. 'I knew you'd be up here!' it crowed, face in darkness. 'You had to come back!'

Sam tried to wriggle from Graydon's grasp. 'Flack,' he squeaked.

'Flack!' Dr Graydon was obviously nonplussed at the other man's appearance. Where the doctor's mania had abated, Flack's mind had obviously deteriorated further. He was wearing a scuffed miner's hat with a light attached, pointing it at their faces, down at the scale he still held.

'You're in on this too, Graydon?' he snarled peevishly, 'they told you everything, and not me? Not nice. Impolite.'

'What are you talking about, John?.' He gestured at the ruin that was Hemming Heights.

'I speak of things hidden. By people afraid of the truth. Rare species! Mysteries.'

Beth drifted behind the doctor, trying not to look at Flack's agitated face. She was tired beyond description.

'They know.' Flack took an unsteady step forward. 'The girl — she gave me this — said she didn't know what it was.' He smiled and lurched at Beth.

Graydon grabbed at Flack's hand, but he was too quick, dancing backwards.

'Oh, no. It belongs to me. The golden thread that connects everything. She *knew* already!! She knew what it was. This is *all* her fault.'

'And the school?' Graydon enquired, trying to block Flack's forward progress. 'They don't need your help?'

Flack shrugged 'Every man has a higher calling. And I have found mine.' He shrieked, a high and aggressive cry.

Sam whimpered.

'Let us go! Run to the house, then!' She stepped forward and jabbed him hard in the chest, pushing him back. 'Go look, just leave me alone. Go up there! Go on. No time to waste.'

Flack never replied. Instead he screamed and pointed. They all turned in time to see an extraordinary sight. Hemming Heights began to swell like a balloon. Houses fell apart or tumbled into dark fissures. Wood splintered, metal creased and kinked and everything seemed to blur, familiar landscapes morphing into something alien. Chunks of hillside peeled away, sliding towards Dairy Road. Through half-shut eyes, Beth saw the top of the hill surge up into the sky.

'An eruption!' howled Dr Graydon, forgetting his interrogation of Flack. 'Run!'

They ran, carrying Sam, carrying the fish. Clumps of rock began to pound down around them.

A jagged rock fell from the sky and shattered on the roadway. Fragments whined past. Flack cried out and grabbed at his knee. blood started out between his fingers. Beth turned to help him, leaving the doctor to lug Sam to safety. Flack writhed on the roadway, clutching his leg and shouting at the rapidly darkening sky. Pieces of Hemming Heights were coming to earth with tremendous violence. The noise terrified Beth.

As she bent to help Flack, she looked up fearing more rock showers. Through thick curtains of rain and dust and smoke, an immense, indistinct form rose suddenly from the hill. Black shadows unfurled. There was too much rubbish in the air to see properly, and her head was far from clear.

A forest of lightning bolts flashed in a circle around the hill, and for an instant, eyes wide and unbelieving, she saw — gold. No shapes, just colour, beautiful, metallic and overwhelming, as if a star had gone nova. She closed her eyes, seeing an incandescent field of pure light. *Goldenscale.*

Then the light was gone and they were in terrible danger.

73

A chunk of rubble the size of a car engine smashed into the recently deserted roadblock. Debris exploded into the air and hummed over their heads.

Goldenscale. I saw the dragon! Awake! He was awake! Through all this strangeness and sensory overload she still struggled down the road, gasping at the weight of her teacher, wishing he'd do more walking and less sagging. All the while he swore and giggled and flung out his hands as if attempting to catch flies. They passed onto Dairy Road, almost past the edge of Hemming Heights. Back into the land of functioning street lights. The road before them was deserted, hazed with thick masses of smoke.

Graydon paused for breath, gently lowering Sam to the ground.

'Surviving?' he asked Beth.

'We might,' said Beth with surprise. 'I didn't think so back there.'

'Astounding,' he puffed. 'Inexplicable.'

Mr Flack fell silent, staring unblinkingly back at the chaos. He held up his hand, examined it, slapped himself in the face. Then again, harder. Tears began to well up in his eyes.

Did he see anything? Beth wondered. Abruptly, he looked across at her, face lit intermittently by lightning and innumerable fires. Despite Flack's tears, he appeared slightly less wild. He seemed to have shrunk. Beth wished she had seen the weakness and hunger in him earlier. 'I'm only a kid,' she muttered angrily to herself.

'So *big*,' Flack hissed, 'putting a shadow over us all. And you thought it belonged to you.'

'*He's* gone,' she replied. 'No-one ever owned him.'

'Let's go,' said Graydon. 'You two can finish this chat later.' He squinted into the gloom and smoke. 'We might be safe on the Arterial. Maybe.' He hoisted Sam onto his shoulder.

'Maybe it's gone, whatever it was,' said Mr Flack with a bitter smile, 'but I still have this.' He held out his precious scale, aglow in the beam of the miner's light.

'What is that thing?' Graydon asked. He reached for it, but Flack shoved it back in his pocket.

'It's something strange our uncle gave us,' said Beth. 'Flack took it. It's not his.'

In light of what she had glimpsed, Beth doubted the dragon's scale would be enough for her teacher, even if it did retain its lustre. She was glad she had returned her own. Her mind wandered. Horatio's bucket was still intact — but did he have enough air?

Her hip, knee and lip began to throb mercilessly. She was forced to let go of Flack and stop again, swaying. As she stood there, she heard a whistling noise and her vision exploded, head kicked backwards by an impact. Retching a bitter mess of bile and blood onto the road, she felt her body collapse a joint at a time. All that was left was a dim sensation of hardness, a dull pain and her thoughts scattering. *I'm dying …*

74

'Beth! Be-ethh!!'

The dragon's taken me with him. I'm climbing through thin air and ice is forming on my skin. I'm cold, but I don't care. What does discomfort mean when in the presence of a god-king?

'Beth. This is your dad. Squeeze my hand if you can understand me.'

I'm flying with the dragon. He swoops low over the ocean, until spray curls back from the wave tops. I can feel his heart beating, and the furnace in his lungs. The king of everything — older than the mountains ...

Her mouth felt dry. Why didn't the dragon let her drink?

He hates our words, our minds, almost everything about us. But does he like me? Will he make some small exception?

Her eyes fluttered, and opened. She saw only light at first, then a strange series of blurs that began to resolve like a camera finding its focus.

Heads hovered far above, floating around like blimps without tethers. She laughed, but no sound emerged. Six familiar heads. Sam, swathed in white bandages. Her parents, crying like fools, and ... Jo and Sarah, eyes wide and shocked. Last, and oddest, a man who looked much like Uncle Henry, smiling, eyes bright with unasked questions.

She was lying at ground level, perhaps on a gurney. A tube had been inserted into her forearm.

'Where's Horatio?' Beth rasped. 'And Freddy?' She tried

to stand, but a man in a dark blue uniform bent and gently restrained her.

'They're fine, darling,' sobbed Abbie.

Nick rubbed her shoulder. 'Don't worry about your coward dog. He ran at the first sign of danger.'

'My head,' said Beth. 'Is it broken?'

'Maybe a hairline fracture. Armour-plated,' said the Uncle Henry lookalike. His voice even sounded the same. 'Got yourself in the way of the last falling bit of Hemming Heights. Messed up your scalp and concussed the hell out of you.'

'*Henry!*' said Abbie. 'Enough detail. They have to take you to hospital now, darling. In the ... ambulance. For a bit of rest.'

People are strange, Beth thought, closing her eyes again. *I don't really need a rest.*

They slid her into an ambulance and began the drive to Goolgoorook Base Hospital.

———

Her head throbbed, but she didn't feel that the pain really belonged to her. She wondered if that was the drugs, and hoped she wouldn't need them for too long. The driver was not hurrying, and she guessed they were heading for Goolgoorook Base Hospital.

'Was anyone killed?' Beth asked the paramedic. He was very young, his skin sallow under fluorescent lights. 'Anyone in Hemming Heights?' This seemed the most important question of all, and she dreaded the answer. *If everyone knew who was really responsible ...*

'We don't think so,' he said, 'the Heights were completely

evacuated after the first big shake. Some sightings of a coupla kids …' He looked at her. 'Anyway, when we found your party, there were no more names on the list.' He fiddled with her drip bag, adding something to it. 'That teacher fellow will need a few stitches. Nasty little puncture wound in his leg. You're the prize of the moment, though.'

Beth's last thoughts before she slipped into unconsciousness concerned the ingratitude of the dragon and a disjointed rumination on the failure of Mara's medicine. If it was hard to medicate a dog, why should a dragon be easy?

75

For the next few days, her parents kept her under close watch, as if she was likely to leap up and run out of the hospital. She was subjected to a variety of scans, the results of which gradually reassured doctors that her brain was no more impaired than it had been prior to the disaster. A nurse came along and picked stitches out of Beth's scalp, distracting her with small talk. Each stitch ended up in a small kidney dish and Beth lost count after fifty. The bald patch around the sutured area was beginning to sprout a spiky field of stubble. Most of her other cuts and scrapes were caused by her fall onto the road after being struck. It was only a week later that her mother told her that she had suffered three hairline skull fractures and experienced a mild brain injury. Moderate bleeding, elevated pressures, probably no neural deficit. *Probably.*

'Would have been good to know this last *week*!' she shouted at Abbie.

'We didn't want to stress you,' Abbie said. 'The doctor said it would be better if you stayed calm.'

'I'm never calm! Especially not now.'

Despite forgiving their children, or even lauding them as foolish heroes for rescuing the fish (which Beth insisted was the only reason for their return to the house, and hoped that Sam was also sticking to that line), Abbie and Nick were not about to slacken their surveillance. Abbie refused to allow TV or newspaper interviews, which was both disappointing and a relief. Beth grudgingly told herself that the world wasn't quite ready for giant golden dragons and trance-inducing scents.

Nick brought Jo and Sarah in to visit and retreated to sit on a plastic chair outside the room, reading on his tablet. Beth felt her formerly rampant sense of guilt returning, but pushed it away. She turned to look at Jo and Sarah.

'Can you get me out of here?' she blurted.

'Uh,' said Jo. '*That's* a prime idea.'

'So you can do it again?' Sarah asked. 'You're already some kind of legend at school. You can take a rest.'

'I've had it with resting,' Beth said. 'I've read too many books, I'm sick to death of television.' She smiled at them. 'Do you to want to see the head thing?' She peeled up enough of her bandages to give them a view of the shaved part of her scalp.

'Jaysus,' said Jo, taking a step back. 'I hope they put the brain back in afterwards.'

The three of them gradually relaxed and conversation began to flow more freely.

Sarah smiled. 'Department of unbelievable stories. You remember how Len had to go up to Ooralloo? Lenny and Jack Netcher are mates, now. No, they are. Jack initiated him into some men's secret business, and he dropped all this white supremacy crap. Now he's probably into Black Power. No BS.'

'Mum's in Fiji,' said Jo, 'though she wanted to come back when she heard about this. She keeps sending me letters to give to you,' she said, drawing a sheaf of envelopes from her bag. Jo showed Beth photographs of her father, smiling in a strained kind of way from some tropical prison cell. 'I'm not sure how the bribery thing is going. Takes time, my mum says. Have to meet the right people, show the right kind of respect.'

Eventually the conversation approached the big events, warily at first. Jo took the lead. 'I don't think many people will leave town. There might be a new suburb down in East Gool-goorook. Rezoning some farmland, or something like that.'

'Did you know Mr Flack's quit?' broke in Sarah, 'sold his house and bought a campervan. What's weirder — he's moved in with Mara, from Ooralloo. Mum says they're having a joint mid-life crisis.'

Beth goggled. She thought for a while, feeling pieces drop into place.

That's what Mara had meant when she said Jack Netcher didn't approve of her boyfriend. And why Flack had never believed her lies. *He must have known almost everything!*

Whatever she had said to Mara went straight through to Flack. She might not have wanted to tell him, but Flack would have been persistent, wearing her down. No wonder Mara had always looked stressed.

Beth made jokes, asked questions and replied to those directed at her, but eventually she began to show signs of exhaustion.

'Visiting hour is up,' observed Jo. 'The infirm must have their rest.' On departure they left her some chocolates and a note. When alone, she unfolded it.

Dear Beth: It was nice to see you, but if you don't tell us more about what happened, we will never speak to you again, or at least not about anything interesting. If you get to dodge massive explosions, rescue a bloody fish and see a whole suburb blow up, then the least you can do is tell the truth. You have a few days to think before this offer expires. Love, your friends.

Beth was still smiling when the nurse came in to check her

temperature and tinker with monitoring equipment. *Maybe I will tell them. Maybe they won't think I'm mad. Or if they do, they will be too polite to say so.*

Wednesday 5 April

Epilogue the First

The doctors said she was more or less better, that her prognosis was good, but they'd prefer to keep her under observation for a little while longer. So far she had been in hated inactivity for *twelve* days

'I'm a fourteen year old,' Beth said, hating them the way a prisoner resents his jailer. 'I *know* I'm better.' She jumped up and ran down the corridor, ran back, then touched her toes. 'See!' she puffed. They promised that they'd think about it in four days.

'Eternity is shorter,' Beth said, but no-one wins an argument with a person in a white suit.

She watched a lot of television, and saw the ragged hole that had once been Hemming Heights: at the edges of the zone of total destruction, roads amputated, trees sheared by projectiles and house tiles everywhere, like fallen leaves.

She also browsed news sites on her iPad. 'Astonishing footage taken in the aftermath of a huge tremor in the sleepy township of Goolgoorook. The worst earthquake in Australian history, but strangely localised. Specialist geologists believe a giant sinkhole collapsed beneath the town of Goolgoorook. An entire housing estate was plunged into a one hundred metre deep abyss. Astonishingly, no deaths were recorded, and very few serious injuries. What could have been a great human tragedy is instead an insurance company's nightmare and a geological oddity. Dr Paul Graydon of the CSIRO has been named as head of a state government-appointed panel of enquiry. His team will consider all possible causes for this catastrophe and interview witnesses and experts.'

Beth lay back. Dr Graydon and science would win out in the end. A coal seam fire or cave collapse or anomalous earthquake would be blamed. If enough time passed, she might come to agree. Very large reptilian creatures could never fly, and even if they could, they wouldn't have enough energy to stay airborne. And as for ability to project flames, use odour to control people's minds and live thousands of years — well, they were without precedent in the natural world.

Diary: Sam doesn't really want to see me at the moment. He's got tiny little burns all over his body. If he was a soldier, they'd call it shell-shock or maybe post-traumatic stress disorder. I think he wants to forget everything — and maybe he thinks D betrayed us. Somehow, I don't feel the same way. D had a right to be free, and he never killed anyone — though that might have been more luck than design. He may have tried to destroy us at the last moment, but I prefer to think he was clearing his throat of the fungus. Burning it out before it could do its work. Or maybe it was all a self-defence reflex.

D's going to need people again. He can't survive without us. Somewhere in the world, in the Amazon or the desert, he must land, and make himself useful — perhaps hypnotise people as he did with us.

There's a nice view from my room up here, a little like the one I had back home. Hard to believe I'll never set foot in our house again, in my room. Sometimes I think I'm there, with my books, then I open my eyes.

Saturday 8 April

Epilogue the Second

Uncle Henry *did* visit her the next day, or the one after that — she was having difficulty keeping track. Hearing of trouble in Goolgoorook, the old fox had returned from Patagonia early. 'Too many mosquitoes and not enough bourbon,' he said.

They chatted about the nurses and the weather, but something about his expression told her he expected the truth, sooner or later. *Get in the queue,* she thought.

'Some secrets are too big for one person,' he whispered. 'I know you had something to do with *that*.' He pointed at the television, and the ruins of Hemming Heights. 'I knew something strange was going on *before* I left.'

'I didn't do it,' said Beth.

Henry passed her a glass of water. 'I don't believe in the world we see,' he said. 'I think there's something stranger beneath the surface. And I think you were granted a glimpse of that.'

She suddenly recognised the envy and regret in his voice. 'I'm sorry,' she said. 'But you were right. It was only a glimpse.'

The last word she spoke triggered a powerful and unexpected memory, words and images floating up. She shivered and spilled half her drink as it was about to meet her lips. 'Moonlight ...' she croaked, dribbling embarrassingly, 'what's the moon tonight? The phase, or whatever?'

'Almost full, I think ...' He consulted his smartphone. 'Here we go. March the fourth. Full moon.'

She sat up straight, ignoring the protests of her hip. 'I have to get out of here tonight, Henry.'

Her uncle opened his mouth, looking dismayed. 'No ... why?'

'Someone made me a promise. I only just remembered. So many things have happened, and I forgot. Can you help me?'

'Your mother ...'

Nick and Abbie were at home with Sam, leaving Beth to entertain herself.

'Henry, it's a part of the secret. Secrets are too big, remember? You want to see what I saw? Then help me, come with me!'

He hesitated.

I'm getting too good at manipulation, Beth thought. *But I learned my tricks from a master.*

Her shoes proved almost impossible to find. Henry spotted them in a bag under a pile of blankets. She shrugged on a jumper.

She finished getting dressed while Henry acted as sentry. All traces of humour had disappeared from his face. 'Your parents will never talk to me again.'

'I'll say I made you do it.'

'Fourteen year old girl kidnaps middle-aged uncle. Yes, I can see that working.'

'Did you want to see the world beneath this one?' Beth asked. He could only nod.

———

Beth left a note on top of her pillow, swearing under her breath that this would be her last disobedient act.

Mum, Dad, back soon. Have gone with Henry to buy ice cream.

The stuff here is rubbish. Love, the Reformed Delinquent. Don't Worry!!

They moved casually down bare and dim hospital corridors, attracting scant attention. The duty nurse didn't look up from her computer screen, and then they were out into the car park.

The night was warm and alive with the buzzing of cicadas. A gentle breeze blew in from the east. Beth felt better than she had in many days.

'A good night for it,' said Henry as he started the car and accelerated. 'Whatever *it* may be.'

Soon enough they rolled to a stop in a roadside rest area. A full moon shone through leafy trees. Beth knew the trail well, and warned her uncle away from low hanging branches.

Pride forced Beth to walk without a limp, and disguise her discomfort. They scrambled across gently curved granite boulders, always moving upward. Henry followed close behind, his breathing a little unsteady. Eventually there were no rocks ahead or above, just starry skies, fields and darkened valleys far below.

Beth sat down carefully, only wincing a little. She was facing west, the lights of Goolgoorook obscured by low hills. She'd never climbed Mount Jugamai at night. By now her eyesight was well adapted to the dark.

Henry grumbled a bit, then sat beside her. 'Very interesting, I'm sure. An absolute surplus of stars up here.' He cleared his throat. 'A little while, that's all, then we *have* to get back. Or my life will be under threat from your parental units.'

'Melodrama,' said Beth. 'We won't have to wait long,' she added with an assurance that she did not feel.

Perhaps fifteen minutes later, Henry grunted sharply, as if he had been hit. He stood and pointed towards the moon, and the eucalypt forest below. 'Something—' he said, but got no further.

A dark form blotted out stars and threw a long shadow over Precipice Creek, scudding along like a wind-driven scrap of cloud. Turbulence carved a vee shaped wake across treetops, branches pushed aside like parted hair.

'It's him,' Beth whispered, too quietly for her uncle to hear. An impulse to run flashed down her spine, but it was too late. Goldenscale dived on them, massive, ancient wings seeming to span the horizon. At a hundred metres Henry uttered something between a croak of fear and a war whoop, and threw himself down, gripping the rock tightly.

A vast red-bronze eye opened, then its pair, and both blinked. *Sam had it right. He saw this somehow.*

The huge scaled belly passed low over their heads, claws throwing lines of sparks as they scraped across stone. A wave of shocked air buffeted them, the wind hot on Beth's face. She drew in a lungful of dragonscent, this time a clean and sharp distillation of ozone and air and water.

The dragon banked and climbed, revealing the tracery of ribs and struts that strengthened his wings and his long tail. Vermilion spines were spaced down his neck, small copper-green horns above his brows.

You can't see colour at night, Beth thought, but that wasn't true. Not this time. For a long moment everything froze and she was able to see all the detail she desired. Each of his scales was distinct, from tiny violet discs near wing joints to yellow-bronze dinner plates along the broad, endless back. Muscles and sinews moved beneath the skin, everything gracefully articulated and perfectly proportioned. His slow, soaring turn threw the moon back in their faces, light reflecting from a million polished facets. *Remember me,* he hissed, laughing.

Goldenscale's wings rose and fell with greater urgency, and he rapidly faded from sight.

Beth knew she would always look for him, for another glimpse of his wings and gilded hide, even if he was merely a far-off wisp over mountains, a phantom late at night. The dragon was back where he belonged — unbound.

Henry sat stunned, watching a blob become a speck become a pinprick become … just another star. Beth stood and brushed down her pants.

'We can go back now.'

The End